Shake Hands
with the
Devil

Tory Gates

BROWN POSEY PRESS

an imprint of Sunbury Press, Inc.
Mechanicsburg, PA USA

BROWN POSEY PRESS

an imprint of Sunbury Press, Inc.
Mechanicsburg, PA USA

This is a work of fiction. All similarities between persons, living or dead is strictly coincidental.

All material written by the author, apart from the selected lyrics:

Aki's Song
Lyrics written by the author and R.K. (Dick) Huntington; music composed by the author, © 2020 Tory Gates Media/BMI.

Love You Like Me
Lyrics by Cheryline "Che'Nelle" Lim Phelps.
All Rights Reserved. Reprinted by Permission.

I'm A Woman
Words and Music by Ellas McDaniel and Koko Taylor.
Copyright © 1978 Arc Music Corp.
All Rights Administered by BMG Rights Management (US) LLC.
All Rights Reserved. Used by Permission.
Reprinted by Permission of Hal Leonard LLC.

Where Did the Time Go?
Traditional; Public Domain.

For information about special discounts for bulk purchases, please contact Sunbury Press Orders Dept. at (855) 338-8359 or orders@sunburypress.com.

To request one of our authors for speaking engagements or book signings, please contact Sunbury Press Publicity Dept. at publicity@sunburypress.com.

FIRST BROWN POSEY PRESS EDITION: September 2022

Set in Adobe Garamond | Interior design by Crystal Devine | Cover art by Mitch Davidson Bentley | Cover design by Atomic Fly Studios | Edited by Jennifer Cappello.

Publisher's Cataloging-in-Publication Data
Names: Gates, Tory, author.
Title: Shade hands with the devil / Tory Gates.
Description: First trade paperback edition. | Mechanicsburg, PA : Brown Posey Press, 2022.
Summary: The third volume in the Sweet Dreams Series features time travelers Aki Sato, her brother Hiro, and their bandmates as they stumble upon a hidden, malevolent force that seeks her power.
Identifiers: ISBN : 978-1-62006-753-6 (softcover).
Subjects: YOUNG ADULT FICTION / Action & Adventure / General | YOUNG ADULT FICTION / Science Fiction / Time Travel | YOUNG ADULT FICTION / LGBTQ+.

Product of the United States of America
0 1 1 2 3 5 8 13 21 34 55

Continue the Enlightenment!

Acknowledgments

WHAT IS ABOUT to pass through your minds, by way of your eyes, and the pages you shall turn, have been written, rewritten (many times), edited, and transformed. I am thankful and grateful you have chosen to again allow your time to be filled with the next chapter in the saga that has become the Sweet Dreams Series.

When I first wrote the rough draft of *Searching for Roy Buchanan* in 2007, I had no idea that it would turn into the story cycle it has. I never expected Aki, her family, friends and all the intriguing characters we have met and will meet would capture people's imaginations. I also never expected there would be three, and yes, more volumes of this series to come!

I started the series with some threads and ideas, and over time, this story and others began to allow me to tell truths about myself, about others, and I hope shed light on not what is impossible but what is possible in literature, art, music, and so forth. We all have a story to tell, and I had to first tell the stories of others to be able to approach mine.

Over the past fifteen years, I have dug into my experiences in my varied careers so I could tell tales as original as I can make them but also make these stories relatable to readers. My hope (as I would do in every book I read as a kid) was that you would do as I did and find that character you identified with, the one you could become friends with, and that they might show you something you needed to know, for your real life.

I am reminded of an interview I conducted for BroadwayWorld.com several years ago with blues musician, actor, and performer Guy Davis. My last question was about how he wanted to be remembered—his response actually scared me because I thought I'd angered him.

"I don't even think I've gotten to where the heck I want to go so I can get remembered," he replied. "I want to be remembered," he went on, "as somebody who overcame his fear of the unknown . . . somebody who scraped the very bottom of his own barrel and found at last some courage. And stood up and showed the world."

That is the gist of his answer. I have never forgotten that experience, and in the years since, that's what I've tried to do. Everything I do in literature, broadcasting, or whatever else, I do because I'm trying to scrape the bottom of my own barrel, and I've not done it yet.

I arrive here, realizing that as difficult as it's been, personally, I continue to create because that is the only way to offer a new avenue, a new method, and a hope that you, the reader, find that thing that lets you escape but gives you something to think about when you come back, and that it inspires or drives you to be more than what you thought you could be. That is how we are going to heal ourselves, first, before we heal our world.

That said, we have made it to the third book of the series, and I believe you will find this another step forward for Aki and the gang. Again, I have endeavored to put out a story that was original enough, strong enough, and good enough for me to be proud to have my name on it. I leave you to be the judge of that.

At this point, I have an awful lot of people to thank:

Jennifer Cappello, for again doing an outstanding editing job and asking me the questions that needed to be asked.

Mitch Bentley, for his talents, his patience, and his eye for what works.

Everyone at Sunbury Press, not the least Crystal, Lawrence, Fen, Taylor, and all my fellow colleagues, for putting up with my ways.

The small town that is the literary, music, and creative community, who inspire and re-inspire me to keep growing my own thing.

And especially to my (hyper-extended) family, who taught me more than I can ever put into words.

TG
Harrisburg, PA
September 2022

Japanese Honorifics (Updated)

IN THE FIRST two books of this series, *Searching for Roy Buchanan*, and *Call it Love*, I have provided a guide on expressions and suffixes, the latter of which, in particular, are integral to etiquette and decorum in Japanese society.

While many of these are a repeat from the previous volumes, there are new words and phrases, with a brief explanation of each.

Included in the more common terms:

-san is the Japanese equivalent of Mr., Mrs., or Miss, with regard to the surname. If it is used with the first name, it is indicative of a closer relationship, either family or friends.

-kun is used when referring to boys and indicates familiarity or friendship. Older men may use the term among their peers; others may use it with a male of lower rank or standing.

-chan would be the equivalent for girls, but it is also used between women if they are close friends. In addition, this honorific may be used for cute persons of either gender, or animals.

Onii-san (or Nii-san) is a term used for an elder brother; An-chan is also used as an affectionate term for an older brother.

Onee-san (or Nee-san) is used for an elder sister.

Otouto is an affectionate term for a younger brother.

Imouto is used for a younger sister.

Itoko is used for a cousin.

Oba is a term used to denote an aunt. In the story, Aki for example might be referred to as "Oba-Aki" by a nephew or niece. The honorific -san would usually be added out of politeness.

Senpai denotes a senior figure, such as a student in a higher grade than the person using the term.

Kouhai is a term used for a junior in the same manner.

Sensei is a term of respect used for educators, artists, or top professionals.

-sama is a term of great respect. It can denote a god or a member of royalty, but in everyday life, -sama shows proper regard for a president, CEO, or some other leader. It may also be used as a flattering expression or a sarcastic one.

(Note: Calling a person by name without an honorific is almost never done in public. To call someone by name only without either permission or a reason to do so would be considered bad form and insulting.)

Common expressions and sayings:

Ohayo means "Good morning." A more formal greeting is "Ohayo gozaimasu." Konnichiwa is the correct phrase for "Good afternoon," and is used from midday until evening. Konbanwa means "Good evening."

Arigato is an expression of thanks. Domo arigato, which was popularized in the West by Styx through their hit song "Mr. Roboto," means, "thank you very much." A more formal way to give thanks is to say, "Arigato goziamasu."

Hajimemashite is a polite set phrase used when you meet someone for the first time. It essentially means "Nice to meet you."

Tadaima is the common expression to say, "I'm home."

Okaerinasai is a response to the above, which means "Welcome home," or "Welcome back."

Moshi moshi is used when answering the telephone. If you are in a business setting, however, it is correct and professional to answer with "Hai," (Yes), and then state your name and/or company name.

Genki desu ka translates to, "How are you?"

Ja ne is a casual way to say goodbye, translated as, "See ya."

Sumimasen is a casual apology, such as to say, "Excuse me."

Gomenasai is the formal way to say, "I'm sorry," although it may be shortened to gomen.

Ano (sometimes spelled anno) is used when someone is trying to find the right word. It can sometimes be seen as the Japanese equivalent of, "Uh," or "Um."

Irasshaimase is a greeting used by shop and restaurant owners to welcome customers. No set response is required; a polite nod or smile to acknowledge the greeting is sufficient.

Kore wa is a phrase that can be used to say, "This is . . ." You would use this when answering the phone, followed by your name.

Sugoi is an exclamation that can mean awesome or amazing. It may also be used to describe the opposite, such as something is awful.

Subarashi is another such word that means excellent, fantastic, or magnificent.

Nani translates to, "What?"

Majide is a way of saying, "Really?"

Moe is a popular term that refers to feelings of affection toward (primarily female) characters in anime, manga, video games, etc. The word has gained such acceptance it may also be used to describe similar feelings toward any subject.

Noh is a major form of classical Japanese drama that incorporates masks, dance, and song and dates back to the 14th century. It is the oldest theater art still performed regularly today.

Puroresu is a shortened term that stands for professional wrestling, which took root in Japan in the 1950s with the rise of Rikidozan as its first native star.

Shojo (also spelled shoujo) is Japanese for "girl." It often is used to describe stories or comics aimed at a young female audience.

Bento is a single-portion, home-packed or take-out meal. While of Japanese origin, the "bento box" is also common in Chinese, Taiwanese, Korean, and Southeast Asian cultures.

Itadakimasu is used before receiving something, and it is important to say before eating. The placing of one's hands together, saying the word, and offering a slight bow before a meal is much like saying Grace in western cultures.

Gochiosama is a polite phrase that means, "Thanks for the meal."

Kanpai is the Japanese equivalent of "Cheers," when making a toast.

Another word about language:

Technically, there are no swear words in the Japanese language, but expletives can be accomplished by using common words or phrases, then adding a couple of words or changing how they are spoken. Caution is advised, for minor alterations can change a slight insult into a rude one. For example: Chikushou; this word translates to a number of these, including, "damn it," "son of a bitch," or "oh, shit."

(A good site to learn about Japanese etiquette and way of life, especially if you plan to visit for the first time, is japan-guide.com.)

1

Sighting

STARBUCKS, TERAMACHI SHOPPING Arcade, Kyoto City. The conspicuous green-and-white logo leaned out over the narrow walkway. Late in the afternoon, the oasis for caffeine and sustenance was in a period of downtime, its interior populated by a handful of customers.

At one of the black metal tables outside sat two girls. Dressed in the blue blazers, miniskirts, and leg warmers of their institution's colors, the two discussed current events over their lattes. They watched the foot traffic of salarymen and their female counterparts, students from their school and others, as well as foreign visitors.

One, her long hair held off her shoulders by a clip, looked up from her iPhone and stared past her friend, who noticed her companion's distant gaze. "What are you looking at, Haruki-chan?"

The one named Haruki made no motion. "Don't turn too fast," she ordered under her breath, "but that woman, coming this way, the one all in black—see her?"

The second girl slowly turned and scanned the walkers. The one described stood out: a young woman in a long leather coat. "What about her?"

"Sarika-chan, doesn't she look familiar?" Pretending to examine her phone, Haruki studied the face, or what she could see that was not hidden by the Ray-Bans sunglasses.

"She looks like someone out of *The Matrix*," her companion remarked.

They watched the woman approach; her pace was fast, businesslike. Everything about her was black but for the face: the long, flowing hair;

the shades; jeans; boots; and turtleneck sweater beneath the jacket were black. She passed through the door next to where the girls were seated.

"Who do you think she is?" Sarika asked her companion.

"That looked just like Aki Sato, the singer," Haruki replied, her excitement just contained. "The face especially." The girls looked through the window and watched the woman approach the counter and make her order.

Haruki scrolled through her phone. "Have a look," she urged.

Taking the phone, Sarika examined the picture, a promo shot of the person in question. She then glanced through the window again. "It looks a little like her," she conceded.

Haruki reclaimed her phone, eyes fixed on the mystery woman as she picked up her drink and approached the door. "This will be a nice shot if I can get it."

She tensed; Sarika looked away, pretending to stare at her own device. As the woman exited, Haruki silently snapped a picture. Cup in hand, the woman slowly looked around her before heading back the way she came.

"Got it," Haruki whispered, even though her subject could not have heard her. Sarika came around to her friend's side to see the result. The photo captured the head and upper body of the woman in profile. Haruki switched between the old picture and this one.

"*Sugoi*," Haruki breathed, "it is her."

"Look at that," Sarika commented as Haruki compared the pictures. "The face is the same," she assessed, "but she looks so thin now. And her expression never changed—she didn't have one."

They looked up. The woman had vanished. "Aki-san dropped off the face of the earth last year," Haruki explained. "It's a shame—I love her voice."

Sarika sat again and drank her cooling latte with dispatch. "So, what did happen to her?" she asked. "I don't pay attention to all that stuff."

"Nobody knows," Haruki told her. "Lot of rumors about her band, *Lotus Flower*, her partner, and all that. My old boyfriend, Hiyo-kun, and I were supposed to go see them; their tour was canceled at the last moment. No reason was given, and no one's talking. The whole thing was strange."

"Well, if that was her," Sarika said, "it looks like she's been sick."

"She was on top of the world," Haruki mused. "I wonder what did happen. In any case," she said as she added text, "this is going up on my feed."

* * *

The target exited the shopping zone and turned onto Teramachi Street. Her pace slightly slower, the woman sipped her cappuccino and regarded the pedestrians about her. Most were headed someplace; others looked into the high-end clothing, book, and related shops here.

She scanned the vehicle traffic: cars, trucks, and bikes of all varieties competed for space. Her gait did not change, but the woman's senses remained alert, watching, listening, feeling; the scents of the city were more than familiar to her, and she quested for any out of the ordinary.

Those two girls were watching her, she knew, and probably got her picture. That didn't matter; she was used to people's eyes being on her; no use trying to stop the typical fangirl.

Two blocks down, she turned onto the wide cement walkway that led to the doors of one of the city's major hotels. She entered through the revolving door and walked through the tiled lobby past the marble-topped reception desk and the fountain in the center of the room, to the rank of six elevators.

At the top floor, the doors opened to a hallway with a burgundy carpet. She looked each way—no one in the well-lit corridor. There were fewer doors on this floor; she walked down one wing to the last, letting herself in with a key card.

A lone light shone off the neutral walls in the foyer. The woman stepped in, removed her shades, and set them on a stand next to an ornate lamp. She cast her jacket onto a velvet-cushioned chair by the door. Sitting, she unzipped and removed her thigh-high boots and tossed them aside. Running her hands through her hair, she then rose and looked into the first room, the bathroom.

Everything was in order, the mirror, tiled walls, and fixtures immaculately scrubbed and shined by housekeeping. The sink, tub, and toilet were spotless, and the hotel's exclusive, thick white towels rested in their places, as did the plush robe of the same color. Satisfied, she switched this light off.

The main room was in darkness, the full-length windows by the bed covered with heavy blinds. Even with just the foyer light, she could see a corner of the king-size bed cover turned down and made ready for her. To her right, the glass-topped coffee table, couch, and overstuffed chairs waited. The wall cabinet that held the television was closed. The closet by the bed had a number of outfits hanging in it; there were personal items on the nightstand, and a small Bose radio player sat on one of the dual night tables.

She pressed the remote control to allow just enough sunlight to filter through the blinds. Sitting, the woman picked up one stack of notebooks lying there and leaned back, her feet on the table. Sipping her drink, she read over some of the written lines and went through them in her head.

After a short while, she put the book aside and went to the bed. On the way, she stripped off her sweater to reveal a black lace brassiere of high quality. She took down her jeans; a matching black thong remained as she tossed the pants on the bed. As she slid her black socks down her legs and to the floor, she seated herself beside them and placed a purple zafu under her buttocks. Assuming the lotus position, she faced the windows and the thin strips of light that peeked through. She took a series of slow, deep breaths, and began to whisper a chant, *"Om mani padme hum, Om mani padme hum . . ."*

Behind her eyes, the darkness gave way to black, white, blue, then purple, which swirled and changed direction in a slow, hypnotic motion.

She saw whorls of light take definite shape, unseen in years past but now revealed. Line and form became a square, then a cube; then more cubes, one, two, four, then eight. These conjoined and chased one another in an infinite loop.

Breaths became deeper, the driving organ pounded, the pulse raced; the woman's closed eyes sought light within the space . . . then, she heard it, that voice, calling to her . . .

Aki-chan . . .

Aki's eyes opened to black. Her breaths short, a hand went to her chest. Heat in the form of sweat escaped her body and beaded on her frame. She looked at the clock on the nightstand; she'd been in meditation for nearly five hours.

Unsteadily, Aki got to her feet and stretched. Her hands again went through her long, thick mane, then down her body. The curves of her shoulders passed through her fingers, over her breasts, and down her torso; ribs protruded not by sight but by evidence of touch; down her hips and to her thighs. She then went to the window where her fingers parted the blinds.

Aki blinked. The city's heart beat as she looked out upon it. The lights were on in buildings all across Kyoto, but to Aki it meant nothing.

She stared out into the night in silence.

2

Mixdown

"*CHIKUSHOU...*" MEGUMI Yoshida-Sato cursed under her breath as she stared at the computer screen. The image upon it held her gaze as she listened to the explanation over the phone, one most insufficient.

"Look," she said testily, after the speaker on the other end was finished, "we pay you to keep things like that *out* of the media, not in it. I know she doesn't give a damn about that, but she shouldn't need to. That's part of my job, and yours."

With her free hand, Megumi straightened the jacket of her black business suit. She took a deep breath and tapped the toe of her Gucci pump. "I know," she replied and forced her voice to a more professional level, "but there's already been enough speculation about Aki-san, and she doesn't need any more. *Arigato.*"

Shoving the phone into its cradle, Megumi sat in her black leather office chair and continued to stare at the screen. The image of the woman in black was displayed on a showbusiness website that dealt in gossip and celebrities captured at their worst moments. The short article below was full of standard idle opinion about Aki's look, where she might be, and what she was up to.

"She looks awful," Megumi commented aloud as she took a screenshot. She gazed past her cluttered desk and around her side of the office. On the wall above the leather-upholstered couch that faced her were three platinum records in glass and metal frames. Behind her, the huge portrait made by her husband showed the Blue Jean Buddhas; the original work adorned the cover of their first album.

To Megumi's right sat the desk usually occupied by her sister and partner. Noriko's space was tidier, and on her side, the walls were decorated with autographed posters, framed documents, and artwork of friends and relatives, as well as other artists connected to the company.

The phone buzzed, and Megumi heard the secretary in the outer office pick up. As she sipped tea from a white mug adorned with Kanji characters (*One Who Smiles Rather Than Rages is Always the Stranger*), the intercom buzzed. "Megumi-san, it's Kojika-*sama* from the label," the secretary called, an apologetic tone in her voice.

Megumi sighed and carefully ran a hand through her long, styled hair. "Thanks," she answered, "I got it. Oh, and Erika-san? When Akito-kun gets here, please send him in."

She picked up the phone. "Shin-san," Megumi greeted, "*konnichi-wa—genki desu ka*? Yes, we saw the photo; no idea where that was taken or who took it. We're looking into it now."

A pause; Megumi drank some more and listened. "I know," she responded, "you've been keeping your superiors off our back, and I thank you. But please remind those guys the contract clearly states that a new album comes *when* it comes, not when they say so. Right now, everyone is scattered to the four winds."

The door opened during this exchange, and a small boy in a black school uniform entered, a leather bag over his shoulder. Megumi smiled and waved to him. "Kojika-sama," she said, "I've got an important meeting that is starting now. Call you back."

She hung up and minimized the picture. Megumi then rose and came around the desk to give her son a hug. "Hey, how was your day?"

Akito leaned up to kiss his mother. "Fine," he replied, "but I think my day was better than yours. The label again?"

"Yeah," she replied as Akito placed his jacket and bag neatly on the couch, seating himself beside it. Sitting with him, Megumi went on, "They want another album; a collection, live tracks, anything right now."

Akito smoothed back his black hair in the exact same motion his father used. Their son was so much like Kenji, she thought: his look, mannerisms, and speech, everything about him, in fact. For a boy of six, his demeanor was as impressive as his vocabulary. "You would think they would leave them, especially *Oba-Aki,* alone."

The combined honorific with the name was informal, but neither Aki nor Kiya minded. "I know," Megumi agreed, "but people still want to hear Oba-Aki sing; yet it's kind of hard to make that happen when everyone's in different places."

"So, Mom . . ." Akito asked as he looked up to her, "does anyone even know where she is? And *Oba-Kiya,* where is she?"

Megumi shook her head and held her son close. "Only they seem to know." Actually, Megumi did know at least part of the answer to her son's question; but the answer could not be believed, even with what she'd learned from marrying into the Sato family.

"Hopefully," she continued, "we'll hear soon." She looked at her gold-accented Seiko and smiled. "Shall we go home? I need to see your father right about now."

Akito grinned. "Sure, Mom."

Leaving the office, Megumi and Akito walked and talked. Megumi listened to her son's summary of his day, but, try as she might, she only had half an ear on the conversation. All she could think of was Aki and what she couldn't tell.

* * *

The snare popped hard in the cramped, enclosed studio, a resounding din of bass and slide guitar unleashed. Hiro snarled into an old, dented microphone; rubbing elbows with him, a shorthaired blond man thumped out a heavy bottom end on an electric-blue Fender Jazz Bass. Almost directly in front of them, two heavy boom mics hung dangerously low over a standard, nondescript drum kit. A black-haired man worked the backbeat in a solid, well-practiced manner.

A set of fluorescent lights was on above them, but they could barely see. No matter; the amps, mics, cables, spare instruments, and gear were cluttered, and the sound waves generated by the three made the scene sound as primal as it looked.

Hiro soloed on an ancient guitar of uncertain make; the length of metal pipe on his little finger scraped across the thick strings. The entire scene was watched over from an even tinier room, into which a control board, racks of processors, a computer terminal, and two reel-to-reel decks were crammed. The lone stool was for the board engineer, while two others stood behind him. They nodded in time and dug the music but all the while awaited their cues.

Hiro brought the blues standard to an end with a screeching flourish, a wash of cymbals from the drummer, and a double bass kick. A long pause, and the board op gave the thumbs up. The person to the right clicked off the tape decks, and the third opened the door and headed into the room.

"Nice work," the young man in black praised. "What you need, James-*Sensei*?" asked the student; part of his duty was to assist his bass-playing instructor and facilitate whatever the session required.

The shorthaired one slid his headphones onto his neck. "Think we're good for now, man," James replied. "What do you think, Fearless Leader?"

Hiro laughed as he set his guitar on a stand, next to the one that held his prized Telecaster. "Was that a good take? Sounded like one."

"Think so," James said as he toweled off in the hot room. "Suya-kun?"

Suya removed his own headset. "Yeah, really good," he agreed.

"Let's hear the playback," James called through the open door.

Hiro smoothed out his thin goatee and removed the elastic holding his long hair. "At least a good demo, but that might be fine as it is," he said as all crowded into the room.

The second student involved in the project rewound the tape and carefully reset the reel, while the engineer made adjustments to the Pro Tools program on the monitor. "Shall we dump it over now?" he asked.

James nodded. "Just label 'em as raw tracks," he replied, "for backup. Let's keep it to tape as much as possible." James then squeezed himself into a position just above the engineer. "I want a rough mix," he said. "Roll it, but make sure 'record' is disabled."

The student double-checked, confirmed, and pressed the play button. All listened on the monitor speakers, while James and the engineer eyed the VU meters and made minute changes to the faders and controls.

Hiro grooved on his one spot; this did sound good. He glanced at his watch; Noriko would have picked up Kala from preschool by now; they should soon be over. The thought of that made him smile.

As the three minutes of the track ground on, James boosted the snare to attain more of the rattle that Hiro and Suya preferred. "How's that?" James shouted over his shoulder.

Hiro and Suya gave approval. "Get some more of you in there," Hiro told him.

James raised the bass level slightly, then added light compression to Hiro's guitar. Once the track ended, James ensured the data was saved to the computer, then said, "Okay, let's clear out and we'll do the mixdown. I think we got it."

The students moved into the studio to leave James and the engineer alone, while Hiro and Suya left the booth and went outside. The door opened into a parking lot on the campus of the Kitaro Conservatory. This portion of the campus was on an isolated section of the property, with the main brick building and offices in the distance. Hiro pulled a pack of Marlboro 72s out of his shirt pocket and offered one to Suya, who accepted. "Tell me the truth, Suya," Hiro asked as they lit up, "is this good or what?"

Suya exhaled the smoke through his nose. To Hiro's silent amusement, his drummer momentarily looked like an Emo-haired dragon.

"Sure is," Suya replied, "but with James it's easy after all this time. You're hitting your spots good."

"Glad to know." Hiro puffed on his smoke and scanned the lot. He didn't see Noriko's car; she must be hung up in traffic. "I needed to get back to this," he said, "and here's the perfect place to do it. Little studio, put it all in one room and just go. I'm loving it."

"Yeah." Suya took another drag and said, "We got a good trio going, but I think we've a lot more practice to get in before we hit the road. That's what you're thinking, right?"

Hiro nodded. "Considering the inactivity," he replied, "yeah. The term's gonna end soon, so James would be able to tour; and he wants to, which is cool. The label said the solo stuff can be worked onto one of the imprints. Nori-chan says we can get it out in the States, too. There's some good labels over there that'll go for this."

Another drag and exhale from Suya. "What's the deal with Aki-chan?"

Hiro looked over. Suya was one of his oldest friends, but even he didn't know the full story. "The whole thing," Hiro said, "it's eating her up, I can tell. Gather you saw that picture of her."

"I did. She looked wrecked," Suya added with concern, "but more like exhaustion than anything."

"I know. What bothers me," Hiro went on, "is what I don't know. It's obvious she's still in the country, but where? Aki-chan's needed time to be on her own, but that always included Kiya-chan, ever since they first met. Right now, I'm not sure if she's handling it."

"Aki-chan's tough, though," Suya said. "Look at what we did the past six years, and the *Lotus Flower* thing."

Hiro agreed, but to him, there were too many things that remained uncertain. "We can only trust Aki-chan," he finally said. "We have to. She'll come around when she's ready. Till then, I gotta do my thing."

"That's it," Suya replied.

Hiro needed to change the subject. "Now, will you have time with what Mika-chan is up to?" he asked. In the years since Suya's longtime girlfriend graduated high school, she'd gone on to art college and founded her own group, which Suya drummed in as well.

"I should. Mika-chan's ramping up some new stuff."

"No more riots for a while, eh?" Hiro chided, and both laughed. Mika's act was certainly original; privately, Hiro saw it as a pretentious art-rock show, mostly due to the woman's onstage antics.

"I hope not," Suya said. "We nearly got banned from Chiba for that one."

"Megumi-san was mad enough to kill," Hiro recalled as he put out his cigarette and replaced it in the pack.

"Well, you know Mika-chan," Suya replied. "That's her alter ego. It gets out there, but even she didn't want that to happen."

Hiro did not reply; he had spotted the black Mazda CX-5 as it turned into the lot. The SUV rolled up to them; Hiro opened the rear passenger door, where a small, uniformed girl with black hair in twin tails was unbuckling her seat belt.

"There's my girl," Hiro said as he lifted his daughter into his arms.

"*Konnichiwa,* Papa-san," Kala replied with correctness unlikely in a three-year-old, "I missed you."

"Missed you, too," Hiro replied as he kissed her. "Have a good day?"

"Uh-huh," she replied as she laid her head on her father's shoulder.

Noriko came around the front of the vehicle in a cloud of black hair, dressed in skin-tight black jeans, a Pink Floyd t-shirt, and spike heels. "I am having a better one now," she declared as she pushed back her shades and gave her husband a kiss.

Suya leaned against the wall and grinned. "Look at you three," he joked. "The rock 'n' roll family."

"Get around to marrying Mika-chan," Noriko cracked back, "and you'll find out how much fun it is!"

Everyone laughed as James came out and said hello to the new arrivals. "We've got a good mix," he said. "Come check it out."

As he carried Kala inside, Hiro thought, *It's not a bad thing, really. I only wish Aki were here. And Kiya; I miss the days when we were all in this together. It wasn't that long ago, but it feels like light-years.*

* * *

Kenji stepped back from the easel and surveyed his handiwork. Today was a day off, but this "work" fueled Kenji's creative side, as it had the past two weeks.

He drank the last of a can of Boss; this one was turning out well. Kenji noted the heavy lines of paint he'd laid down over the edges of the frame and carefully removed some excess with a thin blade. At this point he couldn't do much more, he mused; Megumi and Akito would be home, and he needed to clean up.

Kenji looked around the studio, a room in the house converted for the purpose. The walls and ceiling were a bright blue. Canvases were stacked in three of the four corners; supplies, paints, brushes, and spares, as well as his camera, film cases, albums, books, and CDs were scattered about, which attested to Kenji's need for the space to be his and his alone. The disorderly order was incomprehensible to all but an artist, and the one room Megumi refused to touch. Even the cleaners didn't dare step inside it.

Kenji tossed the can into the recycling bin as he passed through the foyer to the kitchen and removed his paint-splattered t-shirt. Then he stopped; once more, he went back into the studio and again stared at the canvas.

The image was, in fact, two, with a jagged line of orange and red down the center. At first glance it would have looked like the line had been smeared from the upper right corner down to the lower left by someone's fingers, but this was a carefully detailed part of the work. The rest, a dark outline of black and midnight blue, revealed two profiles.

The upper left image was Aki; in the lower right, Kiya. The separation of the two and their faded, abstract expressions felt suitable at this time. Kenji wondered if this portrait could ever be made whole again.

Making it through the kitchen this time, Kenji climbed the stairs. He went into the bedroom and picked up his iPhone. No calls from the Ito Estate; Taru had things in hand.

Kenji then gazed at the photo on the bedside table, of himself, Megumi, and Akito, taken the year before. Knowing they would soon be home, he smiled, but that expression and emotion faded; he wished the rest could do the same.

3

Contemplations

AKI OPENED HER eyes to darkness. She didn't want to move but forced herself to.

She did not need lights to make her way to the bathroom. Eyes closed against the glare when she hit the switch, Aki allowed them to adjust. She washed up, cleaned her teeth, and brushed her hair. Back in the bedroom, she called room service and ordered a pot of coffee.

Aki then picked up a cell phone, one of the cheap flip variety, and speed-dialed a number. She leaned against the headboard in her silken black robe and waited. "Megumi-san, it's me; got your message. Thanks for the heads-up on that program. I suppose I'll watch it, though I could care less what they say. In answer to your question," she went on, "don't worry about the picture. I know who took it; they didn't mean any harm. It's nothing to be concerned over."

A sigh, and Aki rubbed her eyes as she tried to think of something more to say. There was nothing. "I'll call later," she finished and rang off.

The cell clattered onto the nightstand; Aki closed her eyes, rolled onto her side, and lay in the dark, her arms around one of the pillows. She did not move again until a light, hesitant knock came at her door. Aki forced herself up again and went to it, turning on lights as she did this time.

Tying the belt on her robe, Aki unlocked the door and admitted the hotel staffer. One of the older employees wheeled in a cart bearing a silver pot of coffee, plus a tray of sandwiches, though she'd not ordered it. Aki smiled; staying at this place for so long had led the hotel staff to develop their own routine.

Her server poured a cup of the strong blend and placed it on the cluttered coffee table without fuss. Aki signed the receipt and thanked him; the man bowed and left. She followed, relocked the door, and returned to the cart. Aki added a measure of cream, selected one of the offerings, and sat on the couch.

She pulled a notebook from the coffee table to her lap as she ate and examined the lines she'd scribbled in the night. Finishing off "breakfast" without really tasting it, Aki flipped back through some of the pages. She quietly sang some of the lines. *"When we were stars, the world was open to us, all things at our command . . ."*

Taking up a pen, Aki made a note on the page, looked farther down, and sang again. *"Stars are born, stars will fade, stars fly high, come crashing down, stars live, and stars die . . ."*

She stopped. The pen slipped from her fingers; Aki let the book fall to the carpet. She leaned over, her face in her hands.

* * *

Noriko stepped into the parking lot, the buzz of the ongoing session left behind. Cell phone to her ear, she tied the ends of her t-shirt into a knot against her flat stomach. "Okay," she said and took the phone in hand. "You think so, *Onee-san*? Send it to me, I'll take a look at it."

She listened, scanning the nearly empty lot over her shades. "It's going great," Noriko replied. "You have to hear what Hiro-kun and the boys are doing. It's hot; we need to start talking about it, and fast. With the pace they're setting, they could have all the tracks done in a week, maybe less. James-san and his kids will do the mix, but I don't know how long that'll take; not as long as other things."

She pulled a silver case from the waistband of her jeans and again pressed the phone to her ear with her shoulder. Noriko withdrew a Mild Sevens and lit up with the case's built-in lighter. "Yeah," she replied with the smoke between her lips. "I'm as worried as you are. I'll figure it out. Give our love to the boys; *ja ne.*"

Noriko shut off her cell and attached it to the clip on her belt. She took a deep drag from her cigarette and thought about the photo.

A long exhale . . . Noriko didn't want to think of what she saw in it. She also knew she had a long night ahead of her.

* * *

The tall bald man with the goatee leaned back in his chair, his eyes peering through the doorway of his office. There wasn't a door; Zendo removed it when he began working here nearly a year ago. He found the room so small, even the walls were unjustified.

To his left, a black-haired woman in blue jeans, a black t-shirt, and an orange robe sat typing on her laptop. Zendo could only smile; she always made him.

Reaching to his right, Zendo picked up the Taylor acoustic guitar from its stand. Shifting his position in the chair so its arm wouldn't bang against the back of the instrument, he began to play. He sat in a meditative state as his fingers plucked a series of chords.

The woman looked up. "New ideas?"

"Possibly." They shared a smile, and Zendo thought back, again to a day nearly two years ago. The past was a thing no longer existent, but Zendo understood why this part of it returned to him.

From his spot atop one of the rolling carriers, Zendo sat in the lotus position and viewed the impending spectacle of the Summer Sonic Festival. The steel structure over the stage was one of five: while there would be a black backdrop for this central one, the other four held gigantic video screens to give all spectators a full view of the performances.

Eyes closed, Zendo allowed a slight smile as he listened to the moving pieces of heavy equipment and the workers, road crew, and others speaking and shouting in their own languages. He thought of how, in a few hours, the first performers of the big day would take the stage to perform for fans numbering in the thousands.

Aware of the presence at his side, Zendo turned and looked down. Aki, in her old high school tracksuit, her long hair in a ponytail, stood there and peered through her cheap sunglasses. "Surveying the scene?" she asked with a grin.

The one beside her giggled. Kiya, in short cutoffs, a gray t-shirt with a missing collar that showed one strap of her black bra, and sneakers, hair mostly hidden by a baseball cap, held Aki's hand. Despite all the changes, certain things did not.

They looked over the stage, a mass of upturned panels, cables, lighting rigs, and PA monitors. Roadies were hoisting one of the latter into the rafters above the stage; members of other groups and their people milled about, having nothing else to do.

On the expanse of ground before them, barriers were erected and security teams went over their assignments. There would be ten meters of space between front of house and the crowd, due to safety concerns. Behind them, more cables, rigging, and gear led to a specially constructed sound and video tower at the center. This was all connected to the more traditional trucks and units outside the main area. Amid the chaos, Zendo was aware that his mates, Hiro, James, Suya, and others connected to the band, had come out; they talked with their fellows and discussed the coming show.

Among them, dressed in "show black" despite the impending hot weather, was a tall young man with curly hair hidden by his reversed cap, a pass around his neck on a lanyard. Zendo watched him; Koji had risen in the band as well, from a volunteer gear hauler to the Blue Jean Buddhas' chief road dog.

Zendo tensed, and his cousin noticed. "What is it, Zendo-san?" Aki asked.

"I don't know," he replied at length, "but I have had a most singular feeling . . ."

"Hey, who's that?"

All turned to follow Kiya's finger. From the rear gate, a figure entered the grounds. A woman walked slowly but with purpose. Amidst the hive of activity, she passed unchallenged.

"*What* is that?" Hiro asked of no one in particular.

Zendo stared; time, and his heart, stopped.

The woman strode into view. She was Japanese with close-cropped hair. Her nondescript western clothes would have allowed her to pass for one of the workers, but for what she wore over them. The wrap about her was orange and fluttered behind her.

Zendo slid off the box, threaded his way through the scattered gear and workers, and climbed down to the walkway. He effortlessly swung over the barrier; he felt the grass through his sandals, but Zendo wasn't walking. He was floating; at his approach, the woman's eyes widened, and that smile returned as she saw who was coming toward her.

They met in the middle, an island in the war zone. Zendo stared at her; she wore no earrings or jewelry, and the jeans and red cotton t-shirt beneath the robe looked secondhand. Her battered sandals were familiar; Zendo wore the same pair.

The woman smiled and looked up at him. "*Ohayo, Zendo-Sensei,*" she greeted in that quiet voice. "It has been a long time."

Zendo looked up and down the woman, her thin frame lost beneath the folds of her outfit. "Eiki-chan . . ." was all he could get out.

The one long ago known as *Kashoku* stared back. Her expression faded, then turned serious. "*Gomen,*" Eiki said with a nod. "I did not mean to disturb you, but I have returned. I needed to see you."

"What are you doing here?" Zendo breathed. His hands, so adroit when playing guitar or still in meditation, now trembled. They reached out; Eiki's hands met his.

He felt those hands, small, slim but strong, and Zendo looked them over. The nails were clean and perfectly clipped; the skin was soft but bore the feel of work, and the scar of a burn on the back of the right one was the same.

"I resigned the monastery," Eiki was saying, "but do not worry. I left on my own." Then she added with an embarrassed but relieved smile, "I am back."

They came together in an embrace. "I don't need to know the reasons," he said. "Welcome back, Eiki-chan . . . and into my life again."

Eiki looked up; tears formed on the edges of those eyes, but she smiled. "And you into mine." *Eiki never did tell us how she got past the guards, but at that point, no one cared. My family and friends long knew of the nun called* Kashoku, *and what she meant to me. Eiki was welcomed into the family that we, the band, had become.*

* * *

Eiki's return required little explanation. She had done all she felt possible at the monastery and returned to Tokyo to seek her new mission. She'd found it here at the Shambala Center, in Shinjuku. Eiki's job was to coordinate the center's numerous daily activities and programs and to bring in guest speakers.

Armed with that responsibility, Eiki, with ulterior motive, sought out Zendo to request him to speak and teach a Saturday session. He gladly did so, and the directors asked him to join thereafter.

Zendo accepted but first ended the term at Shibuya Ward High School, where he'd met two of his cousins, Aki and Hiro. Zendo continued to teach, even after the Blue Jean Buddhas became prominent. While some colleagues and board members were unimpressed by Zendo's unorthodox methods, the students were. His resignation was accepted but with great sadness by the latter.

Since then, Zendo had become the center's supervisor and oversaw daily teachings and private sessions. The job paid a little less, but as Zendo and Eiki lived together, it made no difference. The money Zendo made through the band also allowed them to live comfortably, without changes to their lifestyle.

Zendo finished off a progression, and the final notes rang. "Do you think," he asked, "you will have the energy to go over some of our music tonight, Eiki-chan?"

Eiki adjusted the elastic that held her shoulder-length hair in place and smiled. "Always." The two sang together while at the monastery, and the couple had formed a folk duo for songs that did not fit the band. They played mostly coffeehouses and small venues; Zendo's position in the B-J-Bs could have commanded a high fee, but he wanted the act to grow on its own. Eiki shared his vision.

She now approached the desk and offered Zendo a proof copy of a brochure. "Here is the plan for next month's retreat," she said. "Let me know if this will do."

Zendo set his guitar aside and looked over the document as Eiki sat on the edge of the desk, and they shared a smile.

"I see no problems," he pronounced. "As long as the guests know what to do at the start, I think we will be fine."

The woman's expression faded. "May I say something on another subject?"

Zendo looked up. "You may, at any time," he replied.

"Aki-chan is on your mind," Eiki said. "You are worried for her, and I, too, am deeply concerned for her welfare, and that of one other." Eiki's tone of voice was to the point and without emotion; that was the woman's style when discussing serious matters.

"I wish I knew the answer," Zendo replied. "I feel only Aki-chan does."

Silently, however, Zendo had made an educated guess, and if true, there was nothing he, or anyone, could do about it—except Aki.

4

Facing the Past

THE TELEVISION CAST its rarely seen glow in the dark room. Aki had decided to chance the program. In her black robe, the remnants of a takeout meal pushed aside, Aki curled into the corner of the couch and sipped a cup of the day's second pot of coffee.

The show on Fuji TV was another of those entertainment programs, with tonight's episode a "Where Are They Now?" special. The hosts, a male-female duo, had been hired more for their looks than musical knowledge.

Seated at a cheaply built desk with the graphics framed behind them on a green screen, the hosts discussed the Blue Jean Buddhas, and more to the point, Aki. "Over the past year," the male host began, "much speculation has occurred with regard to the sudden disappearance from the music scene of Aki Sato and her longtime backing band. While the whereabouts of most of the Blue Jean Buddhas are known, the location of the one fans affectionately call 'Aki-chan' remain in question."

The commentators went on to discuss tired rumors: Aki was in America, working on a new album with another band; troubles in her family; and a split with Kiya. Fortunately, they did not go into great detail on the latter subject.

"From their early rise out of the Tokyo nightclubs," the hostess continued, "the Blue Jean Buddhas were seen by their fans—and always considered themselves—as a family, even after Aki Sato's international success as a solo artist . . ."

That success was as much Kiya's as mine, I will have you know.

Early, shaky footage from one of the band's early shows crossed the screen. Aki smiled ruefully at the low-quality recording. She well remembered the gig, their first before a large audience, and one of the strangest. *Nearly six years ago, and yet I remember it like it just happened . . .*

The opportunity had fallen into their lap at the end of the school year. Despite upcoming final exams—and Hiro and Suya's impending graduation—the band kept up their after-school rehearsal schedule.

By this time, the band had made the jump from house parties to shows at Tokyo-area clubs. The B-J-Bs, as they were nicknamed, had earned a reputation for utilizing the disparate voices of the band as well as their mix of original and cover songs. Blues remained the core of the B-J-B sound, which set them apart from most other groups with a western template.

Megumi had taken on the role of manager and booker while still going to Keio University. She got the band gigs and promoted them, with Noriko as her assistant. Adept at social media, Noriko took charge of the band's accounts, set up an official website and fan club, and organized the boots on the ground. The band's fan base came from the high school, a small army of sorts. Noriko marshaled those forces to post flyers and publicize upcoming events.

That unusual practice of students hanging out in the auditorium after class to listen and watch rehearsals had continued. Their schoolmate Koji became the band's roadie, while Suya's girlfriend Mika handled lighting and offered her artistic expertise for flyers and graphics.

Teardown from the day's rehearsal was nearly complete when Megumi entered the Aud and informed them of the well-paying gig she'd landed them. "Think about this, guys," she said as they gathered at center stage, "a short set for a max crowd of two thousand. How about that?"

This caused excited crosstalk, and all wanted to know where. "Korakuen Hall," Megumi said, "one week from Saturday. They need a forty-five-minute set; they'll supply the stage and the PA."

The venue was known to all. "That's cool," Hiro replied. "Hey, wait a minute—don't they do a lot of . . ."

He never got to finish the thought. Megumi unrolled a large poster; done on a red, gold, and black background, it bore the faces of several men, most of them Japanese and tough looking. The words *NEW JAPAN: RESOLUTION* were emblazoned across the bottom in white characters.

There was silence as the band stared at the poster. "We're opening . . ." Kiya finally asked, ". . . for a *wrestling show?*"

"Yeah," Megumi replied, still in her sell mode. "The son of one of the hall's directors goes to university with me. He put in a good word for us; you're gonna open the show. You wouldn't have to be involved in the matches or get into the ring," she went on. "He says the stage will be set up off to the side where everyone can see and, more importantly, hear you. The idea is to fill the building by offering the music as well as the wrestling."

No one in the band knew much about pro wrestling, or *puroresu*, although Aki recalled her father was a casual fan of it. They did know that results were reported in the media alongside the baseball, soccer, and other sports scores. "Would a wrestling crowd actually care about our music?" Aki asked.

"I can see the fans throwing their chairs at us if we don't go over," Suya quipped.

"And we'll be sharing a dressing room with a bunch of sweaty, hulking pituitary cases," Kiya added.

"Oh, come on." Megumi looked like a miffed girl from an anime as she continued. "Look," she said, "this is a good gig, guaranteed money. I'm trying to help—I won't let you embarrass yourselves."

"Of course not," Zendo replied. "We do not mean any disrespect, Megumi-san. This could be a break for us and," he said and added with a chuckle, "it might be fun."

"It is true enough," James noted, "music and wrestling have worked in the past. I don't see why not again."

Aki and Kiya both went to Megumi. "We're sorry, Megumi-san, we were only joking," Aki said. "In its own odd way, this does sound like it would work."

Megumi was satisfied, and the gig went forward.

Aki smiled at the memory of the odd night; dressing rooms were blocked off for the band, and the female members did have the requisite privacy. The sound check in the arena was before an audience of wrestlers, ring attendants, and TV crews; some of the former exercised and went over maneuvers in the ring during it. The grunts of the grapplers and booms of the mat when a body hit it competed against the PA.

It turned out to be an interesting event, Aki recalled. The building sold out, and the fans seemed appreciative of the music. A number of the wrestlers also came out to watch the show and were complimentary of the band. The B-J-Bs drew an encore, and then they returned the favor to their fellow performers and watched the matches.

From humble beginnings, Aki mused. Her attention returned to the screen as footage from a more cultured appearance was shown, the dealmaker.

We were indeed invited to play one of Mr. Ito's parties at his estate. Kenji was instrumental in the makeover of the land between Mr. Ito's home and that second one. The latter was renovated to a more modern style, and the walkways between were nothing like when Hiro and I were there . . .

The garden party marked Golden Week celebrations, and Mr. Ito christened his newly transformed estate with a traditional ceremony. Aki recalled how certain people could just fit in with the properly dressed "money crowd," as Hiro called them. Megumi and Noriko were as ever turned out, along with their parents; they mingled so easily with associates and friends. Kiya's family as well: Motoko and Claudio knew most of these people, and Kiya, equally dressed to the nines, showed exceptional grace.

Despite their late parents' closeness to the Ito family and others here, Aki felt nervous and adrift. *I had never been to such a formal event in my life; I certainly knew how to conduct myself, yet I felt such a commoner. Hiro was unusually quiet and reserved. Kenji had come in contact with most of the guests; if he did not know them, like our father, Kenji knew how to pick up on another person's "way," and make friends immediately.*

Aki carefully sipped her club soda in a glass that normally would have held alcohol. Her dress was a short, off-the-shoulder affair in blue, which Kiya helped her pick out at the mall. Her shoes, also on the cheap, matched, and her earrings and costume jewelry completed the look.

Kiya held Aki's free hand, her own drink in the other. Kiya made a pretty picture Aki found hard to look away from. Blonde highlights accented her short brown hair, her black minidress glittered, and Kiya effortlessly walked in heels as they waited for their time to play. It reminded Aki of that travel to LA . . .

"Are you all right, Aki-chan?" that familiar feminine voice asked.

Aki smiled and looked into those brown eyes. "Yes, I am," she replied, "although this is an affair I've never experienced before. It's a little daunting."

"Just be Aki-chan," Kiya told her, "and you will be fine. I'm more concerned about our music, but not worried. I'm glad we're being let to do what we will."

"That is so." Some of the individuals in Mr. Ito's circle were in entertainment, broadcasting, and the music business. Aki noted Kenji and Megumi were talking to one such person, a much younger man than she imagined could hold that type of position. Drink in hand, Megumi was doing most of the talking. "Megumi-san is taking advantage of the situation," Aki commented.

"One must seize the moment," Kiya noted, "and Megumi-san surely knows how to do that."

They wandered along the stone pathways, and Aki told Kiya of how they had worked here, back at the beginning of what would become this musical journey. From Mr. Ito's original home, the stones had all been replaced, and ornamental and flower gardens lined the pathway to the new house. In the center stood the gazebo, where they first played, which now held seats of honor for Mr. Ito, his wife, and their young children.

Seating around the gazebo faced a small stage, sheltered from the sun. Religious rites and offerings opened the day, and traditional performers in full makeup and regalia played now. They passed this, and near the standing stone, Aki and Kiya stopped.

Kiya was fascinated by the story of how Aki and her brothers placed the stone, the music played here, and that strange experience. "I feel some power here," Kiya admitted at the end of the tale. "This stone connected all of you to this place, didn't it? Kenji-san found his work, Hiro-kun found his music—how about you?"

"The same," Aki replied, "to an extent. Come with me."

Hand in hand, the two walked down to the new home, which was open for tours, but Aki led Kiya to one of the side walkways. In the shade, the bench remained; they sat down, and Aki told of that moment with Hiro.

Kiya set her glass aside and took Aki's hands in hers. "I see why you brought me here," Kiya said. "This is the place where you came in touch with your grief and pain. I must do that as well one day, but that is for later."

She leaned forward, and Aki took in Kiya's scent, those eyes, and her smile. "For now," Kiya went on, "I can see how far you have come, Aki-chan. All three of you—you are so much stronger. We are here for a purpose, and we've been granted a great opportunity. Ito-sama would not do this unless he felt we were ready. We are—and I'm proud of you, Aki-chan."

Kiya kissed Aki's lips; in this sunken, secluded area, no one would see. "I am so in love with you," Kiya went on, "and, Aki-chan, do not worry. I will look out for you, in any situation, as you do for me."

She is so beautiful. "I am in love with you, too," Aki replied, "and I don't deserve you, but I will do anything for you, Kiya-chan."

"You do deserve me," Kiya countered, "and you deserve all good things. You have worked for them—they are yours."

We kissed again and held one another. I felt something from this place again, and a confidence came from inside me I'd never known before.

Kiya consulted her watch. "Almost time," she said. "Let's do this."

"Yes," Aki replied. "Let's." *We walked back, met up with our bandmates, and went onstage. We played a short set of our best songs; I worried that a band playing the music we did would not go over, but with every song, the applause and cheers grew. We ended with "Singing the Blues" and then called Kenji onstage for "Sweet Home Chicago."*

Afterward, Mr. Ito and his family received the band. His second wife, Katsumi, was much younger; dressed in a traditional kimono, the lady was effusive in her praise. The two Ito children, also in proper Japanese garb, were equally thrilled; in fact, Aki didn't hear a bad word from anyone.

At one point, while speaking with some of the dignitaries, Aki looked over at Mr. Ito. He spoke with Kenji and Megumi—and that man from the label. As if he knew they were being watched, the gentleman turned, made eye contact with Aki and Kiya, and winked.

"I think we're in," Kiya said in Aki's ear.

Aki could only nod and smile.

5
Where Did the Time Go . . . ?

AKI'S ATTENTION RETURNED to the TV screen; the first album cover on the monitor behind him, the male host discussed the band's debut album. The self-titled recording was the surprise hit of the year, "its freshness and eclectic sound ushering in a new style in Japanese popular music."

What? We weren't that revolutionary.

"Touring when some members' school schedules permitted," the host went on, "the Blue Jean Buddhas played across Japan . . ."

We played on weekends and toured during breaks; mostly for Kiya's and my schedule. Kenji, Motoko, Claudio, and the other "adults" wanted us to have as normal a life as possible during that period, and we agreed. I didn't want to have to leave school; off-stage, I just wanted to be Aki, and to be with Kiya, as we'd been . . .

". . . their original style of music, whether playing their own songs or covers of foreign artists, touched a chord with society as a whole."

This is already getting stupid.

The hostess took up the report, talking about how the band sang in both Japanese and English. *Not so unusual; English is understood in our country. Also, a lot of songs don't have the same feel when you change them too much.*

There was more footage of gigs, then clips of fans—including a curious group of kids who turned up at one show dressed like every member of the band. "Spurred by their reputation," the man intoned, "the band remained fiercely independent, self-produced, and refused to change for what label executives and others thought the band should look and sound like."

Everyone thought they knew better than us . . .

They cut to an interview with Megumi; she sat in a room with the obligatory pillar candles burning behind her. "The band, but Aki-chan and Kiya-chan especially," Megumi said, "did not want to be turned into a packaged act. Once they hit, we got so many offers to do TV shows, reality shows, game shows, movies, all manner of things. They wanted to demote the band to studio musicians and turn the girls into a duo, but we said no—rather," Megumi quickly added, "they, Aki-chan and Kiya-chan, said no."

"They're like a cult," Kiya used to say; we never liked girl or boy groups. No matter how talented, they were controlled, programmed, run like robots. Megumi was not going to let that happen to us.

Cut to a tighter shot of Megumi. "Fortunately," she finished, "the label backed off. There's a reason for that, but either way, the band proved beyond doubt they could be successful through their own design."

The next cut was of Zendo and James, seated together in a similar room. "We heard many different 'suggestions,'" Zendo said. He used his fingers to form the quote. "One of those was, 'get rid of the old guy.' I think they meant me."

James burst out laughing, and Zendo joined him in it. Aki had to chuckle at that, too. True, Zendo was older than the rest of the band and, image-wise, he didn't look conventional, *but nothing about us was . . .*

"James-san and I," Zendo went on, "were in the position of having some experience. We knew the pitfalls of the music business and what to watch out for. I would like to think that we did our best to shepherd the others along."

"There was a lot of talk like that," James continued, "but we didn't want to be anything other than what we were. I'd seen all the ways it could have gone. I didn't want my friends to be changed for change's sake."

Cut back to the interviewer, the female co-host: "You are nominally the producer of the Blue Jean Buddhas' albums," she addressed James. "You would have your own opinion on how the band should sound, correct?"

"Yes," James admitted as the camera went back to him, "but as a member of the band, you have a place; as a producer, you have a different one. For the latter, I refused to let my feelings cloud the bigger picture. We all wrote songs; we all had a hand in the production; nobody sat on the sidelines."

There was a cut to a shot of some nameless critic, a short, fat man with graying hair, a terrible five o'clock shadow, and thick glasses. "They were different," this man said in a smoker's growl. "The band worked together to guard their music, their creativity, as well as themselves."

"Indeed," the hostess said, now back live on the screen, "all members maintained low profiles and lived as though they were not rock stars."

"We were never, you idiot!" Aki snapped out loud at the screen. She would have said more, but then came another cut to video, and Aki froze. The clip was from five years ago, backstage at one of the outdoor summer festivals. Another band could be heard performing during the interview.

Aki stared at the footage of Kiya; she looked so cute with her bobbed hairdo. Her black crop top and hot pants outfit was one she chose due to the heat; no one dressed this band.

Kiya stood poised and spoke with ease to the reporter. "We don't consider ourselves pop stars," she said. "We are people who are good friends, who love music, and who love to play it. As long as people want to hear us, and it's fun for us, we'll do it."

She stared at Kiya, her look, her body, and noted with amusement how the camera panned slightly left to get more of Aki in shot, and not just because of the wild tie-dyed dress and white go-go boots she wore. The cameraman had noticed they were holding hands; the extent of their relationship was not yet known.

Shots of the main recording studio at Kitaro, both pictures and video; *we recorded all our albums at Kitaro. James enlisted the aid of his students to produce, and we made sure they all got credited. Our projects weren't work—we had fun, we created, and had unlimited time to record, although we sometimes had to do it in the middle of the night!*

"The Blue Jean Buddhas," the host went on, "made music on their own terms, and their own time. Each of their three albums, released over a span of five years, was meticulously recorded and tapped into different streams of the members' musical influences. Whereas many recordings by bands sound much the same, the surprises to be found on the B-J-B's recordings were many."

A TV variety show performance showed the band playing live; they never lip-synced. The camera was focused on Aki, with Hiro seated at an angle on his acoustic as she sang the song that was their second hit.

"'Aki's Song,'" the hostess said, "was born of one of the first times the Sato siblings played music together. Its simplicity and Aki's unique style made the song a smash hit across the Asian continent."

That simple haiku, and the chords Hiro came up with, took the band to the top of the Oricon charts and was indeed a hit across Southeast Asia. It even gained popularity in China, despite a ban on their music by the government. Zendo had refused to play there, due to the occupation of Tibet, and the band supported him.

Footage of the band boarding a bright purple bus came across the screen, followed by more blather from the hosts. The images made Aki smile again. *We hit the road to promote that first album; Megumi said we'd handle our own travel, at least around Japan, to save money—none of us were ready for what Kenji came up with.*

He took Hiro, Suya, and James with him to an auction, and they drove back in an old Setra touring bus! Some of us, Megumi in particular, were not so sure, but Kenji said, "They were giving it away—we had to bid on it."

Our big brother's genius shone in this project. He gutted the inside of the bus and redesigned it to accommodate the band, our gear, and comforts of home. He overhauled the engine, painted the body purple, and overlaid the Blue Jean Buddhas' name and logo on the sides. We were a rolling work of art.

The sleeping quarters were cramped, but we made the best of it. They were a series of cubicles, with beds and sliding doors so we could have privacy. Kiya and I fitted ours out with as many pillows and cushions as we could find, to reduce the bumps from the road. "The Nest," we called it . . .

Most of our road running was at night; those were among the best, and most romantic times I've ever known. Kiya and I would lie together, look out the windows and watch the nocturnal world go by. Other things happened in that little space too, but we weren't the only ones. Akito was conceived in one of those "nests," and supposedly Kala was too! Megumi and Noriko always denied that . . .

The hosts were again talking about that first album; it had indeed become a hit. Their rendition of Poco's "Call it Love" was the first single; although sung in English, it cracked the top ten. Then came the stunning success of "Aki's Song."

"For a song that's only two minutes and twelve seconds long," the barely seventeen-year-old version of Aki remarked on a talk show (to laughter), "I'm amazed at how it touches people." Aki watched herself continue: "I've long believed that music has a higher purpose, perhaps even a spiritual one. Music of any kind has the ability to not only make us feel happy, or to feel better . . . but to heal."

You think as I do, Aki told her younger self. *We immersed ourselves in the music, to pass time, to stretch, to create, and yes, to heal the hurt inside each of us . . .*

More visions of the past followed. *"Singing the Blues" became my signature song, and we usually did it near the end of the set. I told the others about what I'd dreamed of (but not the Amida), and James's students made it happen . . .*

In a dark Tokyo nightclub, on a stage barely big enough to accommodate the band and its gear, they shot a performance of the song for a video. In a dark indigo velvet dress found in a consignment store, her hair done up, and with long silk gloves on her arms, Aki sang Ruthie Foster's tune to an appreciative audience. *They had six cameras, and somehow, they got all the footage they needed in one take. For the first time, I saw myself not as a girl, but a woman, and my voice . . . I'd found it.*

"'Singing the Blues,'" the male announcer intoned, "was the second number-one hit for the Blue Jean Buddhas, and the successes continued . . ." *We always set aside part of our show for an acoustic set. Certain songs needed that treatment. One of those was "He Left Me His Guitar," Hiro's tribute to Kazu. Already respected as a guitarist, Hiro proved himself a songwriter. The single only just made the top thirty, but no loss of face there.*

Footage from the band onstage interspersed with scenes involving Aki and Kiya, Kenji and Megumi, and Hiro and Noriko. *We were asked to contribute to a compilation of old pop songs, with the proceeds going to charity. Zendo suggested "Nice to Be With You," a one-hit wonder by an American band named Gallery . . .*

The bouncy, mid-tempo tune was a piece of seventies pop history, with verses that largely rhymed. Aki found it easy to sing; Kiya took part of one verse, the band filled in on harmonies, and Hiro (who admitted he didn't like the song) played slide guitar on it and threw enough Elmore James into his part to make it work.

Aki's eyes misted. *The lines in that song, about being lonely, feeling lost, but knowing someone is there for you . . . I got a notion, you're causing commotion in my soul . . . Kiya did that for me, but we framed our contribution more about friendship when it came to us. The love two brothers had for two of our dearest friends—that deserved the spotlight more.*

The obscure tune rocketed to number one and brought in more money than the charity could have hoped for. The single even charted in the States but did not become a big hit. *We never did break into the American market, but in Japan we became even better known. Still, no one knew about Kiya and me . . . the time wasn't right . . .*

Kiya's composition, "If I Could," became the fourth single from the album, and that went to number five. *Kiya was in her element, and her performance was perfection; the ballad always got a big hand for Kiya, and we proved to the public we had yet another talented singer and songwriter in our midst . . . Kiya had more than any of us.*

One more snippet, the single "Nighthawk," which charted at number seven. The simple instrumentation included another video, much like the story of the song: *I sit in my room, a girl writing dreamy love poems, it seems. In the next, Hiro is sitting with his guitar; I come out, he plays, I sing, and the band is overlaid in images of them in each of their homes playing. We also had footage of a hawk from somewhere . . . this showed us as we were, people who made and composed music, then came together . . .*

Aki mused over the comments about the debut album. With five hit singles, it went to the top of the charts and stayed in the top ten for several months. *We had a hit, a big one; our demand and our price went up . . . it really was happening. We toured, took a break, repeated the process . . . and then came the first single from the next album . . .*

A piano intro rolled out in the dark. The lights came up on a Kitaro soundstage to reveal Kiya's hands and face, and the shining silver dress she wore. Aki stared at what she knew would come: her new self. *"You traveled the world, lookin' for, lookin' for love . . . there ain't nothin' out there that you deserve . . ."*

In a shimmering black minidress, her long hair flowing behind her, large silver hoops in her ears, Aki walked in high heels to the lone light that shone on her microphone. *"Tell me, baby, that I know what you're worth . . . and if you're comin' back, 'cause baby I am your girl . . . Can't nobody love you like me . . ."*

The lights went up, and the full band blasted out the rocked-up cover of a Che'Nelle song. *She was a star on the J-pop scene but also made it in America. We opened for her on a Japanese tour, and this song inspired us. We knew we had to do it, and we had to do something else . . .*

A chorus of *taiko* drummers on risers behind the band followed Suya's lead. The sound was stripped down to the music; cameras caught every angle in jump cuts to the beat as Aki sang to the audience—but meant the words for one.

"I'd go beyond the universe, and I'll light the fire inside you . . ." Kiya sang the high parts of the chorus and propelled the band in her own call and response with Aki. *We got as close to modern pop as the band would ever get . . . I never considered myself sexy, despite what Kiya told me, but this time, I took charge of myself and became me.*

Aki and Kiya traded off the vocals in the bridge with the camera shots angling them to sing to one another, lyrics about surrender and how nothing else mattered. The pressure was reapplied with a powerful, blues-drenched guitar solo from Hiro. Aki took the chorus again into her higher range, matched by Kiya and complemented by the band.

We then did what we had to do . . . from the bombastic, over-the-top sound, the music faded again to the piano. The lights went down as Aki joined Kiya. *"Can't nobody love you like me . . . love you like me . . ."*

Kiya played a slower, extended piano roll, and they repeated those words back and forth to one another. On the final note, they kissed.

Aki shuddered and wiped her eyes. The video, and song, never failed to move her, especially that moment. *We made that song the title track: the single started at number one and didn't fall for eight weeks. The video sparked the expected controversy, being banned or edited by most outlets. What we did could have killed our careers, but we didn't care. I wanted everyone to know Kiya was the one I loved, and we also knew that would validate people the world over.*

The support from LGBTQ+ groups worldwide was incredible. We'd made a statement on behalf of millions. Some critics dismissed us as "lipstick lesbians," that we weren't really gay, the usual things. Men trashed us in the media and online, as did some women, but by this time, we were accepted by the fans. Kiya and I knew who we were, and we identified as ourselves.

Aki slowly drew breath. Footage from another video crossed the screen; the black-and-white film, the "burn marks" and cuts, the minor chords and searing, out-of-phase solo from Hiro's guitar . . . *I knew they'd get to it.*

The next single was "Silent Tears." James wrote the song after he learned what happened to Kiya, but he would not sing it. Shot as a *Noh* theatre piece by Kitaro's film students, it drew on a work by Yukio Mishima and depicted Kiya as a young woman in traditional dress. Aki then appeared as a samurai, her long hair tied behind her.

Their interactions involved no spoken words; Aki recalled how she and Kiya re-enacted the latter's confession; Kiya then fled the stage and ran into the street, with Aki in pursuit.

Aki stared; she saw the image of Kiya, now the small child, running in the pouring rain. Then Aki caught up to Kiya, curled against a wall, her makeup running with her tears. Their voices sang the chorus over this: *"Silent tears, fallin' down, comin' down, and they look like rain . . ."*

Aki hit the mute button and remembered: *Those tears were real, and so were mine . . .*

"All right," Aki said, "I'm ready."

They'd come to the conservatory's main recording studio after school so Aki could finish off the lead vocal track. Kiya had already completed her parts, but she came along and sat in the control room with James and Hiro.

After a kiss and a "*gambatte*" from Kiya, Aki went into the vocal booth. There were a couple of false starts, but Aki found her voice and the sensitivity she wanted on the third pass.

As she came out of the booth, Kiya entered the studio, ran straight to Aki, and they embraced. She didn't speak but wrapped her arms around Aki's lower back. On instinct, Aki held Kiya to her and ran her hand through Kiya's short hair as she rested her head on Aki's chest.

Click.

Amidst the studio activity, Kenji was taking photographs. He was on right angles to them, and the picture froze Aki and Kiya in time. *The photo showed Kiya at a vulnerable moment, with me comforting her, as we did one another.*

"What is it?" Aki asked.

"Aki-chan," Kiya whispered, "you nailed it. That was brilliant."

She felt Kiya's body tremble, and Aki held her more tightly. "I did my best," Aki told her. "I remembered how alone and hurt I felt all that time, but you, more than anyone."

Kiya leaned up, and they kissed. "I love you," Kiya whispered as more tears fell.

"I love you." Aki couldn't stop hers, either. *The record company didn't want this as a single; they thought the content of the lyrics and the video too strong. We got our way, though; that picture was the cover of the single, used as a promotional poster . . . and then Kiya went public.*

The critic was back on screen. "'Silent Tears,'" he said, "became one of the most difficult recordings to write about because of the subject matter. The video proved who it was about; Takahashi-san's honesty about being assaulted as a child not only struck the heart of a touchy issue but it also allowed people to discuss it."

Kiya found the courage within her to speak out publicly about the rape. The single went to number one as well and held the top spot for seven weeks; Kiya made the most of its time in the spotlight.

We participated in a march in Tokyo that year, to remember those who were sexually assaulted. No one knew we were there until after the fact. That's what we wanted; the walk was not about us but all those who had been victimized.

Kiya did interviews and spoke to survivor's groups and child victims. I also spoke out about what was done to me, but I let Kiya take the lead. I was never prouder of her.

Hiro popped up on the screen, on that same set, with Suya at his side. Aki tried to refocus as Suya said something about the music. Then Hiro added, "The blues was always the thing for me, and that's at the base of all that I play. Our transition to popular music was not something I was happy about, but for the greater good, I found my way to fit my style into the songs we were doing. You have to listen to other music, other musicians."

Aki looked upon her brother. His hair was longer, he was working on some kind of goatee, but what struck Aki was what he continued to say: "Any musician has to listen, has to know what's going on out there, even if you don't like it. We continued to stay ourselves and let ourselves be open to inspiration."

Suya then added, "Blues fits into all our music, no matter what we do. Hiro-kun has it through his guitar, and we find ourselves—Aki-chan, no matter what anyone says, is a singer, pure and simple. When she cuts loose," he continued, "there's no words to describe that. She stays Aki-chan, but she changes."

Aki thought about that and let the program again fade from her mind. She went back in time again to a strange, dark night in a side street bar: *I don't even remember the name of the place . . . we played a two-a.m. show for a packed square room. In the audience, I remembered seeing a number of Black people, Americans. They looked like musicians; you recognize them . . .*

Onstage, the band had put over a fair amount of their songs but shifted more to the blues tunes they'd stockpiled. Those seemed to energize the crowd, especially the westerners. Sweaty, her short black dress clinging to her skin, Aki looked and felt like the rest of the band, but they drove through the set.

Then, at the end of a song, exhausted, barely able to see, Aki looked out into the crowd. A woman was amongst that group, thick in body and wearing a sequined dress and leather jacket. Her hair was a curly, electric cloud, dyed red. She'd been drinking champagne the whole night, but she wasn't drunk.

Their eyes locked. The lady could have been thirty, or sixty, Aki couldn't tell. She smiled and nodded. *You got this, girl . . . it's gonna be all right . . .*

From her left, Hiro had retuned his Telecaster and played that very series of notes. "Oh, yeah . . ." Aki breathed into her bulb of a mic. "Everything," she wailed, "everything's gonna be all right . . ."

Hiro got the cue and played the line again; Suya built up the drums and the cymbals behind her. "Oh, yeah . . ."

Aki let out a shout; the measure, the riff known even to non-blues fans, was pounded out. The crowd roared, and Aki swayed on her heels. *"When I was a little girl, only twelve years old, I couldn't do nothin', to save my doggoned soul . . ."*

A wave, a black ocean, moved in time to the music, and the floorboards shook. Aki no longer felt hot, or tired; her left hand wrapped around the mic, she set her lips close to it and went with her lower range. *"My mama told me, the day I was grown, she said sing the blues, child, sing it from now on . . ."*

The band slowly moved in time, a slow thrash to a reworked version of "I'm a Man." *"I'm a woman, oh yeah, I'm a woman, I'm a ball of fire . . ."*

Her bare arms and legs tight, Aki brought all her energy through her body; she growled, shouted, and sang with feminine swagger and bravado. *"I can make love to a crocodile . . . I can sing the blues . . . change old to new . . ."*

She kicked out of her heels. Aki leaned into the crowd and sent a sensual, and sexual, message to the house: *"I'm a lovemaker, y'know I'm an earthshaker . . ."*

The audience shouted after every *"I'm a woman."* Standing over her electric piano, Kiya improvised a frenetic solo; Hiro stepped in with a guitar turn, while Kenji sneaked onstage with his harp and blew into Hiro's mic.

At center stage, Aki surveyed the crowd. They were on their feet; with no room to dance, they stayed in place, clapped their hands, shouted, and some raised their cigarette lighters like at a rock concert.

"I'm gonna hold back the lightning, with the palm of my hand, shake hands with the devil, make him crawl in the sand . . ." The primal ritual, a series of sung cries of power and celebration, then the song broke down to deafening cheers.

Aki leaned on her mic stand, barely able to stand. She knew what just happened: *I tapped into my deepest energies, and those of the Amida . . . I never did meet that lady, but she understood, and I unlocked the soul singer inside Aki . . .*

Love You Like Me yielded one more single. Zendo's song, "So It Goes" showcased his vocal and songwriting talents, though Aki and Kiya sang parts. *This one just squeezed inside the top twenty. Kiya and I insisted Zendo sing the lead, though some second-guessers claimed if I sang it we might have had a bigger hit. That wasn't the point; we didn't care about the charts, we cared about the songs—and us.*

More footage and commentary . . . *the third album came the following year and was entitled* Remember. *We delved into our influences for this project and began paying tribute to those who came before, and inspired us . . .*

The screen darkened once more this time to a *film noir* on an abandoned theater stage in black and white. Aki, surrounded by the band, again played the torch singer, to T-Bone Walker's "Evenin'." *Hiro continued to soak up guitarists of every style; this song was spooky to me, and I remember how we fooled around with it on the bus late one night, then added it to our set. This was a song I had to work at; to try to capture a man's tone, his feelings, and how his lover was gone . . . now I know how that feels . . .*

The camera panned over the horn section, three saxes, a trumpet, and a trombone player, all from Kitaro but for one. *We needed horns for some pieces, and we used several different players from the conservatory and our high school band. Zendo dubbed them "The Fighting Spirit Horns."*

Aki smiled as the shot hovered over a tiny girl in an evening gown, her long black hair pinned to the side with a flower as she soloed on tenor sax. *Koji's little sister Hatsue showed up to audition at Shibuya; some of us were skeptical, but Hatsue floored us with a version of "A Love Supreme"! She didn't join the band, but Hatsue got her name on the album and became one of our secret weapons.*

"Evenin'" just made the charts at number forty and dropped off. Aki stared; images, shapes, and a brume shrouded her vision. *Critics ripped us for releasing such a strange song as the first single; some of those armchair experts, just waiting for us to fail, cited that as the beginning of the end. We knew better; we'd all drawn on our influences to make our best record. I, too, felt empowered, Kiya at my side. My voice was never better, and I knew we couldn't be stopped.*

Another TV show, where, at center stage, Kiya sang the song she considered the most difficult, the one about the marionette. *"When I Fall" was the song Kiya put away. We tried to record it for our first album, but Kiya wasn't ready to put that out there. Now, stronger than I had ever seen her, Kiya rearranged the piece, composed all the musical and vocal parts, and we were back on top for three weeks.*

An unplugged set at a jazz and blues festival; seated in their favored configuration, Hiro led the group through "Walkin' Out of San Francisco." Kazu's old song got new life and made it to number twelve on the charts. "I Remember," one of Zendo's initial offerings, and long a stage favorite, was finally recorded and went next. *All our voices were used; we shot a simple video of us in the rehearsal space—the band, our families, hanging out, singing, and playing. We let the Kitaro students walk around with cameras, and the world saw us just as we were. It got us to number six.*

"Did I tell you today, 'I love you'?" Aki froze. *Kiya and I wrote all the time, but we were our own worst critics. I used to say for every ten songs we wrote, one might be good enough to make it to an album. "You Say" was one of those, a conversation between two women, who loved one another so deeply . . . no matter what, that was the one thing that didn't change.*

Seated at the piano, again at Shibuya, on the stage where it all began as girls, two women sat again. *"You say the words so easily, and I know you're telling me the truth, you say 'I love you' without question, 'cause you know it's coming back to you . . ."*

Aki shut the TV off. This was the Blue Jean Buddhas' last number-one, and their final hit. The hosts would inevitably get into *Lotus Flower*, the minimalist recording she'd made with Kiya on piano and backing vocals. They had written a series of songs together, but these did not work for the band. The demos produced by James and Hiro at the conservatory attracted the label's attention and were released as is—to shocking global success.

Aki closed her eyes. With no singles, *Lotus Flower* topped the charts nevertheless, and the subsequent tour took the pair from Japan and South Korea to Southeast Asia, Australia, and North America. They performed mostly in small theaters and venues; Aki and Kiya insisted that the intimacy of the songs be presented in this manner.

The tour lasted six months. They received high critical acclaim from the press and fans alike. Both made clear, however, that they would return to the B-J-Bs.

As Kenji designed the album covers for the band, he was tapped to do *Lotus Flower*. His design, a dark stage with Aki in the foreground, eyes skyward and holding a lotus blossom, with Kiya in the background playing piano, won an award and landed him commissions for similar work.

Aki got up; she shuffled to the blinds, and her fingers let in a little light. She stood and regarded the city's nightlife for a time, then quietly began to sing in a voice she'd not heard from herself in so long: *"Where did the time go? How could it be that long ago? We remember it so well, the stories we could tell, where did the time go . . .*

". . . where did the time go . . ." Her voice broke at the final line. Aki leaned through the blinds against the window, and her body shook.

"Kiya . . ."

6

Remembering

NORIKO SAT IN her home office. Barefoot, in sweatpants and a sleeveless B-J-Bs top, she took a drag of the latest of many cigarettes and set it in the ashtray. A laser print of the photo in hand, she examined its edge with a jeweler's glass. In the upper right corner was a sign atop a distant building. Blurry, but Noriko could magnify this part enough to get some idea of the characters. She checked the version on her computer screen, then compared the print to the image.

"Definitely a business or downtown district," she said to no one in particular. "This building was right across the street." She then went to the bookshelves on the far wall and pulled down a large hardbound volume. Noriko had done her degree in Arts & Humanities at Waseda University. The shelves held a mini library from her course of study, books, periodicals, and publications that made themselves useful in her partnership with Megumi.

Noriko puffed on her smoke as she flipped through the pages. This book included specific works, with an emphasis on commercial art. The design looked familiar . . . Noriko was sure she'd been there before.

She and Hiro had watched the program. During it, Noriko spoke by phone with her sister. Megumi and Kenji were watching as well, and while the treatment of the band's history was decent, there were the usual baseless hypotheses about Aki and Kiya.

"Hiro-kun's not impressed," Noriko said. "It's just a rehash of old stories and a lot of talk."

"That's our feeling, too," Megumi replied.

Noriko then wondered aloud, "What will Aki-chan make of it."

"Aki-chan said she'd watch," Megumi said, "but knowing her, she probably won't say over the phone how she feels."

"I know. I'm still working on the photo; after the show I'll keep at it."

"Thanks, Nori-chan," Megumi said. "It's not much to go on, but I think we all agree we need to at least know where Aki-chan is."

When the show ended, Hiro returned to his home studio while Noriko went to her office. The former Sato family home had undergone changes: after Kenji and Megumi married, they bought a house of their own and turned the keys over to Hiro and Noriko. Renovations included turning Hiro's old bedroom into a home studio, which housed his growing guitar collection and recording gear. Aki's room was split into Noriko's office and a room for Kala. Aki had by that point moved into an apartment with Kiya, so the arrangement worked out well.

Dawn broke through the blinds as Noriko flipped through the collection of books and searched online. She was getting close; Noriko staved off the need for sleep in the hopes of finding what she was looking for.

To Noriko, this was more than locating Aki. Her lifelong friend faced something serious, and while Noriko had no power in the Amida, she understood it.

Even during the years that the Blue Jean Buddhas were at their peak, Aki was not much different as a person after the band became popular and stardom followed. Aki herself made the point early on: she did not want to change, become a diva, or act like a stereotypical pop star. Noriko remembered Aki saying to all who would listen, "If ever I become one of those people, slap me."

To which Kiya replied, with that look in her eyes, "Where *I'll* slap you, Aki-chan, you might like!"

Everybody laughed, Aki the hardest, and the recollection made Noriko grin. *There are some things we don't need to know, girls.*

Noriko recalled that most of the band did not change their styles that much. Hiro, of course, indulged himself in music, particularly guitars and gear. A Martin sent that old acoustic into permanent shrine in the studio, but while Hiro collected axes of varied types, Kazu's Telecaster remained Guitar Number One.

She thought then of Kenji, easily the most level-headed of the Sato family. He continued to work for Mr. Ito, and when Taru was elevated to the boss's right-hand man, Kenji became top manager of the estate.

Kenji's quiet energy radiated in his job, artwork, photography, and also the band. He'd left the group after the first album but still played guest parts, and he applied his artistic skills in the ways best for him. The marriage to Megumi was a highlight of the social calendar, mostly due to the Yoshida family's standing.

Noriko smiled. Held at the Ito Estate, the wedding was western in nature but formal. Hiro served as best man, while Noriko was maiden of honor. She and Hiro tied the knot in a traditional ceremony a few years later. Along the way came Akito and Kala, and the family grew.

As for Aki, what alterations did occur were subtle ones: Kiya had most refined tastes for a young woman, thanks to her parents. Those rubbed off on Aki, and both women exemplified an upwardly mobile look and style, but never did either girl become pretentious with the influx of income and status.

The one thing Aki wanted more than all else, Noriko remembered, was one of those old-fashioned-looking bulbous microphones jazz and blues singers used to use. Shure made one; Aki endorsed them, which led to a signature mic, a marketing campaign, more exposure, and yes, more money.

But apart from clothes, the car Aki and Kiya shared, and the home and property, the couple did not live an outrageous lifestyle. They were not seen in the tabloid papers or on the TV gossip shows. The estate they purchased was a good and smart investment, but it also offered privacy by way of distance.

Noriko lit another cigarette. There was one other change, she thought: Aki had remained herself in public, kind and friendly to people, even the craziest of fans. That endeared Aki even more to her and Kiya's followers, but Aki also feared the attention.

Aki wanted her private life kept private. She did not like being watched, scrutinized, examined; this was nothing new for anyone in the public eye, but living in that fishbowl, Aki detested it. Sensitive, on one level due to her wish to protect Kiya, Aki's moods could change in no time. Noriko saw them as quickly as Kiya did.

The criticism and ridicule came from the media, and pontificators in the press, TV, and online, often not about the music. Like Kiya, Aki was open about their relationship, which brought them disdain from some and open abuse from others.

Noriko took a drag on her smoke and exhaled. Times had not changed much in Japan or much of the world; the girls were slagged in print, online, and over the airwaves, and they were the subject of threats, although none of the latter were substantiated.

This required extra security and vigilance. Aki rarely went out alone, with the ever-fearless Kiya at her side. As she once said in frustration, "I don't want my life dissected by people who know nothing about it."

That was where Noriko and her sister came in. While Megumi was protective of the band as a whole, Noriko assumed the role of one of Aki's guards. There was no doubt: Aki and Kiya were the chief defenders of one another; beyond that, Noriko remained Aki's closest confidant.

Add to it, the Amida. Aki needed to keep people at arm's length due to that. Hiro had tried to explain his experiences in it to her, but Noriko realized you could not understand the Amida unless you'd been through it.

Aki feared one thing more than any other: that someone would see her disappear, and Aki would not be able to account for it. And what if this was captured on tape? Aki had resigned herself to living a double life: having to keep that most intimate part of herself a secret, and yet she had to be out there.

Her eyelids heavy, Noriko rubbed them and continued her search. *I sometimes think we created a monster,* she thought. *We let the band be the band, but was that the right thing to do? We were two kids trying to manage, and we'd never done it before. I want to think we did right by them, but have we? Are we part of the problem?*

Noriko stubbed out her cigarette. She was too ashamed to admit to being angry that Aki did not communicate with her during this absence. Only later did Noriko come to understand Aki did that to take the pressure off her. *I never realized until she went away just how much I love Aki-chan. It's not the kind of love she and Kiya share, but we were sworn friends from the time we were little, and we promised to have each other's backs. It's selfish, but I want—no, I need to see Aki-chan again, to know she's all right . . .*

Then, in a back issue of a magazine, she saw it. Folding over the cover, Noriko held the picture up to the computer screen, then the print-out. The blurred image in the corner and the magazine photo matched.

"Ha!" Marking the page with the laser print, Noriko stuffed it in her shoulder bag and tossed it on the couch as she passed through the living room to the bathroom. She needed to clean up and get moving.

Noriko stripped and stood naked before the bathroom mirror. To her left, Hiro appeared, unshaven and his air askew, in his bathrobe. He smiled as he leaned against the door and watched. Kala was still asleep, so she wouldn't know. "*Ohayo,*" he greeted, "guess you were up all night, huh?"

"Oh, hey . . . sorry, didn't mean to wake you," Noriko replied. She came over and quickly kissed Hiro. "Listen," she went on as she returned to the mirror and brushed out her hair, "can you do me a huge favor?"

Hiro was checking his wife out, which Noriko didn't mind, but this was no time for a show. "Name it."

"Would you see that Kala-chan gets to school today, and pick her up as well? I have to make a trip, but I should be back late in the day or tonight, I hope."

She breezed past Hiro. "No problem," he said as he followed Noriko into the bedroom. Noriko began to dress, and Hiro watched; he found this as a big a turn-on as getting her undressed. "By that exclamation," he went on, "I gather you know where Aki-chan is."

"I think so." Noriko pulled on a black thong and a matching bra. She then went before the mirror and applied minimal makeup. "I may be wrong," she said, "but I'm going to try. I need to make sure Aki-chan is all right . . . if I can find her."

Noriko opened a drawer, pulled out a pair of black jeans, and swiftly put them on. She went to the closet and selected a white silk blouse. "I'll see Kala-chan before I go," she went on. "What's your plan for today?"

Hiro replied, "Once Kala-chan's at school, I'll go over to the conservatory and see James-san. Suya-kun should be there; we'll try to lay down some more stuff."

"How many tracks have you got?" Noriko buttoned her blouse, then pulled a pair of socks from another drawer and sat on the bed as she put these on.

"Seven that are a go," Hiro told her. "We've got one I want to nail today, if I can get James-san to sing lead. After that, we'll see."

"Great. Keep going with that," she urged. "I am convinced the label will get behind it. Right now, those guys want product, but it's excellent music, and that's what matters." Noriko slid into a short black leather coat. She snapped on her Vincero wristwatch and slid a pair of onyx hook earrings into place.

"Better get dressed myself," Hiro said. "By the way, where are you headed?"

"If I'm right," she replied, "Aki-chan's been hiding in plain sight." Noriko picked up a pair of black leather boots and rushed past Hiro. She left these in the living room by her bag, checked she had her cell, and headed into Kala's bedroom.

* * *

Aki sat in meditation, once more in darkness. She breathed deeply and slowly as she gathered her strength.

There is a poem that begins, "I remember many things." I don't know who wrote it. I, too, have many recollections, fond ones of Kiya and my time with her. I know how fortunate I was to have her in my life.

I knew both of us would change as time went on, and we did. Kiya grew out her hair again; I learned that she'd always cut it short after the rape because having it long reminded her of how she looked before it happened. In Japan, cutting of hair signifies a breakup or a broken heart; in Kiya's case, that applied.

Kiya was the love of my life. She was my muse, my collaborator, my partner, and my friend. Kiya stood up for me when I didn't have the strength, and she knew what I needed at those times. It could be nothing more than her touch, her kiss, or her holding me; she knew what I needed, and I would feel strong again.

The creativity between the two of us and the band always flowed. Kiya understood music's healing quality more so than I ever did. We knew we couldn't save the world, but we could make it feel better, for a little while.

The band never tried to image itself as anything other than what we were. So many in the music business, including a number of our friends, tried to look like everyone else. Their stage costumes were outlandish; there were dance routines, light shows, and by then it looked more like a stage performance or worse, a circus. That took away from the music; Kiya and I made it clear that we'd dress the way we wanted, and that was that. Fans often told us they appreciated our honesty in the way we presented ourselves.

Our relationship was another matter; it was no secret Kiya and I were lovers. That caused issues, but they were manufactured ones, usually from more conservative people and some of the minority religious groups in Japan; they considered us bad role models, called our love unhealthy and disgraceful, and accused us of disrespecting our families. We, and most of the public, ignored them. Kiya said it better than I: that was our business and no one else's.

Our intimacy, and our love, deepened. With all the amazing, wonderful people I have met in my life, I have never looked to anyone else but Kiya. I never felt anything for another person, and I've never wanted anyone else.

You learn a lot about the person you love as time goes by. Kiya was completely open about her sexuality, and also her body. For someone who'd been so badly hurt as a child, you'd think she might stay closed off. Kiya was just the opposite, and we explored our relationship in ways I had not anticipated . . .

Aki and Kiya were walking through Harajuku on a shopping trip. In their Shibuya Ward uniforms they attracted the usual attention, but they weren't looking for that. *I was still in my second year, Kiya her first; we'd only just started making a name for ourselves as a band, and we took a rare afternoon away from rehearsals and gigs to be together . . .*

Traveling down a narrow street crammed with shops that hawked electronics, clothes, books, music, and other items, the girls browsed, hand in hand. Then Aki felt her right arm pull backward; Kiya had stopped to look in a shop window.

The window held numerous DVDs and other items meant for adults. Aki wasn't offended but noted Kiya's gaze. *She stared at one specific DVD: it had two women on it, one doing something of a more-than erotic, even graphic nature to the other.*

"What is it, Kiya-chan?" Aki asked.

She turned, and Aki saw the embarrassment on her face. "Gomen," Kiya replied.

"No," Aki quickly said, "don't be sorry. What about that caught your eye?"

Kiya looked back at it. "How I feel," she explained, "I can't speak of in public. I'll explain when we get home."

We later went back to Kiya's; we had a long talk. Kiya admitted to feeling her body was not hers at times, due to the physical and mental pain she'd gone through. I sympathized with that. "I want to know more," Kiya said, "about us. I want to be closer, Aki-chan; I want to be yours."

Aki nodded. "I think I understand."

"This is about trust," Kiya continued. Her eyes peered into Aki's as their hands joined. "I trust you," she said, "with all my being. I have no regrets about loving you, Aki-chan, and I never will. I want to go deeper; I want to love you, and be loved by you, without limits. I want to reclaim what is mine."

I realized what Kiya meant. "You feel," Aki replied, "that we can reclaim our bodies—and ourselves?"

"Yes." Kiya slid her arms around Aki and buried her head into Aki's shoulder. "I love you so; I want us to be one, and I want to show the world that I am a person again. I'm not a victim; I'm taking charge of myself." She looked up at Aki and asked, "Does that make any sense?"

"It does." The two embraced, kissed, and lay on the bed. "Kiya-chan," Aki said, "I don't fully understand this yet, but whatever you need to do, I need to do. And I love you as well."

That part of our relationship remained behind closed doors. Kiya and I went further than I could have imagined, and it sealed our trust in one another. It made love more intense, more satisfying, and I felt completely secure with Kiya.

Behind Aki's eyes, a slideshow played, one Aki had gone over time and again. *Even with our success, we tried hard for a "normal" life. I graduated high school on time, and Kiya followed the year after; valedictorian, no less.*

We were changing; Kiya and Noriko helped me with clothes, makeup, and fashion. I no longer felt the need to be cheap but to treat myself at times. While alcohol and smoking were part of some of our peers' lifestyles, neither Kiya nor I partook; not because we were superior in any way, we just chose not to. And drugs were certainly not something to mess with in Japan.

We became sex symbols as well, although we did not accept a lot of the offers sent our way. Modeling clothes and products we used ourselves, that was one thing. For our own enjoyment, we did a couple of photoshoots, of the kind idols did. Kenji shot them; we chose what to wear, or not wear. We did the photos in a way to show the public and our fans that this was who we were . . . friends, musical partners, but also, lovers. The limited-edition run of the magazines, photo sets, and DVD sold out and became collector's items.

Due to the attention we received from fans, Kiya and I decided to get an apartment of our own. We took one in the same set of towers Motoko and Claudio lived in. We had more security and privacy. Later, we bought the estate, and Kiya and I had a home . . . our home.

Aki recalled the private showing with Kiya, Noriko, and the estate agent. A friend of the Yoshidas, the lady took them on a detailed tour. From the ornately painted gate to the stone walkway, to the wood frame construction, hardwood floors, high ceilings, and other amenities, the house exuded understated luxury. "This reminds me of Ito-*sama*'s second home," Aki noted, "only more modern."

"The house is comparatively new," the agent replied. "Our records show the home was completely rebuilt only two years ago. The owner lives alone and is retired. He is seeking something smaller for himself."

Kiya reminded Aki of a child; eyes wide, she flitted from room to room as if impatient to seek the next chapter of a story. "I love this," Kiya remarked as they passed through the rooms. "It feels like us."

Aki had to admit she liked the home, too. "There's a lot of room here," she noted. *The basement in my old house was nothing but a crawl space, but this one ran nearly the length of the foundation. Our apartment was nice, but after a while, we felt it too small.*

They moved to the sliding door that led to the back deck, the patio, and the green space. A flower garden, well-cared-for, dominated this area. "There's a lot we could do with this," Kiya said. "Aki-chan, come with me."

The two walked to the far end of the property. "Aki," Kiya said, "I feel like this is the place. We can turn the basement into a practice room, have the band over, we can play music as loud as we want . . ."

The two giggled, but Kiya continued, "This is where we can put roots down. I've never felt like I had a home; I love where we live, but the apartment has its limits.

"We have the money," Kiya went on, "and the price is reasonable, according to Megumi-san. Real estate only appreciates, or at least holds its value. We'll never get a chance like this again."

"I suppose not." *I remember looking over the green; my family used to work on other people's grounds to make them look special. We never had one of our own, really. I would like that, I thought . . .*

She turned away. "Aki?" Kiya leaned in. "Am I being pushy again?" she asked. "I'm sorry…"

"No, no." Aki quickly turned and took Kiya's hands in hers. "It's all come so quickly for me," she explained. "I guess I'm just simple and thinking about the cost and everything."

Kiya dipped her knees and looked up at Aki, her eyes big; this usually made Aki laugh, but the expression was searching and sympathetic. "There is nothing wrong with simplicity," Kiya told her.

Aki smiled as Kiya put her hands on her shoulders. "You have sought solitude," she said, "for a long time. You want to stay Aki-chan when you are away from the stage; I don't need to ask, for I know that's right."

She nodded. "Yes. I love all that has occurred, Kiya," Aki replied, "but I also know there is a price. I need to protect myself, and you know why."

"That is only fair," Kiya said, "but we protect one another. I pledged to do that for you, Aki, as you have for me. This doesn't mean we have to cut ourselves off. Everyone deserves a home; and I want one, Aki, with you."

They drew one another close and shared a long kiss. "I want that—no, I need that," Aki declared. "Let's do it." *I did love the home the moment I saw it, just like Kiya. I also wanted some separation so our families could come visit away from prying eyes, and so I could keep others from finding out about me.*

Aki drew a deep breath, and her arms went about her frame. *Our love, the things we kept between us . . . that we could have. I didn't care about the money; we were pretty careful with ours, and Megumi kept close tabs on our royalties, our investments. That meant we didn't have to worry; we could explore our music further, and ourselves.*

I asked Kiya to marry me during the Lotus Flower *tour. We were in Nashville, of all places! The Blue Jean Buddhas never attracted much attention in America, and we only played a couple of shows in Hawaii. But the* album *had taken off in the US, and the response was beyond our dreams.*

We performed at the Belcourt Theater, a small, intimate place. We loved it, and the show went well. Afterward, we went down to a country music bar that doubled as a boot shop! Someone backstage told us about it; he said the boots were half price until midnight, so naturally, we had to go. While a loud country band performed in the same room, we tried on boots along with the other patrons. Kiya ended up buying a pair.

We were in bed at the hotel in the early hours. I remember saying to her those things I've always wanted but needed to say in a certain manner. "I want to ask you something."

In one of her silken French chemises, Kiya blew her hair from her face and rested her head on Aki's shoulder. "Go ahead."

Aki chuckled at that. She held Kiya and felt the curves of her body. "Kiya," she said, "the last few years have been the happiest of my life, and you are a big reason for that. I wonder . . . would you like to do it for all time?"

Kiya took a moment to consider that, then sat up. "Are you asking," she responded, "to marry me?"

"Yes," Aki replied. "I mean, I don't suppose legally we can," she went on, "but I wish to have something that binds us together."

Aki then kissed Kiya's lips and looked her in the eyes. "You are the one I want in my life, Kiya," she declared, "for all time."

"Ohhh . . ." Kiya's eyes welled up, and she buried herself in Aki's arms. "Then I say yes!" she cried. "Absolutely, yes!"

We stayed up half the night talking about how we'd do it; we made love, and we finally got to sleep sometime before dawn. Then we were up a few hours later, and back on the road for the next town. Not much different than with the band.

Our families were supportive of us. It is a strange thing: same-sex marriage is not legal in Japan, but partnerships are recognized in Tokyo. We decided to make it a private affair and would set the date after the tour.

Aki's eyes opened. She sat, wrapped in her robe in the lotus position, and felt empty, weakened, and deflated. *So much for the best-laid plans— Kiya has been lost to me, to her family, and to all of us. That's why I'm here; I can't bear to live in that house again, alone.*

I'm trying not to feel sorry for myself; I feel worse for Kiya, for what happened. I keep thinking it's my fault, and yet I don't know for sure what occurred.

Aki forced herself to her feet. In the dark, she picked her way across the room and made for the stack of notebooks. The one she drew out did not look like the others but more like a thin ledger.

Back to the bed, Aki switched on the bedside lamp and paged through the book. Here, in another hand, were a series of characters, notes, and figures. In particular, Aki focused on one page, which held a singular sketch, plus a formula. *Kiya identified the Amida as a tesseract, or a wrinkle in time.*

The mathematical equations were beyond Aki's skills, but Kiya saw it as yet another language she could speak. *I've rarely traveled in recent years because I felt that using the Amida for frivolous means does no good . . . in truth, I also feared using my power because when I became famous, I was ter-rified I'd disappear in public or at a show. Through meditation, I've become aware of what Kiya was trying to show me . . .*

She returned to her cushion and took a series of deep breaths. Aki focused her waning strength; the universe turned dark, and then Aki entered that space.

Black became midnight blue, then purple, and a combination of the three with a thin accent of white; the stars returned, and Aki floated here. Her efforts, however, to move into the Amida fully, were stopped. Aki continued to focus, to force it, but she could not . . . then she remembered:

We traveled shortly after we got home and before the next Blue Jean Bud-dhas tour; we went back in time, to our high school days, to revisit a place. I wanted to go, to see it. We were looking for certain things, details . . .

How odd, Aki thought, to walk in her Shibuya uniform again, with Kiya at her side. They knew where they were; the walk from school to Uma's, clocking in as if it were yesterday for their usual drinks, then walking into Kiya's neighborhood. All of this seemed so normal, so perfect.

"It's time," Aki told Kiya. They stood at the bus stop by Kiya's apartment building, the very spot where Kiya confessed her love for Aki.

"Okay." *The smile on Kiya's face; so much like the first time I met her, so bright, so cheered to be back here and to know the one she loved was still with her and would always be . . . and then it happened.*

In the darkness, Aki's body convulsed. She'd had a physical hold on Kiya, and she felt them float in space, against this background. Then she saw the figure eight of the cubes, turning and twisting inside of one another, the one to go through presented itself . . .

Aki-chan . . .

Aki wrapped her arms about herself; the cotton of the old uniform was like ice, as were her limbs. Aki's eyes opened, and she saw the bedroom of their home before her. She was seated in the lotus position, as before—only Kiya, who had been sitting across from her, was no longer there.

"Kiya-chan?" Aki called. "Are you here?"

No answer. Aki slid off the bed and turned into the hallway. She walked down to the bathroom and looked inside, but it was empty.

"Kiya-chan," Aki called again, "where did you go?" She tried to stay calm, but Aki's skin crawled from the cold and fear.

She rushed from room to room, then downstairs to the first floor. Aki called Kiya's name again and again; she nearly fell down the basement steps, but a look here showed no one had disturbed the space.

Aki tried not to panic as she climbed the stairs two at a time and ran to the door. She could barely unlock it but did so and threw the door open. Across the porch and out to the carport, the car was parked in its usual place. The front gate was closed and locked. No one had come in or left.

She ran back inside, through the kitchen, to the rear deck. Out here, the patio and furniture were undisturbed. The expanse of enclosed back garden, the grass, its flower garden, and trees had not changed.

"Kiya-chan!" Aki shouted as she raced through the open door and upstairs. She threw herself onto the bed and wrapped her legs back in the lotus posture. Nails dug into palms as Aki tried to control her shaking; she sucked deep breaths and tried to calm herself. She had to get back there, back to Kiya.

It was no use; Aki could not stop the tremors of her body. Water seeped from her eyes, mucus from her nose, and Aki drooled as she tried to concentrate. "Kiya-chan," she moaned, "help me find you . . . *where are you?*"

The dark covered her, and then Aki felt it: in the blackness of the Amida, a rush, not energy but power, flashed, and Aki flew backward, out of the Amida.

Aki crashed to the wood floor by the bed. Pain shot through her body, and she screamed. *I had a meltdown, as Kiya would have said. I must have called someone because when I finally came out of it, Kenji and Megumi were with me. Kenji was holding me and trying to calm me down. It took a long time before I could explain what happened . . .*

* * *

In the present, Aki lay on the thick carpet of the hotel room. The thin slivers of light from the blinds showed the sun had come out, but Aki could not guess the time. It no longer mattered.

Dragging herself to a sitting position by the bedcover, Aki stared at the notebook. She ran her hands through her hair and held herself against the chill. *What happened? I'm still trying to find this out. I fled the house that night; I couldn't stay there anymore; I ran away, not from the problem, but so I could focus on it. My attempts to return to the Amida are being thwarted. I can hear Kiya's voice; she's out there, I'm sure.*

Aki picked up the book, written in Kiya's hand, and held it to herself. "This much I know," she whispered, her voice breaking. "I will find out what happened and who or what was responsible. And I will find you, Kiya; I will bring you back, no matter the cost. If I fail, I must be with you, even if it is for the last moment of my life."

7

Resilience

I'M TRAPPED IN the past. I don't know how I got here—I've got to keep it together. I know I'm alive, somewhere. I need to figure out what to do. I don't have the ability to get back on my own.

All I can do is take stock and find a way to survive until Aki can come for me. That I must do . . . but now, I feel more alone than I ever have in my life; and I am frightened.

The young woman seated in the park hidden behind a newspaper would have stood out anywhere. Bare trees and a cold wind proved the time of year to be fall, and her clothing was definitely out of step with the season—and the times.

She peered over the top of a discarded copy of the *Detroit Free Press*, looked about, and tried to get some sense of the situation. The paper gave her only an idea of where she was, and when.

Kiya realized the travel had gone wrong, how she didn't know. She wondered if Aki was all right and if she would be able to find her. This was a time and place they had no connection to.

She also knew she was cold, and her old high school uniform was a dead giveaway that something else wasn't right about her. There was trouble in the Amida, and Kiya hoped that Aki would be able to deal with it.

Kiya had her old denim school bag with her; inside she found her wallet, which had a few American dollars inside, but not much else. Her driver's license was also there, a card without a picture that listed her as being from Michigan. Her name, however, was the same. *Okay, at least I have an identity here. That's a start.*

She tried to be nonchalant as she walked out of the park, but Kiya knew right away that the eyes of the mostly American and warmer-dressed locals were on her. *I must look like a prostitute in this outfit. I'm going to need a change of clothes and to figure out where exactly I am.*

Kiya turned onto a street that put the river on her left. She guessed this was the waterway that bore the city's name, and she watched an ore carrier slowly make its way southwest. *If I remember my geography, that ship's headed for Lake Erie. That's right, they're called 'boats' on the Great Lakes. Everything seems so old to me; the cars are so big, and the date on the paper said 1969! That joke about being stuck in the sixties is no longer funny.*

Kiya walked on and made her way into what appeared to be a port section of the city. There were a number of old buildings here, and a few businesses. It looked like a village just off the water.

Three young men lounging on the corner took notice of Kiya as she crossed a side street. She saw them but tried not to make eye contact. One stepped out and blocked her way. "Hey," he said.

Kiya looked up. He could not have been more than seventeen but was very tall. He, like his companions, wore heavy wool sailor's coats and caps but looked way too young to go to sea.

"Hey," she replied and tried to pass, but his arm barred her way.

"You want a good time?" His face was dirty, and his eyes were hardly friendly.

"No, and definitely not with you," she sneered and knocked his arm aside.

As she tried to pass, he grabbed her arm. "Hey," he said, "you don't talk like that to me!"

But what happened next likely had never been done to him either, at least not by a woman.

Using her Judo Club training from Shibuya, plus the self-defense skills Zendo had taught her and Aki, Kiya turned and grabbed the sailor's left wrist with her right hand, his thumb with her left hand, and yanked straight back. The boy (his voice was certainly high enough now to be called that) squealed in agony. He'd left himself wide open; Kiya's left foot shot up and kicked him hard in the groin. She closed the distance, then executed a perfect hip throw that left the kid flat on his back.

The other two immediately came to their cohort's aid, but Kiya was already at a dead run down the street. The two raced after her, while the other staggered behind, his good hand holding his family jewels.

Kiya darted in and out among pedestrians and across the narrow streets. *Where are the police? Don't they have any in this town?* Then she had to stop short as a truck turned out of a side alley.

Before Kiya could move, the three were on her. Two of the boys grabbed her arms, and the first caught up to them and drew something out of his coat. "I'll get you for that, bitch," he snarled, and a short blade snapped out of its handle.

The terror of Kiya's past flashed before her. She stared as the creature loomed above her and turned into her father. Kiya tried to scream but couldn't.

"Got a problem here, do we?"

A strange voice had spoken, calmly but with serious authority. Kiya's would-be assailant turned in its direction. In the alley before them was a very large man.

He stood just under six feet, with flaming red hair and an unshaven, weathered face. This man, too, was dressed in a sailor's coat, along with a scarf and cap; he looked the very picture of a man who belonged on the bridge of one of those boats. The jacket did little to hide his protruding stomach.

Standing with him were four boys similarly dressed and as tough looking. "You'll have an even bigger one," the man continued, "if you don't turn her loose and get a move on . . . and I mean *now.*"

The man never raised his voice, but beneath an unusual-sounding brogue was the tone of a man who meant exactly what he said. Kiya was released instantly; the one with the blade dropped it, and all three raced up the street at full speed.

The big man and his crew watched them run away. "Fucking cowards," he growled as he kicked the blade into a nearby storm drain. Then to Kiya, he asked, "You all right, miss?"

Shaken, Kiya managed to nod. "Yes, thank you," she finally was able to say.

A huge paw wearing a fingerless wool glove came out. "Dale McLeod, at your service," he said. "And you are?"

Kiya gave her first name, and her mother's maiden name, which was on her ID.

"Nice to meet you," Dale went on as they shook. "These are my boys," he added as he introduced them around.

Kiya wondered if Dale meant his sons or his gang. "You appear to be in some need," he went on as he removed his heavy jacket and put it over her shoulders. "You'll catch your death out here in that get-up."

Kiya wrapped the coat around herself, amazed at this strange meeting. "Come along, we're headed to the shop." Dale continued, "We'll get you put right."

Despite some uncertainty, Kiya walked alongside Dale. The others provided an impressive bodyguard that made everyone on the sidewalk move out of their way. Kiya noticed they were going down a street named Atwater and asked, "So where are we going? And what is this shop?"

"You'll soon see," Dale replied. He pointed to a metal sign that hung above a set of cracked stone steps. The sign was painted gold, the logo explained by the name that encircled it: *The Black Dragon*.

Unlocking the door with a heavy, ancient key, Dale told the others, "Right, let's get the shipment taken care of while I get Miss Takahashi warmed up."

The Black Dragon was a store as curious as its name. The right side of the narrow building was taken up by a see-through glass counter, an ancient cash register atop it. Comics, books, and other materials lined the opposite wall, and the shelves that held them extended all the way to the back of the store. There were also a number of spinning metal stands that bore similar products. In the far-right corner was an old, roll-top desk and swivel chair, beside it a small table and two folding chairs.

To the left of the desk was a coffee urn on a metal stand. "Max, fill 'er up!" Dale ordered. The smallest of the boys disconnected the unit and took it into the back.

"Coffee is the lifeblood of this business, as it is on the water," Dale commented as he filled the maker's basket from a large can of Savarin. "Sit yourself down and relax. I think we can assist one other."

Kiya took the chair between the desk and table, and she wondered just what Dale meant by that. One of the boys turned on a radio; the guitar riff of "Sunshine of Your Love" filled the front part of the shop via a scratchy FM signal.

Cream was the soundtrack for the beginning of the workday. The boys shed their coats and caps and began opening a series of cardboard boxes. "Shipment day was yesterday," Dale explained, "and we have to get the new product up and out on the shelves."

Max soon returned with the urn, now filled with water. He and Dale set the basket in place, and the boy then went to join the others. Once the urn was switched on, Kiya heard a gurgling sound come from its insides. Dale took his seat at the desk and turned to face Kiya. "Let's now discuss the matter at hand," he said.

"First," Kiya replied, "thank you again for what you did back there. I haven't had anything like that happen in a long time, and—"

"I could tell," Dale said, "if you will pardon the interruption. Don't worry, those guys aren't gonna bother you again. Around here, the going word is, 'Don't mess with Dale McLeod.' That means his friends, too. That being said, I think it is more than fate that brings us together."

Kiya remained huddled in the heavy jacket, despite it being warm in the shop. She merely nodded, and Dale continued, "As I say, we are in a bit of a bagatelle here, or should I say you are. You are in need of a place to stay, for however long."

"I kind of got dumped off here," Kiya said, "and I'm still not sure of where I am at this point."

Dale seemed to accept the answer. "It happens," he replied. "Well, to explain fully, you are in the Motor City. We are right alongside the Detroit River and in the shipping lanes for Lakes Erie and St. Clair. I sailed those waters in my better days."

He then motioned to her clothes. "That outfit," he said, "despite you wearing it well, doesn't really go in this climate. However, I can help you with a rig that'll suit you better, if you're willing to make a trade."

"What sort of trade?" Kiya asked, not without suspicion.

"A fair question." Dale smiled. "In addition to this little enterprise, I have others. I deal in a market involving so-called 'collector's items.' People all over the US and Canada, as well as other countries, write, call, or send me orders for interesting things. My sources are varied, both legal and shall we say, otherwise. Needless to say, your outfit would command a very high price in said market."

"I get it," Kiya replied. "My uni for a set of clothes."

"Right," Dale told her in a voice that was businesslike but still friendly. "I'll pay you a hundred dollars, cash. I get the feeling you could use the money."

Kiya extended her hand. "Small bills," she said, "two changes of clothes, and it's a deal."

Dale grinned and they shook. "We speak the same language, my dear."

* * *

Megumi was working the office phone and discussing last night's program for what felt like the hundredth time. "I do not know if Aki-san watched it," she told the caller, "and at this time, I don't think she is concerning herself with that."

She stood up. "As for the program, I think a lot of what they said was window dressing, but at least they were reasonably accurate. The speculation on Kiya-san I did not appreciate, and I'm sure her family, nor Aki-san did, either. It's a personal matter between the two of them."

Megumi stiffly but politely ended the interview, hung up, and exhaled. She had fielded far too many calls from the music and popular press about the show. According to the entertainment pages, the show scored the anticipated high ratings. That meant the interest in Aki, Kiya, and the Blue Jean Buddhas was still strong.

Looking over at Noriko's empty desk, Megumi wondered where her sister was. She had awakened to a text message; Noriko thought she knew where the photo was taken but didn't elaborate.

That tells us nothing, she thought and sat back in her chair. Aki cagily wasn't using her phone or any email or social media accounts; Megumi only received calls from Aki through burner phones that could not be tracked.

Aki was also secretive about her money. Despite the global use of credit cards, plastic was not so commonly utilized in Japan, although that was changing. Cash remained the rule, Megumi knew from the tutelage of her parents.

While management companies often handled the day-to-day business expenses of their charges, paying their rent, bills, and the like, Aki and Kiya did all that themselves. Megumi oversaw each band member's investments, royalties, and publishing and ensured no one was getting ripped off. Even so, Megumi didn't know everything; Aki and Kiya's spending habits were their own.

The past several months did provide some light to the subject: mail to Aki and Kiya's home had not been stopped or diverted. To keep the curious (and especially the media) off the track, Megumi and Noriko arranged for a trusted neighbor to hold the mail, then hand it off to Erika. She lived in the area, and as an employee of their managers, the woman's appearance did not arouse suspicion.

While sorry to open things she should not, Megumi felt it necessary. Bank and credit card statements showed Aki's accounts were open but hardly used; the last cash withdrawal was a large one from the branch near her home. Anything owed, Aki paid for without leaving a trail.

Even more disturbing: Kiya had no activity at all. Her cell, in fact, Kiya's ID, wallet, passport, everything was found in the house. Like she just vanished, a thought Megumi didn't want to dwell on.

Megumi sipped her coffee. She didn't smoke, but Noriko had regained the habit after quitting when pregnant with Kala. Megumi could use one, or a drink, right now. *I'm worried beyond words, we all are. Neither Kenji nor Hiro could shed any light on the Amida. Kenji surmised Kiya's disappearance is connected, and Aki's reaction could be fight or flight. She must be trying to find Kiya . . . and left to keep us out of it.*

She again cast her eyes on the walls of their office. Yoshida Management was Megumi's brainchild, started out of her bedroom when she assumed those duties. After graduation, Megumi officially formed the business; always her right hand, Noriko became a full partner. Using

contacts from their parents' empires, Megumi found the assistance needed to steer their friends and family in a solid financial direction while
letting them all create in their own ways.

None of this had anything to do with money, a matter Megumi reminded herself of often. *This is about us. We are a family, an extended,
eccentric, and at times dysfunctional one, but it's what we are. I did this
because I wanted to see my future husband and my friends do well; their
music was inspiring, and it came along at a time when the industry needed
something different.*

Megumi had her own motive, as well. She could have had any job
by virtue of her parents (as could Noriko), but Megumi resisted that. *I
started my own company because I did not want what I did not earn. Dad
was supportive, but Mom really wanted both of us in her restaurant business,
to take over for her. She had misgivings but got behind us when she saw how
determined Noriko and I were to work hard and make it happen . . .*

Megumi buzzed Erika and asked for a hold on her calls. Mika was
coming in for an appointment; time to find out what the little lunatic
had in mind for her upcoming club shows.

* * *

Aki remained seated, again before the windows. The sky finally
cleared, and sunlight shone through the blinds. The rays warmed her
nude skin, and Aki drew on that energy.

She had not slept. Aki did not call Megumi about the program; there
was nothing to say about it. There were more important things to do.

One of her notebooks lay on the floor beside her. Aki began to write
again in the night; thoughts of Kiya led her to look back once more to
the time they first met. *"I am searching deep . . . with-inside myself . . ."*

The two words were not meant to be a compound, but they struck
Aki, and so she wrote them out. *"These feelings I feel . . . they are not
fantasy . . . what then, are they?"*

Aki sang them again, in her lower range. It sounded like some of the
Lotus Flower work, slower, with more emphasis on the lyrics. When Aki
wrote, she often heard music; but since she didn't write or read it, she

would hum the idea to either Hiro or Kiya, and they would take it from there.

"What did you see in me . . . ?" The question on Aki's lips passed through; she stared through slitted eyes at the scribbled characters and wondered. She knew what she saw in Kiya and let that image fill her vision.

"What did you see in me . . . ?" Aki's voice remained lower, her "adult" voice, as she called it. This was for a woman, not a girl, to sing; nor was it a plea but a question, and Aki needed to sing this with some power. *"What made you reach for me . . ."*

Aki picked up a pen and scrawled another line under these. The verses were written in a matter of minutes, but now Aki meditated on them. This was the only really good thing she'd written in months—a sign. Perhaps this would bring her closer to Kiya, maybe even help bring her back . . . *bring her home.*

As she breathed in and out, Aki took notice of another sensation, one she'd either not noticed or ignored. When she entered the Amida, Aki could move a certain distance in the direction she needed to go, but again there was this same resistance.

Kiya-chan . . . the message did not change, and Aki hoped that if Kiya were out there, she could hear it. She'd replied before; that voice, either imagined or real, remained a sign to Aki that Kiya was still alive, somewhere out there, in time . . .

The envelope faded, then began to break up like a bad connection. *Something is pushing back against me,* Aki thought, *as if someone is actually interfering with my entrance to the Amida. I've never encountered this before.*

A knock, at first light, then repeated and with urgency, returned Aki to the room. Anger surged in her; she had left the "Do Not Disturb" sign out today. She rose, grabbed her robe, and hurried through the room. The staff never bothered her if the sign was posted, and she was about to give someone on the other side of that door a piece of her mind. That is, until she looked through the eyehole.

Aki gasped then hurriedly unlocked the door and chain. Pulling back the former, she faced the dark-haired woman who stood there.

"Nori-chan," Aki finally stammered, "what are you doing here? How did you—"

"It took a while," Noriko finished for her. "Can I come in?"

Aki stepped back. After closing and re-locking the door, Aki turned to her, and they stared at one another.

It felt like trying to speak to someone she hadn't seen in years. Noriko looked as good as ever, but her eyes were heavy from lack of sleep; Aki knew she was taking stock of her condition.

"I'll explain," Noriko finally said, "but Aki-chan . . ."

The two fell into one another's arms. Aki felt the embrace of her oldest friend; Noriko squeezed her hard, as if Aki might fly away.

"I'm so sorry," Aki said. She felt Noriko's body in her arms and ran her hand through the woman's thick hair, like Megumi used to do, and like Aki did with Kiya. "I'm surprised to see you," she added, "but I'm glad you're here."

Her head on Aki's shoulder, Noriko sucked in her breath and dug her long nails into Aki's robe. Aki didn't feel any pain; Noriko's body shuddered, and she was trying not to cry.

"I've missed you, Aki-chan," she whispered. "We all have."

"I know," Aki replied. "I've missed me, too."

* * *

"*She said I'm not asking you, she said I'm telling you, she said I meant what I said, better get it through your head . . .*"

James belted out the vocal while his fingers worked an upright bass; behind him, Suya locked in with a heavy backbeat. Headphones on, his face intense with concentration, Hiro ripped a blues lead out of his black Gretsch Streamliner.

The students from the day before had manhandled the old upright into the studio and were now behind the board. A quick glance, and Hiro could see they were loving it.

"*Well, that's what she said, but that's not what she said last night . . .*"
The second take was better than the first, and it broke down into a heavy lead riff, a flourish from the bass, a wash of cymbals, and one final heavy note. A long pause to let the sustain die down, and all looked at one other with satisfaction.

A thumbs-up came from the board op, and the three disengaged from their instruments. "That was great," the engineer called through the control room mic.

"Cool," Hiro called, "let's take five."

James and Suya nodded, and the latter joined Hiro outside. In the parking lot, the two smoked and discussed the day's work. "We can over-dub the backtalk part later," Hiro said, "and pull everyone into the studio to make that work. If James-san wants to redo the vocals again, that's fine, but I liked what he did there."

"Yeah," Suya agreed. "That Gretsch sounds really cool for this one."

Hiro took a drag and nodded. "Ever since I saw Zendo-san's axe, I wanted one," he admitted, "but that landed in my lap a month ago. Had to have it."

The pair laughed. "Glad Nori-chan doesn't give you shit about that."

"She's been great," Hiro replied, "but we do have to think about a bigger house. With Kala-chan growing up, we need the space."

"For her toys," Suya ribbed, "and Dad's."

They laughed again. "Well, Nori-chan wants a bigger home office, too," Hiro said. He continued, "This is coming along well, but one of our new ones will be tricky. I haven't practiced it enough."

"'Blues in the Night?'" Suya asked.

"Yeah."

"I wouldn't worry about it," Suya told him after an exhale. "You may want to overdub the vocals for that one since the changes are difficult."

"May have to," Hiro admitted, "but I'd rather not. Keep it raw as we can, y'know?" He checked his cell as he spoke and added when he saw the time, "I have to go soon . . ."

Hiro stopped speaking; he stared at his cell.

"What is it?" Suya asked.

"Hang on," he said, "text from Nori-chan. "'*CALL ME*,' all caps." Hiro pressed the phone icon below Noriko's number. A pause. "*Moshi-moshi*, Nori-chan, what's up? You did?"

Suya watched as Hiro walked away. From the short distance, Suya could hear Hiro's side of the conversation and knew he was talking to Aki.

He lit another Marlboro and leaned against the wall. The door opened and James stepped out. "Hold on," Suya said. "He's talking to Aki-chan."

James nodded. "'Track's ready," he replied, "but that's a sight more important."

8
Captain Ed

FOLLOWING A STRONG cup of coffee, Dale brought Kiya into the back room of the Black Dragon. Here, the narrow aisle was a crooked, twisted path, both sides piled high with boxes and other items stockpiled for uncounted purposes.

"Now," Dale said as they walked, "we'll get you fitted out. I'm pretty good at measurements by eye, so we should be able to find a kit that'll suit you."

Through a door into another room they went; in here, Kiya saw walls lined with clothes racks. "Yet another of my enterprises," he explained without having to note Kiya's curiosity. "We're our own Salvation Army back here."

He began to pass clothing into Kiya's arms. A couple of pairs of blue jeans, work shirts, t-shirts, a scarf, and a pair of fingerless gloves like the ones he wore. "Bathroom's over there," he said, motioning to a door partially hidden by the racks. "Try on some of that, and I'll see about footwear and a jacket."

Kiya went into the space, which had barely enough room for a sink and a toilet. The bathroom looked like it hadn't been cleaned in years, and Kiya didn't want to guess when the last time was. The walls appeared to have once been painted white but were now a dirty gray and covered with graffiti, most of it obscene. A poster of Superman hung on the wall above the sink, along with a Playboy centerfold strategically placed so as to be doing something of an intimate nature to the Man of Steel.

Kiya stripped but decided to keep her underwear at least. The jeans were a little big and meant for a man, but the belt Dale had tossed onto the pile made them fit. An old t-shirt and a flannel with the sleeves rolled up a turn worked, and the rest of the gear would do.

Carrying her uniform and shoes, Kiya stepped out and handed these over to Dale, who in turn passed her a pair of leather work boots. "Guessing your size."

Kiya sat on the floor and tried them on while Dale carefully hung the uniform on a hanger and examined it from all angles. "Yes," he said half to himself, "very nice." Then to Kiya, he added, "Something else for you here."

Dale passed her a black wool pea coat, much like his own. "Little long," he said, "but it'll keep you warm."

The boots fit, and the coat, while on the large size, was in good condition. As Kiya wrapped one of the scarves around her neck, Dale came up behind her and passed her a black wool cap. "The *pièce de résistance*," he declared.

Pulling her hair around to her shoulder, Kiya adjusted the brim of the cap and examined her new look in a wall mirror. Other than her hair, Kiya looked like a boy due to her height and thin build, but this outfit was more practical. The cap was a little floppy, but with the brim pulled low, Kiya liked the look.

"You can pass for a proper sailor," Dale said. "Now, here's another item." He handed her what looked like a long, sausage-shaped bag with a shoulder strap. "Everyone needs a grip," Dale told her. "Stow your extras in there." As Kiya did so he said, "I have a note to write. Come out front when you're ready."

Kiya packed her additional gear, folded up her old school bag, and placed that inside as well. Slinging it over her shoulder, she thought: *This is all so weird; I'm still a little scared, but Dale has helped me. I wonder though, what am I going to do now?*

She stepped out to the front, where Dale was at his desk. He handed Kiya a stack of bills. "As we agreed," he said. "Go ahead and count it; I'll not take offense."

Kiya counted. There were five twenties, as promised. She put these in her wallet and placed that in her pants pocket as Dale continued to write.

"I would assume you'll need a job and a place to bunk, at least temporarily," he went on, "and I think I can help you with both."

"I'm not exactly sure what you think I'm capable of doing," Kiya replied.

"Well," Dale asked with a chuckle, "what did you do before you landed here?"

Kiya knew she couldn't tell Dale the truth, at least not all of it. "I played piano and sang in a band with my, uh, boyfriend," she said. "Guess there's not much call for musicians around here."

"Not for making a living, I'm afraid." Dale signed the note, placed it in an envelope, and handed this to her as well. "I'll have Max take you down to the docks," he explained. "The *Ecorse* is still in port and, last I heard, Captain Ed needs some help."

"Captain Ed?" Kiya asked.

"Ed McCarthy." Dale turned, and his swivel chair creaked loudly as he leaned back in it. "He's the captain, and that's what everyone calls him. An old friend who owes me a favor, let's say. See him; if he doesn't have a spot for you on the *Ecorse*, he'll find you one."

"What kind of boat is this?" Kiya asked.

"I used to sail on her," Dale said. "The *Ecorse* is not exactly the *Edmund Fitzgerald*, mind, but it has a regular run on the Lakes. Small vessel, two hundred thirty-seven feet, give or take six inches. Works in close to a lot of the ports the big boats can't get into. Kind of like a floating delivery truck; her cargo is what's required at any given time. I was Second Mate when Ed signed on," he added. "You will like him. You'll have work and a place to sleep and call home until you're ready to move on. He might even let you stand watch on her in the off-season, which is even better."

"But I've never been on a boat before," Kiya admitted. "Are you sure he'd want to take a chance on me?"

Dale grinned. "Captain Ed will," he told her, "with that letter, of course; but turnover is pretty high. It's an old boat, and better pay and conditions are to be found once a man, or a woman, works their way up. But," he added as he stood, "he's the best man on the Lakes. Stay with him—he won't steer you wrong."

"I don't know how to thank you, Dale," Kiya told him as they went to the door. "You probably saved me from getting hurt back there, and now all this. I'll never forget you."

"Well, do us the favor of dropping by and saying hello when you're in port," Dale said with a smile. "I have a good feeling about you, Kiya, and I think you'll make out okay." Turning toward the back, he shouted, "Max! Get your coat on. I've got a job for you."

As Max came out of the back area, Dale and Kiya shook hands. "Good luck," he said, "and don't worry. Captain Ed will look after you."

Dale stood outside the door and waved as Kiya and Max walked up the street. Stepping back inside, he said hello to a couple of the regular customers and made sure the new shipment of comics was in the right spot on the wall. The radio, now changed to the AM band, keened on, a Who song above the din of the busy store.

The walk to the docks was a short one. Despite his size, Max was a confident companion. He couldn't have been more than fourteen, but he dressed like Dale and the others and walked with a street-smart attitude. Lighting a cigarette as they walked, he said, "Dale's a good guy. He's done stuff like this before, for all of us."

"Really?"

Max took a puff. "Yeah. Since he had to leave the boats 'cause he got hurt, Dale opened up that shop and it's been kind of the home away from home for dead-end kids like me.

"See, my dad's gone," Max explained. "He took off when I was three, but don't feel sorry for me; I don't remember him. My mom, she was doing her best, but she drank too much. Was pretty bad being around that, never knowing which one of her was gonna show up. Mom, or the other one that drinks, understand?"

"Yeah."

"So anyway, a couple years ago I came home from school and Mom went crazy. Hit me in the face with a whiskey bottle. You can see the scar here," he added and pointed to a jagged line under his left eye.

Kiya was about to say how bad it looked, but before she could, Max went on, "I went into the store the next day; Dale took one look at me and got me outta there. Let me sleep in the back of the store for a while, gave me a job, kept me going to school. Mom's okay now; she's quit drinking, but I owe Dale. I'm gonna work for him till I'm old enough to sail. This way now."

Max pointed to a street that led to a docking complex, and they turned down it. "Like I say, Dale's a great guy. He's kept us out of trouble, and in some cases alive. Still," Max said, "what he did for you he doesn't just do for everyone. He saw you in trouble like we've been one time or another, but I think he does like you."

They stopped at the edge of the docks. Down along the waterway, the life of the shipping industry played out before them. Two vessels were tied up here, both being loaded by work cranes and attended to by the crews and dockworkers.

"The one on the end is the *Ecorse*," Max told Kiya. "Just go up and say you wanna see Cap'n Ed and give him the letter. You'll be okay from there."

The boat in question looked like a small oil tanker with the bridge at the aft end. From the rusted, scarred hull, Kiya could tell why people left her; she looked very old and like she had been through more than her share of the business.

Kiya took a deep breath. "Okay. Thanks, Max," she said as she offered her hand. "And tell Dale I mean it; I won't forget him."

The kid grinned. "No problem, Kiya. Good luck." With a quick handshake, Max then turned on his heel and walked away, lighting another smoke as he went. Kiya smiled as she walked down the long dock and threaded her way past the workers, stevedores, and forklifts. On a shipping crate, Neil Diamond keened through a transistor radio turned to maximum volume, a song about a solitary man.

In a strange time, and for her a stranger land, Kiya felt fortunate to have found some of the good people. They were much like those in the time where she belonged and so wanted to be.

Kiya climbed the wooden gangplank to the starboard side of the *Ecorse*'s main deck. A man in a dirty, dark-blue coverall leaned against the rail and watched as a crane lowered a huge pallet of cargo above one of the hatches. Deckhands were carefully turning and guiding it down into the vessel's hold.

Hearing Kiya's footsteps on the gangplank, the man turned and looked her way. He was in his fifties, Kiya estimated, short and overweight. A greasy Tigers baseball cap mostly hid what silver hair he had. He was three days overdue for a shave and looked like he hadn't slept in twice as long.

"Whacha want, uh, miss?" He had realized just in time that a young—and very different-looking—woman was before him.

"Looking for Captain Ed," Kiya replied. She tried to make her voice businesslike, as when she'd cut her deal with Dale.

"Yeah?" The voice was doubtful. "Who sent you?"

"Dale McLeod."

At the mention of Dale's name, the man's eyebrows shot up, and his demeanor changed. "McLeod? Hell, there's a name I haven't heard in a while. So, he set you up, did he?"

"Sure did," Kiya replied. She easily re-adopted the American style of speech, keeping her sentences short and to the point.

The man motioned with his thumb. "Come with me," he said. As they walked aft, Kiya got the sense the boat was much larger than it seemed. She watched as the loading continued and the deckhands secured a series of wooden covers over the hatches.

"Been on the *Ecorse* eight years," the man said as they went. "McLeod was here when I signed on, but he wrecked his back and had to quit. Damn good man; how is he doing?"

"He's fine," Kiya told him. "Got his various businesses going, I guess."

"Yeah, sounds like him. McLeod always had a line on something to make money, and he was usually right. By the way," he said, "Mike Lonegan's the name. I'm chief engineer."

Kiya gave her name and the two shook hands. She then followed Mike up a set of ladder-like metal steps to the wheelhouse. Sliding open the door, Mike announced, "Captain, got someone here to see you."

The man standing next to the wheel turned. Kiya had been expecting to see a man around Mike's age but was surprised when the fellow that turned to face her didn't look much older than she was.

He was in his middle or late twenties, tall and broad-shouldered, and dressed in a heavy coat. An officer's cap was pushed back on his head, which revealed locks of blond-brown hair. He had blue eyes and a square jaw, and while a formidable-looking person, Kiya sensed kindness in his face, especially when he smiled.

"Ed McCarthy," he said as he walked over and offered his hand. "And you would be?"

"Kiya Takahashi," she replied and shook his hand. "Dale McLeod sent me," she added and handed him the envelope.

"Well, well," McCarthy chuckled, and Mike did as well. "So, McLeod's sent us another one," he said. "I do wish he was still out here." McCarthy opened the letter and skimmed through it, nodded to himself, then replaced it in the envelope. "Okay," he addressed Kiya as he put the document in his coat pocket, "know anything about the Lakes? Sailing in general?"

"No, sir," Kiya replied, "but I'll learn."

McCarthy grinned. "No need to call me sir," he told her. "If I may call you Kiya, you can call me Ed, or Captain Ed as most do. We're informal here, unless things get official, if you understand what I mean."

Kiya nodded.

"Okay," Ed went on, "I'm not shipping any hands right now, but I do have a spot. Don't take this the wrong way, but I need a cook. Think you can handle feeding eighteen guys, plus you, three squares a day?"

"I think so," Kiya said. "Depends on what kind of food you want."

"Doesn't have to be fancy," Ed told her, "just good and lots of it. Only order I have for the cook is that coffee be on at all times."

"The lifeblood," Kiya said with a laugh.

"You got it," Ed replied. "Mike, keep an eye on the loading, will you? I'm taking our new cook down to see George."

They went through the back of the wheelhouse, the chart room, and down another flight of steps to the inside of the vessel. The corridor ran across the whole deck, and Kiya followed Ed down to a sliding door. They could hear music, Motown, coming from the other side.

"Galley's here," Ed explained, "dining room's right across. And that," he added as he pointed to the round window, "is George."

Kiya peered through the glass. The galley had a large table running the center of the room, with the washing sinks on the left and the stove on the other side. That was rather less interesting than the man who was dancing around the table, grooving to Martha Reeves and the Vandellas.

George was very short, just above five feet in height with a stocky build and curly black hair. His white shirt, pants, and apron were discolored by grease and whatever else, and he had a deep five o'clock shadow.

Kiya chuckled. "So, that's my assistant?"

"Yep, but not to worry," Ed replied, "he's a good one." He slid the door back, and George turned in the middle of his dance to find his captain and a strange girl watching him.

"Damn!" George reached up and turned down the radio sitting above the stove. "Sorry, boss," he said as his face turned a deep shade of red, "got carried away."

Both Ed and Kiya laughed. "Don't worry about it," the captain said. "Anyway, Kiya, this is George DiCicco," he introduced, then, pointing back at Kiya, "your new cook."

"Hey, good to meet ya," George replied with a decidedly New York accent, and he wiped his hand on his apron before shaking hers.

"Nice to meet you, too," Kiya said.

"Well, I'll leave you to George," Ed told her. "He'll show you to your quarters and the ropes. I'll have papers for you to sign later. We sail at 0600. Welcome aboard."

The door slid shut. "Well," George said, "by the look of it, you're new to all this, aren't you?"

"Yeah," Kiya replied, "I'll need your help for the first few days until I can figure out how all this will go."

"No worries," he said, and then added in Italian, *"I'll make it go smooth."*

Kiya smiled. *"Then we'll get along just fine, George."*

George's jaw dropped. "Holy shit! You speak Italian! I love you already! Come on, let's get your gear stowed and get you started."

As they went through the kitchen and into another cramped corridor, Kiya thought she was now in at least a safe place. *It feels like a whole new life is opening before me. I know where I need to be, but for now, I think I'll be all right.*

9

Direction

NORIKO LOOKED ABOUT the suite as she drank her second cup of coffee. This hotel room had indeed been Aki's home for months. There was a suitcase inside the open closet, clothes Noriko recognized hanging there, along with some others. While the room looked clean enough, there was a chaos Aki normally would not have permitted.

As she sat across from her quarry, Noriko also saw a person she barely recognized, a withdrawn, wounded creature. *She looks ill; Aki's lost weight, and she's hurting; I still don't know what happened to Kiya, but if there's a chance to get her back, Aki will take it.*

"Are you going to tell me how you found me?" Aki asked. She smiled slightly, a glint in her eye that reminded Noriko of happier times. She was about to say it reminded her of the way she and Kiya used to interact, but she stopped herself.

"Wasn't too difficult," Noriko explained, "once I figured out that sign in the cellphone picture. Soon as I got that, I knew you were in Kyoto, and you had to be here. This is your favorite hotel in the city; so, on occasion, your dumb managers can put two and two together."

The women laughed as Aki poured herself another cup. "I never intimated any such thing," she retorted, "and your detective work and intuition combined to track me down. Well done."

"I suppose," Noriko replied. "Now that I've found you, I thought it might be time to ask what you've been up to."

"A lot, and not much," Aki admitted. "I know that doesn't make any sense. I have written a lot of lyrics." She indicated the stack of notebooks on the table.

"Mind if I look?" Noriko asked.

Aki nodded. "Go ahead. The top one is the most recent. Some of it I think is good. I've also meditated a great deal—and searched."

Noriko reached for the notebook as Aki said this. "For Kiya-chan?"

"Yes," Aki replied as Noriko opened the first book and scanned the handwritten pages. The book was typical of Aki's style of writing: lines scribbled, here and there a word crossed out, a correction with a different-colored pen. Then some blank pages and another set of lines and thoughts. "Any luck?"

Aki sighed and put her cup down. "None," she said at length, and she rose to walk over to the windows. "There has been a disruption in the Amida," Aki explained, "which I have never before encountered. I can no longer penetrate the space between the present and past."

"The tesseract, right?" Since Noriko's and Megumi's marriages, they were aware of the power Aki possessed. This confirmed what Noriko long ago sensed about Aki, and she got the concept.

"Yes. Look at that book," Aki said, motioning to the one separate from the stack. "That's Kiya-chan's interpretation."

Noriko dragged the thin volume across the table. Through her reading glasses, Noriko scanned the pages and the notes Kiya had made. "Okay," she assessed, "I understand this, to a point. So, what you are saying is, something inside of this was disrupted, and Kiya was lost in it?"

Aki nodded and continued to stare out the window. "That is my conclusion," she replied. "I have to figure out what is stopping me from moving into the Amida before I can get to Kiya-chan."

"Look, this is a hard question for me to ask," Noriko said as she turned to watch how Aki would react, "but do you believe that Kiya-chan is still alive?"

Aki stared at her reflection in the window, then turned to Noriko. "Yes." Aki's answer was a firm one. "I do, but I admit with every passing day I feel the chances of getting her back diminishing."

She wrapped the folds of her robe about herself and again looked out the window. "I believe, or I want to believe," she said, "that on occasion, I hear her. I want to believe that it is Kiya-chan, hearing me and trying to answer me."

Noriko got up and joined Aki at the window. "Let me get this straight: you have been able to travel before, but now you can't?"

"That's right. I have sensed a presence," Aki said as they returned to the couch, "there is something, or perhaps someone, that is stopping me from entering. I normally can put myself into the time and place I wish to be. Kiya-chan and I did this months ago—you know about that."

"Yeah." Noriko thought for a moment, then replied, "You say this never happened until then. Is it possible you're losing the power, that the Amida is weakening for whatever reason?"

Aki shook her head. "I don't think so," she replied. "I have not traveled since that day. It is true, too much travel in a short time is a strain on my body, but that could not be it," she stressed, "not at that moment."

"What is this presence?" Noriko asked. "Is it a person, a thing?"

"It is a feeling." Aki got up again and slowly paced the room. "I cannot put a name or a face to it," she went on, her voice now fearful, "but there is something there. Something is keeping Kiya-chan and me apart."

Aki threw up her hands. "Why," she said, "I don't know. The thing that I must know is how this has happened to Kiya-chan; only then can I bring her back."

She sat again. "Nori-chan," Aki continued with greater agitation, "you have to understand. That is all I care about. I have to find Kiya-chan and bring her home. She is my responsibility." Aki sighed, and she clasped her hands together; Noriko watched her friend's nails claw at the opposing hands.

"It is so frustrating," Aki went on, and her voice betrayed the emotion. "My life and my career are on hold until I find out. I don't care about that for myself, but I realize that's hard on everyone else—but I have to do this."

"It's not hard on any of us," Noriko told her. "Don't even think that." Noriko moved over and took Aki's hands. "For those of us in the know," she said, "we know Kiya-chan means everything to you, and that can't be overstated."

"I lost her, Nori-chan," Aki whispered, as she rested her head on her sister-in-law's shoulder. "It's my fault. Kiya trusted me, and I broke that trust. I always told her everything would be okay, but I was wrong. I took it for granted that we'd get back, like all the other times."

Noriko stroked Aki's hair with her hand as she held her. "It's okay," she said. "I know what you're saying. I'm here to help you."

Noriko felt Aki mold her body into her own. "I know," she replied. "You have done this before," she went on.

"How's that?"

"You were there," Aki said, "the day we learned Mom and Dad died. You comforted me then; when Kazu-san died, you did the same for Hiro-kun."

Noriko smiled. "It's what a friend does," she replied. "You are my bestie, Aki-chan; it has nothing to do with my job. It's what we've been all our lives."

"That is so." Aki lowered her head and said, "I'm sorry, Nori-chan; if ever you felt left out after I met Kiya-chan. That was not the intent."

"Not at all." Noriko lifted Aki's face so their eyes could meet again. "I was with Hiro-kun," she said, "and we were together. I never stopped loving you as I do."

"And I love you, Nori-chan; and thank you." Aki rested against Noriko and added, "The last person to hold me was Kiya-chan; I've needed that."

It's cool." Noriko kissed Aki's forehead. "As long as you need me, I'm here."

"Arigato. It still does not solve this issue with Kiya-chan," Aki went on. "As I say, the changes in the Amida I cannot account for."

"Did you do anything differently, Aki-chan?" Noriko asked. "Is there a routine? Did anything about that change?"

"No," Aki replied immediately, "there is nothing that I can think of."

"Okay," Noriko said, "then it's not your fault. Either there was a disruption in the Amida that could be explained, or someone did it deliberately." Noriko continued quietly, "If you'd never encountered such a thing before, ever, and it's happening whenever you try to travel now, it would stand to reason there is another force involved here. Someone must be doing it."

"But why?" Aki asked. "The Amida provides an ability to travel," she said, "but it serves as a means of insight, a form of self-education. It helps you see things in a different light." Aki pulled away from Noriko to sit up straight, and she rubbed her eyes. "I'm sorry," she said, "I'm so tired."

Noriko seized Aki's hands again; she was not about to let Aki stop, not at this point. "Could it be a power grab?" she asked.

Aki was about to pull away, but she didn't. "How do you mean?"

Noriko looked. Aki's eyes were heavy, red, and the lines around these, unobscured by makeup, showed the strain not of a young woman but an older one.

"Is the ability you possess something that another would want?" Noriko asked. "To increase their own, or to gain power over others?"

Aki sat in silence, stunned at the question. "I never thought about it like that," she replied. "I've never heard of anyone doing such a thing." Aki added, "It's not supposed to work that way."

"But somebody who has the Amida already," Noriko posed, "could they be trying to steal yours, and use it for their own ends? Could that be done?"

Aki rose and walked toward the window like she was trying to follow Noriko's idea. "You may be right," she said. "Someone must be doing it, but who? I have not met anyone with the Amida who is still alive, at least knowingly. It is not something spoken of; you merely know. I don't know who it could be."

"Since we're talking about energies, it would seem to me that who-ever is doing this must be close." Noriko poured herself another cup of coffee. "Otherwise," she said, "that person might not have as much success in keeping you out of the Amida. Has there been anyone strange around you, anybody you keep seeing? Do you see or visualize someone when you try to travel?"

She turned. Aki was staring at her, but before she could reply Noriko went on, "Look, I want to help you find Kiya-chan. I don't have your ability, and from the look of you, you have exhausted yourself and your options. You have been butting your head against that wall for months, Aki-chan—you need a new tack."

"I do," Aki agreed. "I kept thinking if I did what I knew to do that I could get there," she explained, "and get back to the place where it occurred. I've tried to find Kiya-chan, by sending messages, letting my instinct guide me."

"Have you noticed any irregulars around here?" Noriko asked. "People on the street, guests in the hotel, that kind of thing?"

Aki shook her head. "No," she said, "and I would have noticed. Anyway, this feels more like something that's invisible."

She went toward the bathroom. "I feel the need to go out," Aki said, "and I gather you would like to as well. Staying in here all day wouldn't be fun, would it?"

Noriko chuckled as she followed Aki to the door. "I think getting some real food into you is the first order of business; forgive me, but you look and behave like you've been living on caffeine and not much else."

"Oh, I do eat on occasion," Aki replied, her laugh a sardonic one. "This must all sound completely messed up," Aki continued as she brushed out her hair. "Megumi-san, even knowing of the Amida as she does, would think I've gone mad."

"You're not mad," Noriko told her, "you're in love."

"Hm?" Aki looked over.

"Your love for Kiya-chan," Noriko said as she entered the bathroom and stood beside Aki. "It's been there since the first day Hiro-kun and I saw the two of you together. We knew you were meant to be, to share your lives. You've done that; you all made music together, became known, even famous."

Aki kept working on her hair. "I didn't want that," she admitted. "But Hiro-kun dreamed of it, and we loved the music—I still do. Kiya-chan and I became so many things to different people; we made music they could turn to, we served as role models, idols, even. Kiya-chan handled being popular and known better than I did, but she made it easy for me to adapt. The only thing," she finished, "was that we made each other first in our lives. I needed that more than anything; Kiya-chan's love, and knowing we'd give ourselves to one another, no matter what."

"And now this has happened," Noriko replied. "You are doing exactly what anyone else would do to find the person they loved and needed the most."

Aki thought about that as she stared at her and Noriko's images in the mirror. Megumi's adopted younger sister had grown into a confident, poised, and sexy woman. It would have made Aki smile but for her thin, even haggard face. *I was once like her . . .*

She dismissed the thought. "Yes," Aki replied. "I can't stop until I find Kiya-chan. Until then, there is nothing else."

* * *

"*Kore wa, Satodesu—Konnichiwa.*"

Seated in his office, Kenji surveyed the stack of legal documents before him and the set of work orders and contracts beside them. Both were neatly stacked, but each had a daunting thickness to them.

The answer on the other end made him sit up straight. "Hiro-kun, you spoke with Aki-chan? How did she sound?"

Hiro's reply was distant due to his hands-free unit, and his cell cut in and out. Added to it, Hiro was listening to music as he zoomed about the city in his 350Z. "She said she was okay," Kenji heard him say, "but Aki-chan sounded beat. My guess is she's been trying to find Kiya-chan, and it's worn her out."

"At least now we know where she is," Kenji replied. "The last several months haven't been good to her by the sound of it, and I can understand her reasons."

"I just hope Nori-chan can convince her to come home," Hiro replied. "I think she needs to be around us again."

"I hear that," Kenji said, "but she's going to remain focused. We know how close she and Kiya-chan were. If there's even the slimmest of possibilities she can be found, Aki-chan will explore them."

Kenji stood up. Switching the receiver from one hand to the other as he pulled on his suit jacket he said, "I have to meet with Mr. Ito in a few minutes, but thanks for letting me know about Aki-chan. If you hear any more, call me."

Hiro promised to do so, and Kenji hung up the phone. He adjusted his tie, picked up a leather-bound planner, and checked to see that he had his cell with him. He told the secretary in the outer office where he would be and stepped into the marble-tiled hall that separated the estate's offices from Mr. Ito's private residence.

His shoes echoed as they clicked on the floor. While there were a number of more immediate arrangements to deal with, Kenji would not let his concern for Aki out of his mind. He didn't have to guess what Aki was doing all this time.

Kenji reflected on the past six years of their lives, including the day Taru brought him and his siblings down this very hall, to meet Mr. Ito. He thought of the accomplishments Aki, Hiro and their friends had achieved in such a short time. Then, of his marriage to Megumi, that of Hiro and Noriko, their children, and yes, Aki and Kiya.

In the difficult times, Kenji drew on his strength, mostly the quiet, inner power he inherited from his parents. Yet now, he felt helpless to do anything for Aki. *She will always be* Imouto, *my little sister to me,* he thought. *All we can do is wait for her—Aki would die for Kiya if necessary; I just hope it doesn't come to that, out there in the Amida.*

Kenji reached the double doors that led to Mr. Ito's office. Before knocking, he said a silent prayer for his sister, and for Kiya.

10

Resolution

KIYA PLACED HER coffee cup on the galley table, pulled one of the metal stools from beneath it, and sat down. She rested her head in her arms, and her body rocked to the up-and-down pitch of the *Ecorse* as it crossed Lake St. Clair. The radio above the stove was on low, and George Harrison sang about a floor that needed sweeping.

They'd been on the water hardly a day, but the activity from the time Kiya came aboard was a whirlwind. The new job was a bigger challenge than she envisioned. *I thought cooking for the band was a task, but this is something else.*

The sheer amount of food that needed to be prepared meant being on the go from the beginning. Kiya had been on her feet all day and then a good part of the night to get ready for tomorrow's meals. In between, there was the constant cleaning and keeping the huge coffee urn filled and brewing.

Without George, Kiya would never have made it. He was energetic, answered her questions, and helped in every way. He also did nearly all the serving, so Kiya didn't have to try and make her way through the door, step over the coaming, and then repeat that process to get into the dining room; and all on a pitching, rolling vessel.

She'd seen vague images of the crew, many of them young men who looked fresh out of high school. Then there were a few old-timers like Mike. She had not seen Ed, but Kiya assumed that he'd spend most of his time on the bridge when the *Ecorse* was out.

The door slid back, and the man himself entered. "Hi," he greeted Kiya. "So, how'd your first day, or should I say night, go?"

Kiya lifted her head and smiled. "Okay, I guess," she told him. Noting Ed was carrying a coffee cup, she rose and said, "I've got a pot here. Let me get that."

"Thanks." Ed pulled out another stool and sat across from her. Removing his cap and brown leather gloves, he set them beside himself and ran his hand through his hair.

Kiya poured and set the cup before him without spilling a drop. "No seasickness," she told him, "and George is a dear. He's helped me all the way."

"That's George," Ed said as he sipped the hot brew. "I wanted to give the cook my compliments; your food is superb. I've also heard a lot of good words from the others. Thought you should know."

Kiya smiled as she sat back down. "Thanks, glad to hear it." She turned up the sleeves of her flannel shirt again and added, "It used to be, we'd cook for the band, and I became accustomed to taking care of lots of people. This is a little larger number," she admitted, "but I'm getting the hang of it."

Ed nodded. "You were in a band?"

Kiya wasn't sure how much to divulge, but she'd let that detail slip. "Yeah," she casually replied, "my boyfriend and I were in one over in Japan. There were six of us, and then the attending girlfriends, road crew, and others. We ate together, partied together, did everything together, really."

"What did you do? I mean, what kind of music?" Ed seemed genuinely interested.

Kiya shrugged. "Musically, nothing you'd probably recognize," she replied. "We all had different influences. I played piano and sang a little. We never got famous or anything like that, but we had a good time."

"So, this boyfriend," Ed asked, "where is he—oh, maybe I shouldn't ask, I'm sorry." Ed had detected the change in Kiya's expression; she had to be careful not to drop any more clues.

"No, it's okay." Kiya took a deep breath and clasped her hands around her cup. "His name is Akira," she explained. "He's not just my boyfriend, though; he's my soulmate and my closest friend. The band broke up last year; I came over here because I'm half-American, on my father's side. Akira is going to follow me."

"I see. So, I assume you'll get married one of these days?"

"He's already asked me," Kiya replied as she sipped her drink. "We didn't announce it formally, there's no date set."

Kiya hoped that Ed had not picked up on her lie about Aki. Akira was generally a boy's name, as opposed to Aki's given name, Akiko.

She needed to change the subject. "How about you?" Kiya asked. "I see a ring," she added and pointed to the gold band around his fourth finger.

Ed grinned. Reaching into his coat pocket, he withdrew his wallet and took out a snapshot, worn at the edges by much handling.

Taking the photo in the flat of her hand, Kiya saw an image of Ed in his sailing uniform and a dark-haired woman in a military one. "She's lovely," Kiya said, "and she's in the Army?"

"Her name's Patti," Ed told her as he received the picture again. "She's a nurse. We've been married three years; we met while she was going to school near Detroit, and she entered the Army Medical Corps." Ed paused. "She's in Vietnam now."

Kiya's eyes widened. "Really?" Kiya was suddenly aware that the war was going on at this time; she knew well enough about it from school and from discussions her father and his former colleagues had about it. "What is she doing over there?"

"Well, they needed nurses," Ed explained, "and Patti specialized in critical care. She's in a medical unit; they operate very close to the front line. Their job is to save the wounded as they're coming off of it. Battalion Aid is usually the first stop, and then it's to hers."

There was a silence. "I can only imagine how dangerous that is," Kiya said.

Ed stared at his cup. "Yeah. This job has its own dangers, too," he replied, "but nothing compared to what she's written me about. Patti tries to write regularly but doesn't always have time, then there's the mail service. What little she tells me is enough to know that war is a thing I don't want to ever have to deal with."

Kiya nodded. "So, we both miss someone," she said, "don't we?"

Ed smiled sadly. "Guess so. The way you spoke just now, I can tell Akira means the world to you. Patti means the same to me."

Kiya nodded. "Yes. I wait for the day I'll see him again. I just have to be patient and do the best I can until then."

"Same here." Ed stood up and put on his cap. "Would you kindly refill me, please? I must get back to the bridge."

"Of course." Kiya turned and picked up the pot. As she filled the cup, Ed pulled on his gloves and said, "Thanks, Kiya. Hey, if you get time, come on up. You ought to see the lake this time of night. It's a lovely sight."

Kiya smiled. "Perhaps I will," she replied. "Of course, feeding all you guys is my priority right now."

Ed chuckled as he passed through the door. "And you do it well," he said, "steady as she goes."

The door slid closed. Kiya topped off her cup before placing the pot on its burner and adjusted the metal rods, known as fiddles, to keep it from sliding with the motion of the boat. There wasn't going to be much time for sleep, she thought as she sat down again. She reached up and retied the red bandanna around her head, which kept her long hair behind her.

She liked Ed; Kiya guessed by his manner, and the respect accorded him by senior colleagues such as Mike and the younger men, that he was a good captain. Kiya also believed that what Ed shared about his wife was not something he would do with just anyone. She realized she was not alone in her feelings for Aki; Ed felt the same way about Patti.

We miss our lovers as much as the other, she thought. *As sad as that is, it's good to know he understands. He seems, like Dale, to understand a lot more than either one lets on.*

The radio segued to another song as Kiya got up. Taking a broom from the corner, she swept the floor in anticipation of the next meal, as Bob Dylan asked questions and wondered where to find the answer . . .

* * *

A lone overhead light illuminated the booth as James rolled back the tape. Suya knelt beside him as the two mixed the rough track they and Hiro laid down before the latter left to pick up Kala.

"This needs more," Suya suggested. "Second guitar, you know? Doing the rhythm while Hiro-kun does that hammer-on thing."

"Yeah." James thought about it further as he restarted the track. "I'm thinking something more as well; listen to this part."

The track was a slow blues with minimal percussion and bass. Hiro's rhythm included a choppy hammer-on technique on certain strings: *"It's another night, on the razor line, you step to the edge, see the other side . . ."*

"Right there," James said over the backing track's volume, "I'm hearing piano. You know, almost like jazz piano, down in there."

"Yeah," Suya replied after considering that. "I hear a Strat for the rhythm," he suggested, "while Hiro-kun does lead. That was only a scratch track; he'll want to do it again, anyway."

James stopped the tape and leaned back. "That's good," he said. "I know who to get to play on it, seeing as how you-know-who isn't available. I wonder how Hiro-kun will be on that."

"All you can do is ask," Suya said as he rose. "Anyway, I'm gonna head home. Mika-chan's probably wondering what I'm up to."

James chuckled as he pulled his suit jacket off the back of the chair. "What's she doing now? More performance art?"

"We have some new songs, plus the other stuff she was doing before," Suya explained. "I know most of it, so playing is no problem. She was supposed to see Megumi-san today about the idea and try to get some more shows booked."

"Without the riots, I assume," James added.

Both laughed, but it hadn't been funny at the time. James spun the tape off the reel and carefully placed it in its box while Suya normalized and shut down the board and the computer. "Tomorrow then?" the former asked.

"Yep," Suya replied. "So, you're thinking about Ri-san to do the piano?"

"Bingo," James said as they walked out the side door. They made sure the locking bar caught, then James continued, "She teaches here, and Ri-san can play anything, though I wonder if Hiro-kun will be able to stay with *her*."

Suya laughed as they walked across the lot to their cars. Having graduated from the conservatory himself, Suya knew the woman in question. "That," he declared, "will be fun."

* * *

"Asahi, with a glass," Noriko ordered as she scanned the menu.

"A pot of green tea, please," Aki said to the waitress. Once alone, the two scanned the menus in the corner booth of a restaurant near the hotel. "This is on me," Noriko said, "so order something food-like, okay?"

"I aim to," Aki said with a laugh, "and thanks for finding me, Nori-chan. I suppose I needed it."

"We all did," Noriko said, and she put her menu aside. "Life goes on, you know, but without you, it's a little sad. Kala-chan really misses you."

Aki smiled. "I'm sorry I've not been there for her, and Akito-kun. So, Kala-chan asks for me?"

"Often," Noriko said. "She wonders where Oba-Aki went off to. She's the same way about Kiya-chan as well."

"I hope to have an answer for her," Aki replied. "I believe you have given me the insight I wished for a long time ago."

"In what way?"

"I think," Aki said, "I am going to need to seek some help in this matter. But first, it's time to go home."

"Home?" Noriko asked. "You mean, home-home?"

"Yes," Aki replied as the waitress returned with their drinks. Serving these, the waitress then took the meal order.

"It's time to go back to the source," Aki continued after they were alone again. "Home is where Kiya-chan and I made it; I couldn't handle being there without her, that's why I fled. But," Aki went on, "it will be more familiar. I'll be around all of you again, and there is a place I must go as well."

Noriko took a long drink of her beer and poured the rest of the bottle into her glass as she listened. Noting Aki's expression, she said, "You are resolved. You sound a little better than you did a short time ago."

"You opened a door for me, Nori-chan," Aki replied. "I'll pack and check out when we get back; where is your car?"

"Left it at the train station," Noriko said, "but I'll ride back with you."

"I'll drop you off there, then. There is," Aki said, a determination in her voice not heard in too long, "one place, that he, she, or it cannot keep me from going. It is there I may find what I need."

Noriko looked to Aki in curiosity. "What place is that?"

"The Summerland."

Across the street from the restaurant, a man stood on the corner. He was out of the line of sight of anyone who might have casually glanced out the windows of the establishment.

Dressed all in black in a long leather coat, he did attract some attention from those on the street. So much else about him was neutral, however, and only the most perceptive would have taken more careful notice of him.

As he fingered the silver crucifix that hung about his neck, the man stared at the building and smiled a thin smile that had no trace of humor, nor for that matter, any other emotion.

11

Confrontation

FROM AKITO'S PERSPECTIVE, his mother was in a much better mood than he'd seen her in some time. Seated in his usual spot before her on the office couch, he had learned to gauge Megumi's level of stress.

At home, and elsewhere, Akito noted how Megumi shifted gears. She reminded him a lot of his grandmother; always on the job, remembered people's names, talked correctly, and recalled even the tiniest details.

Akito now watched and listened to Megumi speak on the phone. Based on the conversation Akito walked in on, it sounded like Noriko had located Aki; perhaps she would now come back home.

Akito naturally wondered if Kiya was coming, too, but he guessed not. *Mom and Dad have kept it quiet,* he said to himself, *but we know what's going on. Oba-Aki's got some sort of power to go places; kind of like what the people in that anime Kala-chan likes can do. But it's all a big secret.*

I don't know how it works, but it's gone wrong, and Oba-Kiya is in trouble. Everyone's afraid for her, and I am, too. What is sad, as Dad said, is there's nothing we can do about it.

Megumi hung up, and there was a big smile on her face, which her son reciprocated. "That was your aunt," she said, "and another one's coming home."

"That's good news," Akito replied and slid his feet to the floor as he saw his mother picking up her own bag and jacket.

"Yes. It's about time."

"Is Oba-Kiya coming, too?" he asked.

Megumi's face fell; Akito quickly went to her and nodded. "I'm sorry," he said, "I shouldn't have asked that."

"No, it's okay," she replied, and she ran her hand through his hair. "I was hoping that, too. But not yet; at least Oba-Aki's coming back. She's going one step at a time," Megumi added as they left the office. "The steps for Oba-Kiya come after that. We have to be there for her, you know?"

Akito nodded. "I do." *More than you know, Mom.*

* * *

Aki and Noriko stepped into the street. "I have to get a few things together," Aki said as they walked. "I don't feel ready to do music again, at least publicly, without Kiya-chan; but I do want to start beating some of the lyrics I have into a workable form. When she returns, I'll have something to show her."

"What I read up there was interesting," Noriko replied. "That song about stars had some good lines to it, and I like the one about seeing."

"That one feels good to me," Aki said, "but it has a long way to go."

Noriko was watching Aki. Hands in her pockets, head down, Aki looked in thought, but over her shades, Aki scanned the block. Her eyes swept each pedestrian, car, and bike. Aki felt she was entering the Amida, but no, that feeling, coupled with the one of months past . . .

Aki slowed her pace as they approached the corner. "Don't look around," she said quietly. "Across the street . . . he's here."

"Who?" Noriko asked. She stared forward but let her peripheral vision work behind her shades.

"There's a man in a black coat like mine," Aki said. "It's *him*."

He was leaning against the wall and looked to be waiting for the bus or someone else. Like Aki, he dressed in black: black boots, pants, a collared shirt, and a long leather trench coat. His hair was black and cut short; his face was of a mixed background, Japanese and possibly Chinese. Sunglasses obscured his eyes, but Aki could guess what was behind them.

"What do we do?" Noriko asked as the lights changed and they crossed.

"Let's find out what he wants," Aki said.

Noriko slowly inhaled. "Do you know what you're doing?"

"No," Aki admitted, "but if he has anything to do with Kiya-chan's disappearance, I'm going to find out."

As they reached the curb, Aki suddenly turned and ran down the street at the man. He'd been looking right at them as they crossed. When he saw Aki turn, he broke into a run in the opposite direction.

Aki tore after him and left Noriko in her wake. The target handily dodged fellow pedestrians; though older, he had good speed. Aki saw him make a right turn about a block ahead. Running into the street, Aki paid no heed to where the cars were, found the turn, and made it.

The alley was shaded from the sun by the closeness of the two buildings and a third at the end. The usual garbage, cans, and dumpsters were along the sides, but the man was nowhere in sight.

Aki removed her shades and scanned the alley. She couldn't see him, but he had to be here. She moved forward slowly, one step at a time, looking in each direction, as well as up.

"I'm over here."

Aki whirled and found the man standing behind her. About four meters separated them; she was boxed in by three walls but felt no fear.

She stared at the man. His athleticism belied his age; the face, sharply cut, had deep lines; his thin smile showed a man at ease with himself, but Aki also sensed uncertainty. "I am impressed by your courage," he went on in a neutral voice. "It is very few that would challenge me in such a way."

Aki placed her hands on her hips, her coat open before him. "If that's what you want to call it, fine. You've been around for a while," she said. "How about you tell me what you want—and a few other things."

The stranger adjusted his leather gloves. "There is only one thing I want," he replied. "You have it; the essence, the power that I seek, which will allow me to return."

"The Amida," Aki said.

"Yes. I have searched for many years," he explained in that measured, calm manner. "You, Aki Sato, are nearly pure in its origin, usage, and application. It is what I must have."

"The Amida is not for sale," Aki told him. "I have never been under the impression that it is a commodity." Aki tried not to let her anger show, but she knew this man could sense it. "I know what you have done," she finished.

The stranger's slight smile remained. "I am not here to fight you," he replied. "I have no intention of harming you, either. You would still be alive and well, and able to continue your career, with your beloved Kiya-chan at your side."

"Then you know." Aki reached down and grabbed a long metal pipe that lay near her feet. She took one end in her hands, felt the balance in the weapon, and swung it casually but expertly; Aki did not take kendo classes in school for nothing.

She did not advance on the stranger but kept a defensive posture. "Where is Kiya-chan?" she demanded. "And what do you really want?"

The man didn't flinch. "Your anger is turning to rage," he said. "That is not good. Suffice to say, I could disarm you if you advanced upon me, and hurt you quite badly. I would rather suggest a trade."

"What kind of trade?" Aki was not about to let her guard down, and she wondered where Noriko was.

"A fair and even trade." The stranger opened his gloved hands in a gesture of offering. "The Amida; your Amida for Kiya-chan. You will have her, she will have you, and all things will be as they were. Only you will not travel."

Aki did not answer. "Is this not reasonable?" he asked, the voice still neutral. "That thing you have that I desire, for the one who you desire more than anyone?"

"That is blackmail," Aki returned, her voice low, "and I won't do it. The Amida is a part of my mother, a part of my soul. I will die first."

The smile faded and the expression of the stranger turned downward. "How disappointing," he replied in a patronizing tone of voice. "Like so many, you are emotional. Believe me, I can take your power from you now, or at my leisure. It isn't as difficult as you may think. In the end, you will have nothing."

He took one step forward, and Aki took a side-step. The pipe was heavier than a staff, but she realized it might not work with someone such as this. The man's eyes were cold, like the rest of him. Aki was no match for this man.

"*Chiang!*"

The voice came from above and behind Aki, and it sounded too familiar. The man looked past her, and she watched his expression change. It was a look of surprise, then for the first time, on his face there was fear. His aura had changed as well; where once Chiang exuded a smug confidence, there was now a weakness and something darker.

Chiang slowly backed away. "I will deal with you later," he warned. "Your friends will not be enough to stop me." He turned and ran past Noriko, who had finally caught up to them.

Aki now turned to see who had run Chiang off. Standing on the roof of the one-floor building that turned the alley into a dead end was a man. He, too, was dressed all in black, down to the leather trench coat.

She stared. This man was small, not much taller than five feet in height; his long black hair flowed behind him, and he had a black Fu Manchu mustache and goatee.

Noriko ran up to Aki, breathless. Aki dropped the pipe, and they watched as the man turned and crossed the roof. He leaped off the other side and was gone.

Aki did not move or speak for several moments. "Did you," she stammered, "did you see him?" She pointed up at the roof.

"Yeah," Noriko said, still trying to catch her breath, "but who was it?"

"That looked like Kazu-san." Aki was certain she had just seen the younger incarnation of her brother's teacher and her mentor.

"But Kazu-san's dead." Noriko took Aki's arm and said, "Come on, let's get out of here."

"I know now what happened to Kiya-chan," Aki said as they walked back down the alley. "That man Chiang either has her or sent her away. He wants the Amida in me. You were right, Nori-chan," she added, "he wants what I have, and he is holding Kiya-chan somewhere in the hopes of gaining my power."

Noriko stepped out into the street and signaled for a taxi while Aki took a hurried look around; Chiang was nowhere in sight. "Okay,"

Noriko called over her shoulder, "this thing is getting crazier than before. Let's get back to the hotel and look at the big picture."

Aki nodded as a cab pulled up. Both climbed in the back, but not before Aki took a long look through her shades at the driver. He was a younger man and looked nothing like Chiang.

The cab turned around. Her hands stuffed into her jacket pockets, Aki stared at the back floor of the cab. *So Kiya is still alive. Chiang is the key to that, but I'm not going to be able to get her from him, not yet. I have to go to the source; it's the only place I can go that he can't keep me from. I only hope I can find the way, and hopefully the strength, to stop him and get Kiya back.*

Her hands balled into fists, Aki closed her eyes. *I'm coming, Kiya. Please hold on, wherever you are.*

12
The Source

THE BLACK BMW pulled out of the garage beneath the hotel. The 335 rarely left the garage during this time, apart from occasional trips. Aki felt excited to be back behind the wheel—and to be going home.

Noriko helped her pack and check out, the sizable bill covered by the company. Aki didn't need Noriko to pick up the tab, but the latter insisted, and Aki did not argue the point. After a friendly thank you and goodbye from the manager and hotel staff, the car was loaded, and they were gone. Bruce Cockburn's "Lovers in a Dangerous Time" played on the radio; Aki kept it down as Noriko was on the phone with her sister; the road trip would be a long one, and they wouldn't make it back until evening. There would be time to talk, catch up, and, already for Aki, to think clearly again.

Aki pulled onto Sanyo Expressway, gave the car gas, and cut into the fast lane as Noriko rang off. "Okay," she said, "how's about a little welcome home dinner tonight, at your place? Megumi-san's headed there now."

"That would be good," Aki replied with a grin. "I'd love to see everyone again. By the way, I didn't even ask what is up with the house?"

"No one's there, if you're wondering," Noriko explained. "The neighborhood association is sworn to secrecy. We left the A/C at a reasonable temperature, and the lights are on timers. We've been looking after the mail; Kenji-san sends a crew from Mr. Ito's over there every two weeks to do the lawn and any other work. Megumi-san has the cleaners in as well, and she's ordered them in today for your arrival. She'll make sure there's food there, too. We took the liberty of clearing out the fridge after it was clear you weren't coming back for a while."

"That's fine," Aki said. "Right now, I have to plan. I'd like to find an accompanist, at least for a while, get in touch with the others, and find the answers."

"You will be busy," Noriko said as she leaned her seat back.

"That's all right with me." Aki passed a slow-rolling semi and moved back into the travel lane. "It's time to get back to it, but the real work is finding Kiya-chan—and I will do it."

Noriko put her arm behind her head and closed her eyes. She said nothing more as Aki turned up Cockburn and put on more speed.

* * *

The *Ecorse* cruised at its maximum twelve knots across Lake Erie. The little vessel was scheduled to make its regular port calls along the lake's western edge. They would clock in at exotic locales such as Gibraltar, Estrel, and Woodland Beaches, the Luna Pier, and then down to Toledo. November had begun, and the season neared its end. This would be the final run for the *Ecorse* before it tied up for winter at the dock where Kiya first met the boat.

Despite the late afternoon and the cold, windy weather, Kiya sat on one of the wooden hatch covers in the lotus position. There were snow flurries, but bundled in a heavy sweater given to her by George, her scarf and wool coat, her cap pulled low, Kiya felt warm enough. The chilly weather and the wind helped clear her mind, especially after weeks of being cooped up in the kitchen.

The past months were an adventure, Kiya reflected. She'd learned much, and the life was exciting. While she didn't see a lot of the shipboard activity, she certainly heard it: boots clumped along the steel deck above or through the corridor, and the men talked about subjects such as the weather, the boat, what port they were headed to, and their families. Just overhearing such conversations took her mind off the routine of work and sometimes even distracted her from how much she missed Aki and everyone else.

Kiya had a routine of her own, sandwiched around her workday. After the final prep for the morning, Kiya would retire to her tiny quarters.

The space held just enough room for only a bunk, locker, and a chair, with a 60-watt bulb overhead. Then, Kiya didn't spend much time here; she pretty much lived in the kitchen.

Fortunately, George was a steady backup. They'd become good friends and often held long conversations in Italian. Other than Claudio and Motoko—who became fluent in the language—Kiya never had anyone to speak it with.

Kiya discovered George was a lot deeper than first glance provided. He was intelligent, well-read, and when not on duty he could be found in his bunk with his nose in a book. Then there were his people: Kiya was invited to his home in the city one evening when the boat was in port for a couple of days. She hit it off with his wife and two young daughters, but especially George's aged mother, who spoke almost no English. The lady was delighted to learn Kiya spoke her native tongue, and they, too, had a long discussion that night.

Dale was right about turnover on the Lakes and the *Ecorse* in particular. This season alone, Kiya counted at least a dozen men who joined and then left the boat for varied reasons. Ed told her that number was pretty normal for a season.

While Kiya had not gotten to know many of the regular crew well during these last months of the season, she at least knew most of their names. They were White, Black, and occasionally other ethnicities. Several were from Detroit or the outlying communities, some lived in Ontario, and one fellow called Wales home. Not a few were intrigued by the young lady who worked below decks and kept them fed.

One or two of the young men seemed interested in her, but Kiya was able to brush them off. Later, she found through George that Ed heard about these overtures; he quietly made it clear to the men that the cook was off-limits. With Aki, and those around them, Kiya had felt protected; she was glad to have that here.

Beyond that, the guys seemed all right with the one who made their meals, and there were no complaints about that. She remembered what her cowboy friend Randy told her and Aki when they'd traveled to Alberta some years ago. *Don't mess with the cook,* he'd said. Zendo held that job with the trail-riding gang back then, and Kiya found the principle was the same on the water.

Kiya was glad she got along with everyone, and that Captain Ed was behind her. He'd informed her earlier in the day that she had landed the job of winter watch on the *Ecorse*. This guaranteed Kiya a place to stay, as well as work, over the winter. "It's about as boring as it gets," Ed warned her, "but," he snickered, "at least you'd only cook for yourself most of the time."

She would not be completely alone. The *Ecorse* was to undergo an engine change over the winter, so Mike, other engineers, contractors, and workers would be around for part of the off-season. Beyond that, Kiya's job would be to keep an eye on the vessel through the frigid months.

"The boat will be connected to shore power," Ed explained as he stood watch on the bridge earlier in the afternoon. "You'll do a little of everything: keep a pathway shoveled from the gangplank to the deck, check for leaks, radiotelephone traffic, mail, correspondence, and make sure no one sneaks on board to steal stuff. You'll have it pretty much to yourself, though there will be port security and police around if you need help. They're just a call away."

Kiya was visibly relieved. She was glad to have a place to stay at season's end, although she had hoped to be gone from here by now. "I appreciate your trust in me, Ed," Kiya told him. "I do need a place to stay, and honestly, I consider this boat home."

Ed smiled. "I felt you did," he said. "You've done a fine job, Kiya; and I want you here for the next season, that is, if Akira doesn't show up."

Kiya didn't respond but turned to look out the window. They were standing to the right of the wheelsman near the bridge wing door, which was partially open. He could not hear their conversation.

Her silence reminded Ed that "Akira" was not someone she liked to talk about. His hand rested on her shoulder. "Sorry about that," he said. "I get the feeling your fiancé is a little hard for you to hear about, considering how far away he is."

"It's all right," Kiya replied, "don't apologize. I miss him, that's all. Things will be the same when he comes for me; that I am sure of. But . . ." she paused.

Ed turned to her after a scan of the horizon with his binoculars. "But what?"

"I have to tell you," Kiya said as she looked up at him, "I'm going to find it hard to leave here. I've enjoyed being on the *Ecorse*; the sailing, seeing the Lakes, the little towns and cities we call in at, all of it. I grew up in Japan, so I never spent much time in America, and I've needed to know what my father's homeland was like. It's also been good for me to be on my own," she added. "I never really have, as I think of it."

"It's a good life," Ed replied. "This is all I've ever wanted to do. My father sailed, my grandfather and great-grandfather did, and I love it out here. I wasn't pushed to do it; I turned this way easily. As I've said, there's danger, and you've been through a couple of the storms. But this," he finished, "is what we do."

Kiya thought about that conversation as she meditated on the hatch; her body moved with the pitch and roll of the vessel. While in this time frame, she was secure in the knowledge she would remain here and in place for Aki to come. Now, Kiya wondered, could she influence that?

As she'd done nearly every night, she closed her eyes and sent out a message. *Aki-chan . . . I am here.* She didn't know if Aki could hear or sense her, but Kiya hoped that by sending out her mental energy, it might help.

Her eyes opened just slightly. The cold and wind were starting to penetrate Kiya's clothes; she had been out here a while. Time to go back, as George would need her.

"Hey, there." The man himself had come out and was leaning against the hatch, a heavy coat over his kitchen rig.

"Sorry, George," she said as she stretched out her legs and got up. "Didn't mean to leave you alone so long."

George gave a wave of his hand. "Forget about it," he replied, "we're cool. Cap'n Ed was watching you; he thought I better bring you in before you freeze or get swept overboard."

They laughed as they walked aft. The snow picked up, and the seas had as well. "So, are we doing the pasta thing tonight?" she asked.

"You planned the meal," George said, "but I got twenty-five pounds of sausage ready to go. Good thing there's no vegetarians on this boat."

Kiya chuckled as she climbed the back ladder to the deck, George behind her. "By the way," he added, "I hear you got the winter watch. Congrats."

"Thanks," she replied, "I needed a place; this is home, at least for now."

"Yeah, it's like that," George said as they removed their foul weather gear and hung it by the door. Motown was playing on the radio, and the upbeat girl-group sound spurred them into action.

Funny, Kiya thought as they prepared for the upcoming meal. The radio was such a lifeline here for people. With no Internet, cable, or satellite TV, radio stations, especially at sea, sounded like distant outposts. Whether another boat, a weather station onshore, or one of the commercial outlets, it brought the world in, yet it sounded so primitive to Kiya.

As Kiya was in here more hours than she cared to remember, she found herself listening to area stations to figure out what they were doing. Certain ones had news of the world and the local area, and she began to know which were which, not by their call letters but by dial position and also the voices of those on the air.

The newsreaders, the fast-talking deejays, and the hosts of jazz, classical, and public affairs shows became familiar voices to Kiya. After a while, she felt like they were friends, always there at the appointed times. Remembering interviews she and Aki had with reporters in America during the *Lotus Flower* tour, so few of them sounded like these people.

Here in this time and place, Kiya found it old school. These people knew their stuff; they rarely made mistakes, tripped up on their words, or were at a loss for something to say. The only difference was the lack of women; there were few female voices on the air here.

Then there was the music; the popular sounds of the 1960s were so different, but Japan had its own version back then. Kiya remembered seeing pictures and films of the groups that tried to copy the look and sound of American and British stars. The power-pop scene the Blue Jean Buddhas broke into was almost exactly the same . . .

Kiya reached up and moved the AM/FM button and turned the dial. The pop stuff was getting a little boring, and one of the few FM stations they could get always had intriguing music. They didn't just play hits, but deeper tracks, and even full album sides. "That's more like it," George called from the other side of the galley, as "You Shook Me" growled out of the speakers.

For George and the others, this was a new, heavy sound for rock 'n' roll. Robert Plant's north-of-London wail and Jimmy Page's guitar profile heralded the bridge between Chicago blues and the new rock of what would soon be the seventies. Led Zeppelin was a name that had only been around about a year, but already they'd radically changed the face of music. *So odd to be here,* Kiya thought, *right as this band and so many others are making that impact.*

As she tossed some salt into a big steel pot of water on the stove, Kiya wondered about her own music. She wrote down lyrics, thoughts, and progression ideas in a small notebook; she hadn't been able to play piano, another thing she missed. Kiya often found herself exercising her fingers on the tabletop. She wondered if Aki was writing, what the band was up to, and whether they'd get back together.

Even more, Kiya missed her parents. *What they must be going through; but there was no way to tell Mom and Dad about Aki and what she can do. I have no idea what Megumi and the others have told them—they know it would not be like me to just disappear. Mom, especially, must be fearing the worst. The one who never left me . . .*

Kiya shook herself. *That's all too far ahead. I have to get back there first, or Aki has to get here. I'll keep trying, as hard as it is for me. I sometimes fear I'll never get home, but I can't think like that. I believe in Aki, and I must believe that she will get to me. Every day, I remind myself: that belief alone, plus the feeling I get every time I think of her, gives me the strength I need to move forward in this world. I must hang on until we meet again . . .*

* * *

Zendo sat in the main meditation room of the Shambala Center. The center was closed for the day, and Eiki was finishing up some last-minute work before they left. Zendo took the time to practice guitar in the room alone, and to sit.

He felt Eiki enter the room and place her briefcase on the floor. She sat beside Zendo in silence. "Are you waiting for me, Eiki-chan?" he asked at length.

The laugh, that light sound Eiki made, came to his ears. "Not at all," she said. "I am ready whenever you are, but there is something to bring to your attention."

Zendo opened his eyes and looked at Eiki. "And that is?"

The woman grinned. "Guess who's coming to dinner?"

Zendo smiled. "Let me guess: the name starts with an 'Ah' and ends in 'ki'?"

Eiki laughed. "Yes! Aki-chan's been in Kyoto. Nori-chan found her today, and they are on the way back. Dinner is at her house tonight, and we're invited."

"Wonderful." Sliding into their shoes near the door, Zendo set the security code on the alarm system, and they stepped out into the late afternoon sun.

"I have detected seriousness about you today, Zendo-san," Eiki said as they walked to their car. "Is there something that troubles you?"

Zendo placed his guitar case in the back seat of the Yaris and climbed in on the passenger side. "That is so; it has come upon me," he explained, "and Aki-chan's return appears connected to it."

Eiki put the car in gear and slowly pulled it up to the street. "Then this also would have to do with Kiya-chan's absence," she observed.

"I am afraid so." Eiki pulled into traffic, and Zendo continued, "I fear there will be danger in the coming days, for Aki-chan."

"You fear for her." Eiki glanced at Zendo. "How dangerous will this be?"

"I cannot say," Zendo replied. "Aki-chan has suffered terribly; she has from a distance emitted great sorrow over Kiya-chan's loss. She blames herself, but that is not the case. I feel it as I would feel pain in my own body."

He stroked his graying goatee. "All any of us can do, Eiki-chan," he said, "is be prepared to act if necessary."

"I know," Eiki replied, "that you would do anything for your cousin, or any of your family. I would as well. Is it selfish of me, however, to wish it would not come to that?"

Zendo shrugged. "It depends on how you define the word."

Eiki braked the Yaris at a stop sign. While waiting for the traffic to pass through, she turned to Zendo. "I know enough to know," she said. "I leave it at that."

The two leaned toward one other and kissed. "We must," Zendo replied, "for now."

* * *

Aki turned down the street to her old neighborhood. She took it slow, despite her excitement.

Stopping only for fuel and coffee (plus a smoke break for Noriko), the trip went fast. Aki dropped Noriko off at the train station, and she now followed behind in her own car. The houses hadn't changed; still here were unique designs, tiled roofs, gates, and shining nameplates. The vehicles, too, were a step higher than Aki recalled before the days of success; mostly Japanese makes, but a few BMWs like hers, a Mercedes or two, and some American models.

The overhead light was on, as were the welcome lamps on the posts at the gate. It looked the same as when Aki had left—well, fled it months ago. Along the street she saw Megumi's Beamer, Hiro's Nissan, Kenji's pickup, and others.

The gate was open, the space where she and Kiya always parked waiting for her. Aki pulled in, backed the car around, and climbed out. She removed her shades and took a long look around. She took a deep breath and drank in the house and the atmosphere. She was home.

Noriko came across the lot to her. "How does it feel?" she asked.

"Great. Thanks for keeping it up," Aki replied. "It's nice to come back to this."

They stepped onto the walk. The door opened, and two small children rushed out. Akito and Kala hurried down the steps, and Aki bent down to grab both of them into her arms. "*Okaerinasai!*" they shouted.

Aki held both of them close and kissed each one. "Look at you both," she exclaimed. "You've grown so much. I am so happy to see you!"

"So are we," Akito told her.

She looked up. Hiro had just come out; his hair was a little longer and he hadn't shaved, but the grin was the same. Aki went to him, and they embraced. "Welcome back, *Onee-chan*," he greeted and squeezed her to himself. "Been too long."

Aki could feel the tears coming, but she didn't care. "I know."

Inside, Aki was reunited with Kenji and Megumi, as well as Zendo and Eiki. For the first time in too long, she felt warm. The house was lit up inside, and smells of food came from the kitchen. But Aki heard something more: coming from the basement stairs, she could hear the piano. "Who's that playing?" she asked.

"James-san is down there with a few of the usual suspects," Megumi said, "plus someone you might like to meet."

Heading downstairs, Aki stepped directly into the carpeted practice room. This portion of the basement was rectangular in shape and had a low ceiling. The room was outfitted with a grand piano; Kiya's synthesizer was to the left of this, racked against the wall. The high stool Aki would sit upon before Kiya was still there; in this place, so many of the *Lotus Flower* tunes, as well as later B-J-B songs took shape.

The clubhouse atmosphere ruled in those days; the whole band would have spare amps, gear, and other equipment strewn about the room, on the floor, and against the soundproofed walls. The sound of the piano and Suya's unmistakable percussion were another homecoming.

Back into this world, Aki stepped as Suya put aside his djembe to come over and give her a big hug and welcome her back. Mika, in Gothic black from head to toe, did the same, as did James. After these pleasantries, the latter turned toward the one who had risen from behind Kiya's piano. "And here is our guest," he said. "Aki Sato, meet Ri Hanagawa."

The woman who approached intrigued Aki. Ri looked to be about thirty-five; tall and broad in her upper body, Ri was carried by a pair of muscular legs mostly covered by a long black skirt. A black silk blouse covered her large bust line, but Aki was drawn to Ri's face.

Under the long black hair was a face that was Japanese but with a distinctive western background. The dark brown eyes were direct from behind a pair of wire-rimmed glasses, but like her expression, they were warm. The large, bejeweled dragon she wore around her neck completed a look that reminded Aki of Mika but of an appearance that was taken much more seriously.

"*Hajimemashite.*" Ri greeted and bowed formally, her voice low but feminine. "I have anticipated this meeting."

Aki smiled and returned the pleasantries. "You honor me," she added. "I've heard your music, but much more from our friends about you."

Ri taught at the conservatory and had a stellar reputation, both as an educator and musician. Ri had recorded two CDs, one a series of variations on Bach and Mozart pieces, and a second of her own compositions. Kiya owned both; Ri had earned her fellow pianists' respect.

The reunion dinner was large and long, as everyone filled Aki in on their doings. She kept answers to questions about her own activities to a minimum. Those informed of the Amida knew she could not say much, especially about Kiya.

On the patio after dinner, Aki found herself sitting beside Ri. All were having coffee or tea, and some smoked off to the side, while Akito and Kala played in the green space. Ri began their conversation: "James-san and Megumi-san tell me you're interested in having someone accompany you, at least in terms of working on new music. I would be glad to do it, if you are agreeable."

"I am," Aki replied. "I have a lot of new ideas more than songs. I will try to put those into verse. It's hard to explain how Kiya-chan and I used to work."

"I understand," Ri told her. "You two have your own dynamic. I don't want to try and change what you do. Nor will I try to be Kiya-san; I can only be myself."

Aki smiled. "That's all you can be," she said, "and I expect no more than that." Her smile went away. "Please understand, Ri-san," Aki continued, "this is going to be difficult. There's a lot I must do in terms of music but also to deal with Kiya-chan not being here. I'm still trying to track her down."

"I am certain," Ri replied as she looked at Aki directly, "and that is only proper. It shows how much you love her."

That expression—Ri is looking right into me. There was a connection being made, but Aki did not feel uncomfortable over it. She felt reassured, though in a strange way.

The moment passed; then, Aki had an idea. "Hey," she called, "what do you all say to playing some music?"

The jam session that followed went into the night as everyone sang or took up instruments. Songs from the Blue Jean Buddha albums, covers, and even some of Hiro's new music came up.

Suya and James were as ever solid and behind Hiro's rhythmic, blues-inspired guitar. Ri added a rocking piano to the mix, and everyone sang backup, clapped hands, or added sound with Aki's old djembe and the numerous other instruments scattered around the space. For a little while, Aki forgot all she'd been through; she hoped these energies would reach Kiya and reassure her.

13
Time Won't Let Me

THE SESSION RAN late, but no one cared. Akito and Kala went to sleep upstairs in a spare bedroom. Their mothers looked in on them from time to time, but at one point the two sisters found themselves in the kitchen with Zendo.

As he poured himself a cup of coffee, Zendo said, "Being home is the best thing for Aki-chan. We have you, Nori-san, to thank for convincing her to come back."

"That was Aki-chan's decision," Noriko replied. "I think she's going on a new method of finding Kiya-chan."

"That is good," he said. "Here is a place of warmth and strength," Zendo went on, "and it will be easier for Aki-chan to search from this base. I do think, however, we should be careful: let us not try to overprotect her or be too willing to stay close to her. Unless, of course, that is what Aki-chan wishes from us."

Zendo added cream to his coffee and silently took his time to stir it. He turned back to them and said, "Aki-chan must have her privacy, still. This is a neighborhood where residents watch out for one another, and the media or strangers will be conspicuous. Aki-chan must be allowed to walk her own path. The music will come, but she has much more to do in terms of finding Kiya-chan. As I say, we need to be careful, but no one has to tell Aki-chan. She knows."

"A lot is riding on this," Noriko said. "You've seen how she looks. I think Aki-chan will feel better being home, but I have to tell you, she is focused, even obsessed. She is going after Kiya-chan, and . . ." Noriko stopped. "Look, I have to tell you this. Let's go outside."

Megumi and Zendo followed Noriko out front. The porch and gate lights were on; anyone stepping past the latter after a certain time would trigger security lighting. "There is someone else involved in this," Noriko exhaled and said quietly. "I still don't understand it, but I am afraid for Aki-chan."

Megumi and Zendo stood on either side of her, aware of her concern but also the fear in Noriko's voice. "Who is this person?" Zendo asked as she lit a cigarette.

Noriko described the incident in Kyoto with Chiang and the man who looked like Kazu. "I didn't hear all of the exchange," she said, "but I'm afraid Kiya-chan is caught in the middle of this. It has to do with the Amida; Chiang knows where she is. Aki-chan doesn't care; she's going after Kiya-chan, no matter the consequences."

Megumi didn't know what to make of it and said so. Zendo, however, remained quiet; his head turned slightly as his eyes scanned the neighboring homes and up and down the street. Both Megumi and Noriko wondered what he was looking at, or for, but then Zendo gave a nod.

"Aki-chan can handle this." Zendo kept his voice quiet, but the gravity within the tone he did not disguise. "This person is presenting himself as someone more than what he is. I would not worry, but be there for Aki-chan if she needs you. I will do the same. Let us speak no more of this tonight." Zendo turned and went inside.

"This is fucked up," Megumi said in a hushed voice. "Nori-chan, who is this Chiang, or what is he?"

"He has the Amida," Noriko replied as she smoked. "I don't think he's a threat to any of us; he is to Aki-chan, but there's more to it."

She exhaled away from her sister. "*Onee-san,*" she whispered, "I love Aki-chan as dearly as you do, as much as Kiya-chan. I am scared to death for her. Zendo-san's right, all we can do is be here for her, but we can't fight that guy. No one but Aki-chan can, but I don't think she's strong enough to take him."

"I get you." Megumi put her arm around her sister. "We have to be here," she said. "We'll need to keep close to Aki-chan and watch for her. That's all we can do."

They went inside. From downstairs, they heard Zendo's familiar guitar strum. *"I remember, all the days of our lives . . ."*

The song was played from the very first gig. Zendo's heavy strum of his Taylor propelled the track; James followed with his high harmony vocal, one of the minor signatures of the B-J-Bs, and they heard Ri play an underlying rhythm on piano.

"Yes, I remember, those nights when you were here . . ." Aki had taken the second verse; the band members often traded them off, *". . . moments like stars they are there, it seems, but less than meets the eye . . ."*

Megumi and Noriko listened. Somehow, the songs the band came up with over the years, either theirs or someone else's, seemed to tell a story, often the most immediate one.

"Remember the times, the good and the bad, remember the tears and the laughs that we had . . ." Zendo, James, Mika, and other voices joined in the chorus, a reminder of these past years. "We're all still family," Megumi noted.

"We are," Noriko said, "but there's a big part missing. Part of Aki-chan, part of her heart and soul is gone."

They went downstairs in unspoken agreement to hold these feelings in. Sitting on the basement steps together, the sisters watched the gathering. Everyone sat in the few chairs or on the floor. Aki reclaimed her high stool before the piano; there was no denying the happiness in Aki's eyes. She was home again.

"I got one," Hiro called when they finished, and he played a series of notes. Suya clicked his sticks, and the band rushed into "Time Won't Let Me." The band often played the old Outsiders tune onstage, and they put a live version on the B-side of the "If I Could" single.

Moving in time on her stool, Aki leaned into her stage mic and took the lead. As she sang about not waiting, Noriko knew who she sang it for. The younger teenage Aki returned on songs like these; she smiled, projected more, and reminded them of who she once was.

Voices were raised for the chorus; the band had played the song so many times they just picked it up again. She knew, however, that Aki, the girl she'd known all her life, had changed.

Like them, Aki had grown up. She'd stayed the same person, even during the years of the band's success and then the stardom that followed with *Lotus Flower*. Still, there, too, were changes: age, the stress of being a frontwoman, the attention (mostly unwanted), and certainly the Amida had made Aki no less a person, but Noriko now saw how it wore on her.

"Managers manage," their father Shinjiro, often told them, "but it is important to let people do their work." In that capacity, the sisters did all they could to make it easier on their friends, letting the band create and make music, without having to worry. They also tried to shield their charges, especially Aki and Kiya.

Noriko knotted her fingers together on her knees as she watched her husband play a non-blues solo. *This industry eats people alive; we've seen it. We weren't about to let anyone take advantage of them; some don't like working with us because Megumi knows what our people want and demands it. That's not to make us rich. We do it because we saw a chance to help our friends, and it goes way beyond music.*

She cast a glance at her sister, the one who from the start believed in the music Aki, Kenji, and Hiro created, and how she eventually found her purpose outside the Yoshida family's influence. Their mother, Yukari, never forgave Megumi for not joining her in the restaurant business, Noriko felt. She sensed the lady's disappointment in her as well, but to a lesser extent.

Their father's entrepreneurial spirit and their mother's drive; Megumi and Noriko had that in abundance. Two females, one still in high school, managed a band and turned it into a successful business—both parents (one, grudgingly) could not but be impressed with what their kids had done.

Noriko again watched Aki; her voice still had that practiced form but was thinner from lack of use—though no non-music person would notice. Looking at Aki now, despite the joy of being home and with family and friends again, the strain showed through. That existed as the band became prominent, and heightened by the pressure to perform, and to keep her secret.

Kiya was the one that relieved it in Aki, they were the safety valve for one another. Without her, Aki fell apart—a perfectly human thing, as the bond with Kiya was so deep. And she ran away, to try to save Kiya, and keep the family out of harm's way.

But Noriko also noticed what everyone else did. At Aki's core remained a strength she admired and a courage no one else she knew possessed. Just watching her sing this song, more than any, they saw her sister-in-law, the before, the now, and what was to come.

"She is the toughest of us all, isn't she?" Megumi said into Noriko's ear.

"Kiya-chan's coming home," she replied. "Aki-chan will find her."

* * *

Kiya looked up from her notebook as a song for a winter's night played on the wheelhouse radio from a Canadian station. She slid off the high wooden command chair bolted to the deck, left of the wheel. Turning up the collar of her sweater, Kiya stepped to the rail and looked out; she hummed the melody of the tune, recorded in '67. Sarah McLachlan had gone on to cover it, Tony Rice as well, and others. *Barely two years ago,* Kiya thought, *at least in this world . . .*

The rigging lights of the *Ecorse* reflected off the white flakes of snowfall and ran the length of the ship, despite her being in dock, hemmed in by snowdrifts and ice. The latter hung down in huge, dagger-like icicles. The deck below was covered in the white stuff but for the path from the bridge down to the hauled-up gangplank. Kiya would have another day of shoveling tomorrow, but at least she would have something to do.

Kiya drank down the last of her lukewarm coffee and put on her scarf and jacket. She would do her final walk around the boat before calling it a night. Kiya moved to turn the radio off, but her hand stayed. A segue followed by the voices of a group from the south shore of Lake Erie; the propulsive rhythm and lyrics about not waiting made her listen . . . Kiya didn't hear the man singing anymore—instead, she heard Aki over the radio, as their version of the song and the original became one . . .

The song over, Kiya shut off the box. She pulled on her gloves and picked up a heavy flashlight. Two feet long and made of steel, the item doubled as an excellent club, should it be required for such use.

That, however, was unlikely. Since the *Ecorse* was tied up for the winter, there were no uninvited guests. The only visitors Kiya saw besides the port officers were those involved in the overhaul. Mike was here most days to assist and keep an eye on things, but no one else from the crew turned up.

There was little other work during the day. Kiya didn't have to feed the renovation crews, but she made sure coffee and snacks were on tap for them. She also dealt with various shipping documents and supplies, made sure personal mail got to crewmen who had left the boat, and took occasional calls over the radiotelephone.

Technically, Kiya was on the clock eight hours a day, but her pay included extra for being on the boat. If she needed to leave for any reason, she would contact the port office and let them know the *Ecorse* was on its own until she got back. The office would step up patrols on the dock until her return.

Kiya made her way through the starboard side tunnel beneath the main deck; she shone her light along the hull as well as the deck plates. She never detected anything unusual, but this was protocol. Down the ladder into the empty cargo holds, her boots echoed as she walked through the freezing, cavernous bowels of the vessel searching for leaks or cracks in the hull; tonight, she found nothing out of place.

On her first rounds, Kiya was surprised to find a distressing number of rivets lying in the bottom of the boat. Mike told her not to worry; boats as old as the *Ecorse* often popped them by the bucketful, and welding had replaced riveting. That did not amuse Kiya; the pressure of the ice against the hull often caused creaks and groans, but she found no more errant pieces of metal. Like all else, she got used to it.

Kiya entered the engine room, where the vessel's heart lay in pieces, large and small. Mike told her the overhaul of the *Ecorse*'s engine was on schedule and should be completed by the New Year. Testing and trials would take place in March, as soon as the breakers could deal with the ice.

Back on deck, Kiya crunched forward through the crusted snow. With the buildup, she could now lean against the rail of the bow with her hip. Before, her head barely came above it.

She looked over and down into the dark, past the dual anchor chains. Beneath the drifts was three feet of solid ice, and a sea of white surrounded Kiya and the *Ecorse* except for where humans such as she had cut into it with their feet and tools. The snow was falling a little harder now, and the wind started to pick up as well.

Kiya stared out toward the river, and she imagined the inland sea of Lake Erie beyond, which probably looked much like this. She was alone and felt lonely, yet Kiya knew she could not have it any other way, not at this time.

She thought about her friends here: she wondered how Dale was doing, and that odd coterie of kids. Kiya dropped into the Dragon whenever she was in town, and they were always glad to see her.

George had taken the family to Florida for a vacation and sent her a postcard. He had not been around otherwise, but who would want to be here after living on the boat for nearly nine months out of the year?

Kiya's thoughts then went to Ed; she got a call from him before a trip to California. He hoped to meet up with Patti if she could get leave. Ed spent most of the off-season at the company offices in the city, "sailing a desk," he joked.

Kiya wondered how Ed dealt with Patti's absence, without a boat and crew to think of all the time. *He could well be like me; we carry on, day by day, minute by minute, hoping to hear from our loved ones that things are all right.*

The snow began to fall heavier now. Kiya closed her eyes, and despite the bitter cold, she stood there at the bow and sent her energy out. Then Kiya sang, a lower, slower line than her world knew. "*This now is the love, where have you been all this time, find us, here and now . . .*"

Kiya quietly sang, as she and Aki had shared it, and felt the disconnect and distance of decades. "*Love comes soft and sweet, and sometimes hard, oh so hard, when the one you love leaves . . .*"

Years of being alone, never able to find the one person she could be open with. Then came Aki, and Kiya risked being rejected again . . .

"*You must find the light, the light that's all around you . . .*" Kiya went into her higher range and sang against the coming storm. She found herself singing mostly to keep her vocal cords limber rather than to show off. She received a lot of compliments for it from Ed, George, and the like. Kiya stuck to songs from the radio, or tunes she knew were old enough—she could not possibly let them hear anything the band had done.

"All is not in vain . . ." Kiya turned toward the city and made her appeal to the moon, which revealed itself through the cloud cover. In the shadows, Kiya thought she saw a form . . . a woman . . .

"Reach across all time, love will always find its way . . ." Kiya kept the lyrics in that sensual, mystical tone she and Aki had discovered to make the song their own. Her eyes widened; the shadow seemed so real against the moonlight.

But this was not Aki, Kiya realized—the body and silhouette were not the same—still, Kiya somehow felt a familiarity. Who could she be?

"Find us, here and now . . ." Kiya wasn't sure she sang at all now as she reached out and the shadow withdrew.

"Find us, find us now . . ." The song and the light went out; the harbor and city offered a moment of silence, and Kiya was alone in the frozen wasteland. She wanted to go home, but this now was home. She could only wait, here in the ice, cold, snow, and storms. No one in the physical world heard Kiya, that she knew, but her voice and its vibrations carried. She believed Aki might hear, but there was no way to know.

Tears freezing on her cheeks, Kiya turned and walked back the way she came, down the snow and ice-covered deck. She was alone and could not go home.

14
Kind Woman

MIDMORNING SUN FILTERED through the blinds as Aki awoke in her bedroom for the first time in months. She lay on her side in a red silk chemise, arms wrapped about one of the double-sized pillows. She'd done this involuntarily over the past several months, wishing it to be Kiya.

She could smell the coffee from downstairs. Several guests had crashed, as the music ended late, and Aki could hear moving about on the floors below. After washing, then sitting for a short time, Aki pulled on a thick black robe and descended the stairs to find Suya passed out on the couch, Mika asleep in his arms. She smiled; inseparable since high school, the couple was one nearly as long as she and Kiya had been . . . *and will be again,* Aki resolved.

In a borrowed nightgown and an apron, Megumi was in the kitchen frying up a western-style breakfast. "There you are," she welcomed over her shoulder from the stove. "Hiro-kun and Nori-chan took the young ones to school; Kenji-san sends his apologies, but he had to get home and to Mr. Ito's."

"I'm not at all upset," Aki replied. "People have things to do." She went over to Megumi and gave her a hug from behind. "Thank you for all this," she said. "You're the best."

Megumi turned and wrapped her arms around Aki and kissed her cheek. "I would say the same for you. You sounded awesome last night, and I can't wait to hear your new stuff."

Aki sat at the high kitchen table as Megumi poured each of them coffee. "Ri-san and I are going to meet up at the conservatory tomorrow to go over some of it. I also want to drop in on Hiro-kun and the guys. I'm impressed by what they've come up with."

"Speaking of which," Megumi said, "I gotta give those two a kick." She went into the living room and roused Suya and Mika.

Over breakfast, Aki learned of the remaining guests' intentions. Tomorrow night was Mika's return to the stage, as she, Suya, and their group would open for some American nu-metal band at a downtown club. "They just got signed," Suya explained, "and they're being pushed as the next big thing." Suya and Mika's dual expression was one of, *yeah, right*, and it made Aki laugh.

"We once were like that," she recalled. "Ironic now that we are barely adults and I feel the music scene has passed us by.

"In a way," Aki went on to her friends' inquiring looks, "that's good. We got a chance to do something very few do, and I don't regret any of it. But I don't want to think that's in the past," she continued. "We've grown as a band but also as individuals. We have so much more to create and accomplish."

"How do you want to do that?" Suya asked Aki. "Do you want to do the band again? No one's forcing you, but I have to admit," he added with a chuckle, "that was a hell of a lot of fun. We've got the blues thing, but James-san, and especially Hiro-kun, we don't forget where we came from."

"That's the thing," Mika added. "I've watched all of you, Aki-chan— no one could have predicted how the band was going to take off. You were all doing something different, and it touched people. It inspired me—I know that."

Mika leaned across the counter. "The other thing," she went on, "is everyone has such respect for you, Aki-chan. You became the voice of the band, and its face, but you didn't forget us. You brought us along, but without you, without Kiya-chan, it's no band."

"What Mika's saying," Suya added, "is that the B-J-Bs are one, the sum of its parts. If you don't feel it, if Kiya-chan doesn't when she comes back, then that's okay. Every one of us is important, and that includes you two. If it's over, then fuck it—we had a great run. We'll still be friends and family."

Aki pushed her empty plate aside. "I really appreciate that." Cradling her cup in her hands, she sighed and thought it over. "I'm so thankful," Aki finally said. "Without you, and I mean all of you," she declared, "this would never have happened. All of us, our combined talents, our energies, that's what made this band. I claim nothing more than what I offered."

She put her hands out; Suya and Mika each took one. "Thank you both for saying what you have," Aki said. "I never once have overlooked your contributions, and I never will. As for now, I have to catch up to Kiya-chan," she continued, "and see if it feels right again. I'm also out of step with the times, but I'll get back into it. I don't want to speak for Kiya-chan, but I think she will want to."

"Why don't you come out, Aki-chan?" Mika suggested. "I have some new work to put over on the crowd—it'll kill 'em."

Aki smiled. Mika wrote some interesting lyrical poetry, albeit on the angry side at times. She wove it into her own songs and others, and her stage get-up was a shade sexier—or raunchier, depending on perception—than how she usually looked. So funny, Aki thought, how the tiny, demure girl she'd met back in high school morphed into a local scene performer and made a name for herself. Then again, Aki had no indication of what was in store for herself, either.

"If I can," she said, "I'll be there."

"Cool," Suya added, "and we'll make sure you're safe backstage. I think people would freak if they knew you were out and about."

"That would be good," Aki replied. "I'd rather no one knew, at least not yet."

"We have another show to check out," Megumi said. "Zendo-san and Eiki-chan are playing tomorrow, too—Uma's, of all places."

Everyone chuckled. Uma's coffee shop was right up the street from their mutual alma mater. Uma was still alive and well, serving Shibuya Ward students and others his unique brand of java, as well as Japanese and American sweets and pastries. In recent years, he'd expanded the shop and added a small stage for acoustic sets.

Hiro played solo there some years ago, and Mika was a regular at the poetry slam events. "That's going back in time," Aki said, "but we should hit that, too." Then she added as an afterthought, "I must also go visit Kiya-chan's parents."

The others nodded. Motoko and Claudio were stunned to hear of their daughter's disappearance. Aki spoke with them on occasion, but she was too wrapped up in her own difficulties to communicate much. Sadly, the truth could not be told about the Amida; Aki struggled over whether or not to reveal the secret, but in the end, she was not sure they would believe her. She dared not demonstrate the Amida to them either, for fear of what might happen. "They must be hurting more than any of us," Aki continued. "I will call them today."

After breakfast, her last guests left. Aki smiled and waved from the porch as Megumi drove off.

The smile faded once Megumi's BMW was out of sight. Aki returned inside, locked the front door, and then went around the house to make sure all the doors and windows were secure.

Dressing again in black, including her leather coat and boots, Aki sat in the lotus position on the deck. One of the reasons she liked the home was that out here no neighbors could see, and the prying eyes of the paparazzi could not either.

She began to breathe, slowly and evenly, as Aki set her thoughts on a place. She was headed for the Summerland and, she hoped, answers.

* * *

"Kick out the jams, motherfucker!"

Kiya entered the Black Dragon to find Max and three other members of Dale's staff air jamming to MC5. The former was standing on the counter in a wide stance, holding an old cane like a mic stand. The others were "playing" bass, guitar, and drums respectively, and the few customers in the store were enjoying the show. Kiya stood off to the side and grinned. She'd done the same as a little girl—and then later, of course, for real.

The exhibition ended when Max glanced out the window. He jumped down behind the counter and immediately turned down the radio. "Dale's comin'!" Everyone busied themselves, and Kiya tried to keep a straight face but couldn't.

"I know what you were doing," Dale said with a knowing look and tone of voice as he entered the store. "I could hear that noise all the way up the street. Now get caught up."

His temperament altered when he turned his attention to the customer. "Ah, Kiya," he greeted, "long time, no see." Dale gave her a big hug and said to the store at large, "Good thing for you she's here. She has made my day."

The two got cups of coffee out of the urn and took their regular seats. "Update me, how's the old *Ecorse*?" Dale asked. "Getting re-engined, I hear."

"She has been." Kiya reported that the overhaul was completed ahead of schedule, and preliminary tests and inspections showed the vessel ready for sea. "She should make fourteen knots, sixteen if we push her," Kiya said, "according to Mike."

"Lonegan knows his stuff," Dale replied. "I'm sure he could make it do even better, but that'd cause a stress fracture in the old girl. One thing the company needs to do," he went on, "is to replace some of those ribs down in the hold. There any leaking in the plates?"

"Not that I've seen," Kiya replied. "Ed told me to keep a sharp eye out for that, but so far nothing. No more missing rivets of late either."

"Good. Problem with a lot of the smaller, older boats," Dale explained, "is the companies don't want to spend any cash on 'em. Run 'em 'til they drop, only hoping they do it either in dry dock or aground. He took a drink of his coffee and went on, "It's been a little better of late, since the *Cedarville* went down."

"What happened there?" Kiya had heard about the boat, but only bits of information from Ed and her fellow sailors.

"She went down in the Straits of Mackinac in '65," Dale explained. "Bunch of damned bean counters for US Steel ran that ship to uselessness, then ran her some more. They let the boat go to pot, put a yes-man in charge, and overloaded her like every vessel in the fleet. They ran full speed in the fog, steamed out of the shipping lanes to save time—you name it, they did it."

Kiya was on the other side of the coin, she realized. Ed ran the *Ecorse* by the book; he double-checked everything, especially his plotted courses. He kept the boat up to code and its crew in line.

"She finally ran out of bounds too far," Dale went on, "and collided with a freighter. Lost ten men that shouldn't have died. A damned scandal."

Dale's voice and expression were bitter, but they softened as he added, "I was pretty lucky. I've worked for lines that treated their ships and their people a bit better. Ed, as you now know, is one of the real captains."

Kiya nodded. The thought of what little she knew on top of the details provided by Dale showed her how bad things could get. "I consider myself lucky, too," she said. "I have had that on my side a lot lately. Your story reminds me of that."

The door had opened during the last exchange, and a new character entered the store. His head nearly struck the top of the door, he was so tall, but he also was extremely thin.

"Jeff!" Dale called out. "Come back here, meet a good friend of ours."

The man strode back to the desk. Clad in an old Army parka, blue jeans, and sneakers, he couldn't have been more than twenty. His blond hair hung long past his shoulders, and his pointed beard extended down to his chest area. "Kiya, meet Jeff," Dale introduced, "folksinger extraordinaire."

Jeff laughed at the adjectives as he shook Kiya's hand. "Good to meet you," he said; Kiya noticed right away his piercing blue eyes and the strong scent of marijuana. "What's been going on?"

Dale filled Jeff in on matters of varying sorts as he opened his case and produced a battered six-string. "Jeff plays around the area wherever he can find a gig."

"Yeah," he said as he tuned up, "gotta make a living somehow. Dale told me about you," he added to Kiya, "says you sing. What do you know?"

Kiya shrugged. "I don't know if you'd know the stuff I do. You'll have to try me."

Jeff grinned. "Okay." His long fingers worked a couple of licks and he launched into a Gordon Lightfoot song about a black day in July. The radio was turned off, and those in the store continued to work or shop, but Kiya saw all were listening, and some came over to hear.

The song dealt with the city's race riots, which were only a few years from this time; Kiya remembered reading about the subject in history class. Jeff's interpretation brought out a voice in him that didn't sound like the way he spoke. His pipes were deeper when he sang.

A less whimsical tune, Lightfoot touched on the heart of the riots, haves and have-nots, and how the latter reached but never seemed to quite get theirs. The lines about being brothers, finding peace . . . not much, Kiya realized, had changed.

"Let me try one on you," Kiya said after the applause ended for Jeff. "Do you know 'Four Strong Winds'?"

"Ian Tyson, sure!" Jeff slid his hands down the neck of the guitar. "I'll transpose; let's do it."

Kiya hadn't sung the song in a long time, but as Zendo had said about himself, it was one of those tunes that sang to her and was never forgotten. She and Jeff harmonized on the bridge and chorus; the store remained silent, and the customers stopped shopping. They'd all heard Jeff before, but Kiya was a new experience.

A huge round of applause was the response as the song ended; Jeff stuck out his hand to Kiya. "That was cool," he said, as he shook hers. "You got a great voice."

Kiya smiled with satisfaction. The trading off of songs went on for a while, tunes from the radio and others. As it began to grow dark, Kiya stood up and said, "I must get back to the *Ecorse*." Shaking hands with Jeff and the others, she passed her thanks around and got a goodbye hug from Dale.

As she walked alone through the darkening streets, gloved hands in her pockets, Kiya thought of how good it felt to sing again. It reminded her of the early days when everyone gathered at school or someone's home or apartment to play, eat, and have a good time. It also reminded her of how much she missed Aki, her parents, and everyone at home; but friends such as Dale made it okay for now.

Stepping onto the dock, Kiya thought of Aki and began to quietly sing one of the tunes she and Jeff had done. "Kind Woman" wasn't as big a hit for Buffalo Springfield, but Kiya heard it on the radio now and then.

With thanks to one of the patrolmen, Kiya climbed the ramp to the *Ecorse*'s deck, then dragged it up behind her. The officer then headed for warmer places.

Moving through the two inches of new snow collected on the walkway, Kiya made her way aft. *Another quiet night; at least tonight it will not be so bad. I wonder where my "Kind Woman" is and when I will see her again.*

15

The Black Watch

A WARM BREEZE greeted Aki's senses, and slowly she opened her eyes. She was sitting in the lotus position on a hill. Grasses grew tall around her, and she noted she was still wearing the clothes she'd "left" the house in.

Aki stood up. The fields below stretched onward for as far as she could see, with the shadows of mountains in the distance. She saw no buildings or structures of any sort. There were no humans or any other beings in sight. *The Summerland . . .*

Instinct told Aki to move in the direction of those mountains. Well-worn paths led down the hillside; this place was a spot traveled to often.

Aki knew there was much to do in the mundane world, but this was crucial. The answers she sought were here, and yet she'd not thought of it until recently.

As she made her way to level ground, Aki noted the grass in this area was much shorter, to calf level. There were no fences, and the field stretched to the left and right as far as Aki's eyes could take her.

She walked slowly, feeling a strange sense of calm take her over. *It's so peaceful, idyllic here. Will all who have gone before me be here? People I don't expect? Or will there be those I'm meant to see?*

Looking up, Aki realized she was no longer alone. Against the background of the blue hills and mountains, she could see two specific forms. They were still too far away to see clearly, but Aki knew they were coming for her.

They were a man and a woman; the former seemed to be gradually outpacing his companion as they approached. Both were dressed in black, as she was, down to their leather coats. Aki wondered if her recent choice of clothing was not a completely conscious one.

She stopped. Aki suddenly recognized who was before her. The woman, whose long black hair flowed behind her, had stopped about twenty meters away; the light breeze blew the mane about her, but Aki remained focused on the man, as he walked up until he was arm's length from her.

Aki could not speak. This was the one who stood up to Chiang during her confrontation.

Kazu reached out and took Aki's right hand in both of his. "Good to see you again, Aki-chan," he said with a bow and that familiar smile. "I'm sorry I didn't properly reintroduce myself the other day."

This was the younger version of Kazu, the one she'd been with on that travel to San Francisco. "This is so strange," Aki finally was able to say, "even though I know this is what I should expect in the Summerland."

"That's all right," Kazu replied. "I was most surprised myself when I got here. We are all in this place for varied reasons.

"But now," Kazu added as he turned slightly, "there is someone I know you would like to see again."

Aki looked past Kazu to the woman, and for a moment thought she was looking into a mirror. *She looks like me . . .*

Then the voice, a voice Aki hadn't heard in years, spoke: "It is I, Aki-chan."

Aki ran past Kazu to the woman, who caught her in her arms. Her strength failed her; Aki's legs buckled, and she was eased to the ground.

The woman knelt in front of Aki, who looked up through blurred vision into that kind, smiling face.

"Mom . . ." she whispered. "I want to believe it's you."

"Believe it, my child," Hiroko Sato replied. Her hand slowly brushed away Aki's tears; the touch felt to Aki exactly the way it did when she was little. "Circumstance has brought us together again."

"All this time," Aki gasped, her body trembling, "I needed one thing—the one thing I never thought I could have."

Hiroko held Aki as she wept aloud. "Let it go, Aki-chan," she whispered. "You are safe with us."

Her mother sat down in the field and drew Aki into her arms. Kazu moved off; Aki rested her head against her mother's chest and let herself be held.

"It has been so long, Aki-chan," Hiroko said sometime later. "Your father and I have watched all our children from here."

Aki looked up. "Where is Dad?" she asked. "Is he here?"

"He is not," Hiroko told her. "Yujiro-san is in the Summerland, but we are of the Amida. This meeting is for us alone, and there are matters to be dealt with."

Hiroko again drew Aki to her. "For the moment, think of this time together as I do: an opportunity that may never come again."

Aki's mind slowed, as did her heartbeat. "The Amida," she said, "has shown me so much. I never thought it could do this."

"There is much to learn," Hiroko replied. "The Amida is boundless; its expanse goes beyond our comprehension. But now I must speak to other things."

Aki sat up, and the two faced one other. Her mother looked more like an older sister here; she guessed that Hiroko had chosen this age or aspect of herself upon entering the Summerland.

"As I say," Hiroko continued with a smile, "your father and I have watched you grow. I suppose we did well by you; you picked yourselves up after our passing and made your way. We are immensely proud of all our children."

Aki smiled and rubbed her eyes. "To hear that from you," she said, "makes me feel good. We often wondered about you and Dad, and what would you think of us if you could see us."

"But we did see you," Hiroko replied with a laugh. "You could not know that; at times we were certainly worried about you, as parents shall always be. We also knew that you would make the decisions necessary for your lives. I'm especially happy to have heard you sing."

"I never expected that to go the way it did," Aki said. "I never wanted to be famous, but that seems to have happened."

"What I am most proud of," Hiroko replied, "was how none of you gave up your true selves. You moved up in the world, as westerners might say, but you did not change and were not consumed by your stardom."

Aki shrugged. "There was no need," she said. "I didn't want to be anything different, and we all agreed we would become who we would. The money we made offered us a little more freedom, a little less worry in that way, but it was all about the music and the fun we were having. Our audiences were enjoying themselves, too, that was more important. We were helping them, Mom; we entertained them, but some of our songs have gone deeper, which is what I hoped for."

"They have." Hiroko nodded and stroked Aki's face. "You speak of music being a healing thing," she said, "and it is. Hiro-kun healed himself through music, as you have, and Kenji-kun, in his own way. With all that occurred to you, and to Kiya-chan, you rightly turned to the place to heal those wounds, but you gave back."

"We tried." Aki sighed and rested her hands in her lap. "Kiya-chan entered my life and loved me," she said, "and never was I happier than with her. Not only the music, but the person Kiya-chan is."

"I understand," Hiroko replied. "Your love of, and for, Kiya-chan," she went on, "is why you are here."

"Yes. Mom, I have to find her," Aki said. "I owe her my life, this life I've had. Without her, I would not be what I became, and I would not know real love. I am responsible for her and what happened to her, and now there's this Chiang, and all these things are happening."

Hiroko stood up and helped her daughter to her feet. "That is why we are here," she said as Kazu approached them again. "As well, there are others who shall remain nameless. We are part of what is known as the Black Watch. We are guardians of the Amida."

She took Aki's hand, and the three walked toward the mountains. "We must discuss the matter involving Kiya-chan and Chiang," Hiroko explained, "but this is not the time or the location. We must go to sacred space."

Aki nodded but said nothing. They walked together, Kazu a few steps behind, as they closed in on the edge of the field.

The bluish haze that blurred the contours of the mountains took them in, and soon they began to climb a long, winding stone path. The temperature cooled, and there was a mist that obscured the area, like that of early morning.

Aki became aware of the voices, numerous voices, male, female, young, and old, as they chanted, sang, and spoke a universal language. It sounded like *kirtan*, Hindu lyrics and verse. Zendo had long been attracted to it, and he often used and infused it into his practice and song.

Even with the darkness, Aki and her companions walked without fear of stumbling. The chants and voices now were augmented by percussion, ancient sounds that heralded an arrival—but to where?

Ahead, how far away Aki did not know, an orange-yellow light flickered in the distance. Fire, a small, weak one, and the smell of smoke came to her. The chanting faded slightly, as did the drums, and Aki saw they were headed toward a space ringed by stones. It reminded her of the ruins in Northern Europe and Greece, which she and Kiya had viewed when they visited there . . .

Another verse and the voices rose; the drums remained, a steady beat with a minor delay. As they walked on, Hiroko stared ahead, past Kazu, toward the arena. Her face was impassive; she said nothing.

Aki now saw a tower of sorts, which presided over this open space. They then passed through a broken arch, and the music stopped.

The three entered a space before this larger one, nearly covered by the overhanging trees. Here now was the fire, which burned within a stone circle.

Kazu stirred up the embers and the few pieces of wood that remained. Once these were active, he placed more fuel on the blaze and gradually brought the flames up.

Hiroko led Aki to the circle, and they took seats on a pair of stumps. There were eight of these planted around the circle. Kazu sat on the other side of Aki, and the three warmed their hands before the flames. At length, Hiroko said, "Aki-chan, we must explain to you the situation you find yourself in, and also the dangers."

"Dangers," Aki repeated. "I have felt danger, from my meeting with Chiang. Yet it came before, and it has stayed with me since. Who is he? Why does he want the Amida from me? What has he done with Kiya-chan? I have feared she is in some terrible place, and I cannot get to her."

"Finding Kiya-chan," Kazu replied, "is, at the moment, secondary, if you will forgive my saying. We will do our best to help you retrieve her if we can. For now, Chiang's power is such that we must wait for a weakness in him before we can act."

"Chiang is, like Kazu-san and me," Hiroko explained, "already dead. Little is known of him, except in life he was a minor figure, a soldier, in organized crime."

Kazu then took up the story. "Chiang was murdered while protecting his boss's family," he said, "and so found his way to the Summerland. He bore a terrible anger and hatred for his killers, and Chiang resolved to find a way to return to Earth in order to have his vengeance."

"Chiang was aware of the power of the Amida within him," Hiroko said, "and he began to experiment with it. He used it to travel, but as Chiang learned how to harness his power he began to steal from others. He is known among us as a soul-taker; it is a mental, or psychic, form of assault."

"He spoke of my pure power," Aki replied. "Is that why he wants it?"

"Yes; Chiang believes that your Amida, because you used it only on occasion over the years, bears more strength," Kazu said. "He reasons that the purer the power he gains, the more opportunity he has to return and do what he will. He is responsible for the disruptions in the Amida—and for Kiya-chan's disappearance."

"But Kiya-chan is not lost." Hiroko placed her hand on Aki's shoulder. "Kiya-chan is alive, and safe, for the time being," she said. "Do not be worried for her, Aki-chan; rescuing Kiya-chan, however, can be done only when Chiang is weakened. He has such moments; we know of them, and of these you will learn. The important thing, Aki-chan, is to be aware, and to take action when it is called for."

Hiroko and Kazu then rose, as did Aki. Each took one of her hands in theirs. "There is now," Kazu said, "one more place you must be made aware of."

The scene vanished from Aki's eyes; it felt as though they were indoors. As her eyes adjusted, Aki looked down; they were standing in a circle lit in green from beneath the floor. They were in a room, but Aki could see no walls and no ceiling.

"Where are we?" she asked, and her voice echoed and reverberated.

"This," Hiroko explained, "is the Last Battleground. Remember this place, for it will become necessary, and important, if you are to achieve your goal."

She took Aki's hands in her own and led her into the center of the circle. Hiroko then looked into her daughter's eyes; Aki met her mother's gaze. The irises of her brown eyes opened, and Aki saw her own do the same in reflection.

Silver now were the mother's and daughter's eyes; the two connected, and Aki felt her mind absorbing Hiroko's energy, and her mother taking in hers. The light took many shapes, slowly at first, then with speed. Silver, gold, and white in patterns Aki could not follow flew back and forth between them. The transfer electrified her body, but Aki felt no pain. Around them came the stars; that space Aki had traveled through so many times, the tesseract.

Hiroko's voice then brought Aki back to her. "You may only receive one opportunity to rescue Kiya-chan from the past," she cautioned. "When it happens, you will know what to do. Kiya-chan's insight and intelligence taught you a way to understand the Amida and to navigate it. All the same, your personal instinct, especially through the tesseract, you must rely upon. As for us, we will do what we can when that time comes, if we are able. This we do."

She felt her mother's arms go about her; Aki returned the embrace; Hiroko's strength, so unique, took her in. *You are brave, Aki-chan, and powerful . . . you will do what you must . . . we shall be here for you . . .*"

Aki opened her eyes. She was back on her deck, still seated.

Slowly, she managed to get to her feet. With difficulty, she walked to the sliding door, removed her boots, and left them there.

The cool rooms of the home welcomed Aki in, but she barely felt anything. She stumbled upstairs, shed her coat, and threw herself on the bed. Grabbing Kiya's pillow, Aki held it to herself. She ran over the experience in her mind again, trying to remember all the words as well as the images.

Aki's breathing labored and sweat burst from her pores. *That was it—after all the past months of stress, sadness, and searching, I went to the place I needed to go all along. I didn't know what would be there, but it's where I had to be . . . with my mother.*

She sat up and locked her arms and legs around the pillow. Aki felt her strength return. *Even if the Black Watch can't protect me, I know I must act when that moment comes to hand. Even though Chiang is dangerous, I will get through him and whatever he throws at me.*

Aki set her teeth and glared at an invisible point. *I will bring you home, Kiya-chan . . . I vowed I would do so, and I will.*

16

Long As I Can See the Light

A DECADE HAD ended, and a new one began this night. From the starboard bridge wing of the *Ecorse*, Kiya could hear the steam whistles, car horns, and revelry of a city celebrating the New Year. Everyone was having fun, but Kiya wanted no part of it. Christmas had come and gone; the quiet time on the docks suited her.

She spent the holiday at George's and had baked a special cake as a gift for the family. A good time was had, with much of the conversation in Italian. Since then, Kiya kept to herself. She was aware of a stirring of sorts, and she wondered if Aki was coming. In that case, Kiya wanted to be in place and ready.

The snow fell lightly now, and Kiya went inside. She slid the bridge door closed, sat again in the captain's chair, and listened to the radio traffic. Most of the conversation was between the nearby Coast Guard station, the icebreakers, and other vessels. Few boats were out on the Lakes, most of them in the bigger bodies of water and a long way from Detroit.

She picked up the binoculars and scanned the horizon. The way the *Ecorse* was berthed, Kiya could see downriver on a line from northeast to southwest. Her point of reference was the slowly turning beacon from the lighthouse on the point. The light turned, blinked, then turned and blinked again without a stop. *The lake's heart is beating,* Kiya thought.

Restless, Kiya stepped out to the port wing and watched the distant light for a time. Looping the binoculars over her neck, Kiya pulled her ponytail out of the strap, draped it over her shoulder, and adjusted her cap and jacket. The thermometer showed the temperature was nearly zero, and the wind made it feel even colder, but Kiya was used to it. Somehow, the cold insulated her from certain feelings.

She thought about what Christmas must have been like at home. Although not a regular churchgoer, Claudio would have gone to Midnight Mass. Motoko might have gone, too, despite being non-religious. Kiya liked to go when she was younger, as she loved the music and the singing.

Christmas Eve was a date night in Japan; Aki and Kiya would go out, sometimes with their family and friends, unless of course there was a gig. The Sato family celebrated the day at one person's house; this came about after Kenji and Megumi were married and everyone went their separate ways. Last year, Hiro, Noriko, and Kala hosted; Kiya recalled a time of gifts, food, singing, and being together. *Aki and I were supposed to do it this year; I wonder how it went and if Aki even did it.*

The light blinked again, and Kiya began to hum the keyboard line of a song she heard on the FM. She knew it well—but how strange, again, that this song was still considered new—lyrics about a candle in the window, being gone, but as long as one could see the light . . .

Kiya sang the CCR tune in her lower range, and without John Fogerty's gospel-blues shout or vibrato. True, his soulful rendition was superior, but Kiya liked to try a less-is-more approach with tunes such as these. 'Sultry,' Aki had called her voice, which made Kiya red in the face, but she loved the compliment.

Being alone in this place, Kiya felt she could stretch her voice and her feelings; she didn't feel so lonely after that. She recalled how, when she was younger, she enjoyed playing before others. Singing, on the other hand, was hard for her. Kiya had joined the band partly because she wanted to be with Aki but also because she had to learn to play music with others.

After that, Kiya never had a problem singing in public. Still, she was glad that Aki did most of the lead vocals in the band and later on the *Lotus Flower* project. She guessed being behind the piano shielded her to an extent. *Aki used to say that having me there gave her more strength than she could bring out in herself. She did that for me as well; I never played or sang better than with her around. If—no, when she comes for me, I wonder if we can get that back?*

And if so, Kiya wondered, what would they do? She didn't know if Aki wanted to do another solo project. *Lotus Flower* was an experience they needed, to be on their own, and while they enjoyed the tour, it took too long. Both missed the band—had they moved on, and what were they all doing? *I know what Aki's doing,* Kiya told herself, *and I have to believe she is trying to get to me. It gets harder every day, but I have no choice. When you love someone, you have to be patient, you have to wait, and you have to hope no matter how much it hurts.*

Kiya sang the chorus once more and drew out the final line. For a long moment afterward, she stared out to sea.

"That was lovely."

Kiya nearly left the deck in surprise, and she spun around. Leaning against the bridge door under the dim light, in his sailor's greatcoat and officer's cap, was Captain Ed, whose gloved hands applauded politely.

"How long have you been there?" Kiya demanded, but she smiled as she said it.

"Just long enough to hear that song," he replied. "I was taking in the New Year's festivities, and I thought I should pay you a visit."

"You look like a nautical Humphrey Bogart," Kiya said, "standing like that."

Ed smiled and cocked his cap to the side. "Well, sweetheart," he replied, "all I'd need now is a cigarette, but I don't smoke."

The two laughed and met each other halfway. "I've missed my captain," she said. "I wondered where you'd been."

"A lot of places." They stepped to the bridge wing and looked out. "I was in San Diego for vacation after we tied up, as you know. Spent a couple of weeks quite literally on the beach. Nice time."

"Did Patti get leave?" Kiya asked.

Ed shook his head. "No, she couldn't get away."

"I'm sorry."

"It's okay," Ed replied. "I gather Akira has not arrived, either."

"No." Kiya stuffed her hands in her pockets. "I have heard nothing," she said. "All I can do is wait."

"Same here. Oh, I ran into Dale this evening. He wishes you well."

Kiya smiled. "Dale's a great guy. I drop in on him at the Dragon every so often."

"Been there once or twice," Ed noted with a chuckle. "Not my scene, but he seems well."

"Mind if I ask you something?" Kiya turned and looked at Ed. "Dale says you owed him a favor," she explained, "and that's how I ended up here. Is that true?"

Ed looked across the water. "I owe him my life."

"You do?" Kiya was genuinely surprised.

"Yeah. Up at Port Sanilac, this was years ago." Ed leaned on the rail as he explained, "We were loading cargo, and despite being a third-generation sailor, this young and newly minted deckhand didn't know his ass from his elbow. I was walking along the deck, not paying attention to what was going on, and the netting around two tons of canned goods broke. I was right under it."

Kiya's eyebrows raised; having watched the perilous business of loading and unloading many times, she could imagine the situation. "What happened?"

"Dale was there," Ed said, "and he threw himself into me, knocked both of us right through the hatch, all the way to the bottom. The cargo spilled mostly on the deck. I'd have been killed if he wasn't there."

Kiya followed Ed's gaze. He told the story quietly, without any heroic-sounding words. The way he said it was enough. "Wow," she replied.

"Of course," Ed went on, "given the distance we fell, I ended up with a separated shoulder, and Dale messed up his back badly. He was out most of the season, and when he returned, he was still in a lot of pain. He stayed on for a few more seasons but finally had to quit. I don't forget what he did."

"Sounds like the kind of thing Dale would have done," Kiya said.

"Yes," Ed replied, "Dale was, and is, that man. The things he's done for those kids, for you. Of course, if you're involved in some of his other businesses, that may be a different story. But I know nothing about that, so don't quote me."

The two shared a laugh, and Ed put his arm around Kiya's shoulder. Kiya found herself putting hers around Ed's waist. "You are a lot like

Dale," Kiya told him. "You are a fine captain, based on all I've heard and seen; but you are a fine man as well."

Ed blushed, even with the cold. "Thank you," he said, "and I think very much the same of you, as a woman."

He stared into her eyes. Kiya felt he was thinking hard about something he had to say. "I know," Ed went on, "how much you care for Akira, and you know how I feel about Patti. If the circumstances were other than they are, I would find myself very fond of you. Not just as a cook, or as a friend, but more. Don't get me wrong," he then added quickly, "I'm not trying to make a move here."

"That's all right," Kiya replied. She placed her other hand on his shoulder. "I know what you mean. Akira is all I have in my life; he is my one love, and the only one I'll ever have. But that doesn't mean I can't care about other men. I care for Akira's brothers, I care for Dale, and I care about you, too, Ed. You feel for Patti the way I feel for Akira, that's clear."

"I think that's it."

An awkward pause, then a cold breeze whipped through the wing of the bridge. On instinct, Kiya moved close, and Ed took her in his arms. "*Anno . . .* sorry."

"No, don't be." Ed held Kiya securely, but the captain handled her as he would his dividers and compass in the chart room.

Kiya looked up to Ed, and he to her. Without words, the two embraced. Kiya closed her eyes and let her captain, the only man since Claudio, to be close.

Gloved hands dug into the arms of Ed's coat, and Kiya rested her head on his shoulder. She felt his strength, the consideration he showed his fellow officers and men, and the kindness toward her. Kiya thought of this moment, the man in uniform holding the woman, barely out of being a girl, alone on a boat on the water.

For a long moment, the two held on and said nothing. "I've missed Akira so much," Kiya said. "I have felt you miss Patti in the same way."

"I do." Ed kept Kiya in his arms. "For just one moment, I need this—you do as well, right?"

"Right. You know," Kiya said, "Dale's right. You are the best man on the Lakes."

"I have a long way to go before I'm that," he replied. "But," he added with a smile, "I appreciate that I'm on the road to it."

Back on the bridge, Ed took his seat in the chair and the two discussed the refit and plans for the coming trials. They were back to business; under the circumstances, they knew their significant others would understand.

* * *

Aki sipped the strong espresso as she relaxed in the plush armchair. "I am amazed, and perhaps it is wrong to think this way," she said, "but I was fearful you would be angry with me."

Motoko Takahashi-Paganini smiled. "I can see why you would be concerned," she replied, "but, Aki-chan, there is nothing for us to be angry about."

The two were seated in a private meeting room at a downtown Tokyo social club. Neither woman was a stranger to such places; the club was a modern world of its own with a restaurant, a main bar plus two smaller ones, and a theater and performance stage. For those so inclined, there were also more traditional rooms laid with *tatami* mats, low tables, and *kotatsu* in colder weather.

Motoko had invited Aki for lunch at the club, where she and Claudio were members. The latter was teaching at the university this day, but Motoko offered his regards. "I am most happy to see you again, Aki-chan," she said. "What occurred with Kiya-chan must still be painful for you as well."

"I admit to that." Aki set her cup in its saucer. "I wish I could explain in more detail," she went on and tried to choose her words carefully. "It is exceedingly complex."

Aki thought Motoko looked well, but she was appreciably thinner, and her black hair had many strands of gray. She wore her typical business suit, black slacks with a matching jacket, and a red blouse. She looked at Aki from over her gold-framed spectacles, her brown eyes worn from care. *Just like me; we've both lost sleep, and weight, and quite a lot more.* "There has still been no communication?" Motoko asked.

Aki shook her head. She decided not to tell them about the Amida, but Aki sensed that Kiya's mother suspected something out of the ordinary. "I firmly believe Kiya-chan is near," Aki said, "and I am searching for her. I can't do it the way others would, such as hiring a detective. I don't want to do that because it would attract public attention. Kiya-chan doesn't want that, and I don't either."

"I understand." Motoko nodded. "Claudio-san and I are of the same mind. Kiya-chan will return when she is ready."

The quietude of the club seemed to diminish even further. Aki became aware of a presence, a mixture of light and dark, which competed against itself. "Whatever the case," Aki went on, "I have to decide what direction I will take. Kiya-chan would want me to do this. When she returns, we will see where we are. I would like for us to pick up where we left off, in our lives and our careers; but it would be too much to ask that things be exactly as they were."

"You will have a lot to catch up on," Motoko agreed. "And yes, it is inevitable you will have both changed in each other's eyes; but the love that is at the center of your beings, that will always remain." She checked her watch. "I must apologize, I have to return to work, but I do thank you for coming, Aki-chan."

As she walked with Aki to the main entrance, Motoko said, "The mother in me would say you look well but tired. I won't say the other things Hiroko-san might have, or what I would tell Kiya-chan."

Aki laughed as they waited out front for the valets to bring their vehicles around. "I would not be offended," she replied. "Please give Claudio-san my love."

"I shall."

Aki's BMW was first out of the lot, and the valet swiftly pulled up, got out, and stepped aside for her. "Until next time, Motoko-san," she said with a bow, "*arigato goziamasu.*"

"I thank you as well, Aki-chan." Motoko bowed and waved as Aki drove away.

As Aki pulled into traffic, she saw him. Standing on the corner, in the same black outfit she'd seen him in before, was Chiang. He tried to make himself unobtrusive by standing on the other side of the transit shelter, but she knew he was there, watching as she drove by, the silver cross that hung about his neck in his fingers.

Aki could care less at this point. *If I faced him now, I know I'd be afraid, but I would do it. I also know that when that time comes, or is meant to come, I will take him on.*

She then thought of something else. *A strange thing, that cross he wears; I saw it in Kyoto. Despite the feeling I get that he has no morality or conscience, he must have one that's buried deep. Otherwise, he would not wear it.*

Aki thought no more of him. As she drove, a song came over the radio, a familiar one about seeing the light. With that came a vision of Kiya.

She and Kiya were connected again.

17
When We Were Stars

THE WOMAN IN a long purple silk shirt and black tights sat in a small auditorium of the Kitaro Conservatory, on the left side of the room, two rows from the front. She listened but also watched the young man onstage at the piano.

Ri studied the student's body language. She felt it important to see, as well as hear, what a musician was doing. Ri took no written notes, merely made a mental checklist of what she would need to address.

The student's short black hair would have made one think of an office worker, but the green and white stripes dispelled that right away. The thick glasses and fuzz-like beard did the same. The Lip Cream tee under a white, striped collared shirt and the black bondage pants completed a look that was incongruous to the jazz composition he was winding down.

At its end, Ri stood up and applauded with deference. "First of all, very original," she praised as she climbed up the steps in a pair of thigh-high boots with three-inch heels. "The composition feels solid, based on what you've shown me."

The young man smiled and nodded as Ri clicked across the stage and pulled up a chair to face him. "Now, the coda will need tightening up. The time changes from verse two to the bridge are unusual, but I can see where you're going. Big thing," she continued, "is your feel. You're pushing a lot through your hands. That's good, but you must do this."

Sitting straight up, Ri placed her hand on her stomach. "Keith Jarrett learned to play from the gut," she explained. "It's like singing: from the gut and the diaphragm. Bring the energy out of there, let it transfer from there through your hands. It takes time to learn how to do that, but it's good practice."

The student nodded. "Let me try with part of this," he offered.

"Pick a spot," Ri told him, "anywhere within the piece. Go slower if you need to." She got up and walked around the stage as the student began to play again and tried to bring up the feeling that Ri had explained.

"Good," Ri called as she saw the back door to the auditorium swing open. She waved at the new arrival as she continued to study the actions of her student.

A shoulder bag over her leather coat, Aki walked down the center aisle and took a seat in the middle section. Ri had indicated she would be working with a student; Aki watched this fellow in action and thought back.

She'd watched and heard Hiro and Suya during their matriculation here; both grew not only musically but also from the academic side. The young musicians, artists, filmmakers, and performers astounded Aki . . . *and yet, I'm one who lived their dreams. I resolved every time I went onstage to never forget these people and to let them know, if I can be this, they can be anything.*

The student finished the piece and asked Ri, "How was that? I could feel it change a little."

"Better," Ri replied. "Don't overdo and you'll be all right. My next client is here," she joked as she motioned to Aki to come up. "See you next week."

The student exchanged bows with Ri. He stored his sheet music in a battered case and pulled on a brown suede jacket. He nodded to Aki as they passed; he did not recognize her.

Aki climbed the steps to the stage, and the women greeted one another. "A protégé?" she asked.

"One of my many students," Ri said as she took his place at the piano bench. "He has most intriguing music coming out of him."

"I would say so," Aki replied as she removed her jacket and tossed it over the folding chair. "That was a little hard to follow, but I liked it."

"What do we have?" Ri ran her hands through a short classical piece to warm up as Aki opened her bag and took out a clipped stack of pages.

After yesterday's meeting with Motoko, Aki spent much of the night organizing months of accumulated notes to find her best song ideas.

"I have two in particular I feel good about," Aki said. "I hope," she added with polite embarrassment, "you can look past my musical shortcomings."

Ri laughed. "Don't worry," she replied. "Many of the finest musicians I know cannot read or write music; each has a language unique to them. The trick is to learn that language yourself, then speak it."

The way Ri said that, and her gaze, made Aki relax. "Do you want to run through some established music to start?" Ri now asked. "I am familiar with most of what you've done, or we can go on to the new stuff."

"Let's go new," Aki replied. "I feel I want to get these out."

"Good."

Aki pulled her chair over, and the two went through the lyrics. As she did with Kiya and Hiro, Aki explained what she "heard," and began to hum the melody.

Ri played along with the first idea, then shifted to different keys to see what would work. Aki made notes as they went along, and soon a chart began to emerge for one of the new songs.

"*When we were stars, the world was open to us, all things at our command . . .*" Aki tried singing with her middle range as Ri played chords on the bottom end with some slow right-hand arpeggios. Aki nodded as they continued into the chorus, and Ri's chords were more accented.

"*Stars are born, stars fade, stars fly high, then come crashing down . . .*" Ri carried on with some additional improvisation, and Aki continued through the song. For the first time, Aki knew that Ri "found her," as musicians called it. What Ri was doing reminded Aki of Kiya's ability, yet Ri's own style came through.

"*Stars burn hot, then fade to dust, in the end, I wonder, were we ever stars at all?*" Aki stared at the floor; she listened to the silence.

"Excellent," Ri praised quietly. "You found the range for that one."

There was no response at first. Aki then raised her head. "I like what you did, too," she replied. "I don't know what else the band would do with this, but as Hiro would say, 'throw it against the wall and see what sticks.'"

Ri laughed, and Aki did as well; Ri had apparently never heard the expression. "All right then," she finally said, "but seriously, sounds like highly personal lyrics. Thinking about the days of the band, or was that more from the *Lotus Flower* train of thought?"

"A little of both," Aki admitted. "It seemed like we could do no wrong for almost six years. I'm amazed at what we accomplished; but it all flashed past, and yet I remember little things as if they'd just occurred. After *Lotus Flower*, Kiya-chan and I were 'it,' I suppose.

"I have never been comfortable with being a star," Aki went on. "I, and Kiya-chan as well, tried to stay out of the spotlight. To us, that is for *when* we take the stage. We don't perform twenty-four hours a day like others pretend they do. We had such a normal life together away from that, and we took pains to make it so."

Ri nodded in understanding. "Your brothers and their wives have done well to keep their children out of that."

"They have. They are protective of Akito-kun and Kala-chan," Aki explained, "but they're brought up like normal kids. They're not spoiled, and I don't think they are aware of how big we were, or perhaps still are. Hiro-kun certainly enjoys our success, but not in a negative way. He's proud, like our father was of his accomplishments, but never foolish about it."

"That's one thing I respect all of you for," Ri said. "You enjoy your work, but you don't see it as all there is. You have your home lives, your families, and your interests. It's the right way to be. Speaking of which, I have been asked to drop in over at the Pit later for your brother's session."

"The Pit?"

"Our nickname," Ri said with a grin, "for the studio."

Aki chuckled. "It fits," she replied. "I remember now; James-san wanted you to add piano to one of the tracks."

"I'll do it if it works," Ri told her, "but I will not barge in there and try to put my mark on someone else's music. Same as I'm trying not to do here."

"Don't worry," Aki replied, "you are not, Ri-san. This is going well, and I've no concerns. If I do, you'll hear them."

The two shared a smile; to Aki, a comforting one. "That's good," Ri said. "Shall we have another go?"

Aki nodded, and Ri began again. *"When we were stars . . ."*

* * *

Kenji leaned against the back wall of the studio; he nodded in time to the music coming through the speakers. James and Hiro were seated before him with two chairs crammed into the space as they continued the mixdown.

He'd taken Saturday afternoon off from the Ito Estate. He'd seen Mr. and Mrs. Ito off that morning; they were flying to Singapore for a meeting, then would take a working vacation in Bali.

Megumi was picking up Akito from school, and her parents would watch him and Kala tonight, as everyone was going out. After an early dinner, they would repair to Uma's to see Zendo and Eiki's performance, then to the Imperial for Mika and Suya's opener for that band no one could seem to remember the name of. Kenji realized he hadn't gone clubbing in years; it would be a fun night out.

He watched as his brother ran the track back and discussed the mix with James. Hiro was as focused as James was when it came to the music, but Kenji understood it. He felt the same about his artwork.

Earlier that morning, he'd called Megumi into the studio to show her the finished split portrait of Aki and Kiya. Megumi well knew her husband was as unpredictable in his style and subject matter as Mika was in her performances, but Kenji could tell this one really surprised her.

She stared for a long time at the work. "Hmmm . . ." Megumi leaned in close for a period of time as she scanned it, then took another angle, like a collector sizing up a buy. "Kenji," she finally said, "this is incredible. Your brush strokes are strong and assertive—the dark areas especially."

Kenji nodded and smiled. "Thanks."

"And . . . I see a lot of pain." Megumi noted the facial expressions of Aki and Kiya. "Neither one is showing that much emotion," she went on, "but I see it. It's like you knew how they felt—or feel."

"Yet I did not see Aki-chan until after I did that," Kenji explained as he set his brushes and tools aside for cleaning. "I imagined it, and surprisingly, what I saw of her the other night is what was already here."

"I'm serious," Megumi said as she came over and kissed him. "This is brilliant. You have got to show this stuff someday."

Kenji chuckled. "Who," he asked sardonically, "would want to see it?"

"Me," she replied, "and a whole lot of other people. Now, the rock art is one thing, but the other stuff in connection? Hell, I'm surprised Ito-*sama* hasn't asked to look at it."

"Actually, he has." As they walked into the kitchen where Akito was finishing breakfast, Kenji explained, "Mr. Ito, of course, has seen the album work because of his kids. The other things," Kenji added with a self-deprecating smile, "he sounded impressed. I don't think he wants to purchase any of it, but he was encouraging."

"Ito-sama knows his art, Dad," Akito remarked in an aside.

The parents chuckled, but Akito had visited the estate before and noted how Mr. Ito knew a good thing when he saw it.

Kenji thought back to that conversation. Megumi had a showing in mind; there were certainly plenty of galleries around Tokyo that would be interested, but Kenji still wasn't sure he was ready. Then again, Megumi would never let him not be.

When it came to the management of the band, Megumi handled the money and the contracts, and Noriko did the go-between work. His sister-in-law was a big influence on Hiro, and Noriko knew from early on in their relationship when to push and when not to.

Kenji found himself thinking about the past six years. His direction, as the B-J-Bs evolved: Kenji played harmonica and added flute on some of the tracks of that first album but opted out apart from guest appearances on the next two. Artwork, photography, and album design became his main contributions, ones he was much more comfortable with.

From this angle, Kenji was able to stand on the outside and look in. He had a unique perspective from which to watch his siblings and everyone else. Hiro had found his career in music and would not be denied, but both were surprised at how Aki not only found her voice but herself.

Kiya provided the spark, Kenji thought; she would gently nudge Aki in the areas she needed, but never too hard. And to see Aki in love, as Kiya was with her, was wonderful.

Being brothers, and older, both Kenji and Hiro felt the need to look out for Aki but learned they didn't need to. *I sometimes worried about their being so open about their love, but that was where Aki showed herself and her character. She is one of the sincerest people I know; everyone, from family to the fans, loves her for that because they know where they stand with her.*

Kenji looked over the studio, watched Hiro, James, and the others, and thought of all those who'd come into the family's lives. *Since the days of our parents' deaths, I now see how our friends rallied around us. We pulled together, the three of us, but without those friends, Megumi, Noriko, Taru, Mr. Ito—I know we would have survived, but would we be where we are?*

"Hey, *Onii-san.*" Hiro leaned back and asked, "What do you think? If Ri-san gets here soon, I'll overdub the lead on this and we can wrap it up."

"That works," Kenji said, "and I'll tell you what, this back-to-the-blues thing is sounding really cool."

They stepped outside so Hiro could smoke. "It's been a blast," he said once his cigarette was lit. "The three of us, and maybe a keyboard player doing some club shows? It'd be awesome."

"Megumi-san says they're going to shop it to the blues labels in the States," Kenji replied. "How will they take that here?"

"Unless they want to get on board with it," Hiro said, "it's hands-off. They might not be interested, but we have the option of doing solo work on our own. I like it better this way; no interference. While we're at it," Hiro went on with a sly grin, "we would not mind hearing you on a couple of these upcoming tracks."

"I wondered when you would ask," Kenji replied. "If you want me, just say the word. A good blues album has to have a little harmonica in it."

The brothers laughed, and Kenji posed the question, "Now that Aki-chan's back, will you work with her again?"

"Absolutely." Hiro took another drag. "I'll do it," he added, "if Aki-chan is up for it, but you know? This session is the most fun I've had since we were playing together back then. I mean, what we did in leading up to the first album was good, always was." He shrugged. "Somewhere along the line, it all changed."

"Did it stop being fun for you?" Kenji asked. "The band, I mean? You were all about the blues at the start, but you rolled with how the band went."

Hiro nodded. "I know what you're saying," he replied. "I didn't want to be a blues purist," Hiro explained. "I realized that music only attracts a certain population, but what remains is at the root of it all, at least to me. I found plenty of spots to put my influence in; it's all good."

"Very mature of you," Kenji complimented. "Another thing," he continued, "you have chilled out considerably from our younger days."

"I'm aware of that." Hiro leaned against the wall and stretched his shoulders. "Nori-chan is the one who calmed me down; Kala-chan, too. I learned to think twice when it came to her."

The two shared the laugh. "Same here," Kenji replied. "I remember Dad sometimes doing that, taking a moment before saying what he was going to say."

"Yeah," Hiro said. "When the music came, I channeled that energy into it, and suddenly I felt like I had control of things again. At least when I play guitar, and now do the music I can do, I feel myself."

Hiro stubbed out his smoke and replaced it in the pack. "No regrets, but even with this, I wouldn't mind getting the band back together again."

"I know you don't think this way," Kenji said, "and Aki-chan never did. But once she began to attract the attention, the band became more about her. Then later, her and Kiya-chan."

"I didn't need center stage," Hiro replied. "Like I said, I made my own mark."

"You did." Kenji looked across the lot. "Speaking of which, there they are." Aki and Ri were walking in their direction, and the former waved as she approached.

"Ri-san and I got some stuff started," Aki reported as they exchanged hellos.

"Cool," Hiro replied and motioned inside. "Wait till you hear some of *this*."

"Ah, competition," Kenji joked.

All laughed and they headed inside. An electric piano was squeezed into the corner by the techies, and Ri sat behind it and powered up. "My old Hammond might do better," she suggested, "but let me hear this. Piano or something else?"

Hiro shrugged as he strapped on his Tele. "We all thought piano, but do whatever you feel works," he said. "We can do at least a run-through before everyone gets here."

"Sure." Ri put on the headphones that rested on the instrument and began working with an electric piano sound. Once Hiro was ready, he nodded to James and the tape rolled.

In the booth, Kenji whispered something in Aki's ear. She nodded and smiled.

18

The Storm

"ENGINES AT IDLE, Captain," the wheelsman called and checked that the telegraph arm was set in its proper position.

"Very good." Standing on the starboard bridge wing, Ed gave the signal to cast off. Dockworkers unraveled the heavy lines fore and aft and tossed them free of the posts that had held the *Ecorse* fast to the dock for the past several months. As the deckhands quickly pulled them aboard, the captain stepped back inside the wheelhouse and scanned ahead with his binoculars. Picking up the radio mic, he pressed the button to transmit. "*Mackinac*, this is Captain McCarthy. *Ecorse* ready to follow you out."

Some scratchy feedback, and the reply came: "Roger that. Ready to steer one-zero-zero."

"One-zero-zero, understood." Replacing the mic in its hook, Ed ordered, "Dead slow." He then picked up the telephone to the engine room. "Mike," he called, "we're heading into the channel now. How goes it down there?"

Over the sound of the refurbished engine, Mike returned, "All systems go, Ed. The inspectors haven't reported anything; we should be in good shape."

"Right, thanks." Ed hung up and looked out the bridge windows. The *Mackinac* was now well ahead, cutting a path through the remaining ice to the river. While March was a rough month, the last ten days were warmer than normal, and the icebreakers moved apace. With that in mind, the company ordered the *Ecorse* out for its required trials and first pickup of the new season.

Ed turned to Kiya, who had brought the bridge crew a round of coffee. "Feels better already," he said. "Engine's purring like a kitten."

Her hand wrapped around a cup of her own, Kiya nodded. "It sounds healthier," she agreed. "What is this trial going to be like?"

"We'll go straight downriver into Lake Erie," Ed elaborated, "and conduct tests on the way to Pelee Island, do the loop around, and check in there. We'll pick up the first load, head for Put-In-Bay, Toledo, and back up the coast. Starts the year off right."

"Then I better get below," Kiya said. "George and I need to get back in the swing of keeping everybody fed."

"Thanks for coming up," Ed replied. "Good seeing you and everyone again." He raised his cup and added, "Here's to a good season."

"*Kanpai.*" Kiya clicked her cup to his and headed down.

Ed sipped the black brew as he went into the chart room and checked the plot. The course was one he'd mapped out and followed numerous times before, but he liked, and needed, to be thorough. He took one final look at the forecast mounted on the wall above the table: *Mostly cloudy through the afternoon and evening; chance of snow flurries and squalls. Winds out of the NE, 25-35 knots, shifting to E-SE by tonight. Swells 3-6 feet this afternoon and evening, with light-to-moderate chop.*

A little heavy weather was possible, Ed thought, but not unusual for early spring. Good thing he'd ordered the ballast tanks filled; without cargo, the *Ecorse* could get banged about the lake if things got hairy.

Down below, the voice of Marvin Gaye blared through the radio as Kiya stepped into the kitchen. George was stacking a large set of white towels on the galley table. "Just in case things start bouncing around," he commented.

Kiya nodded in agreement as she went to wash her hands. In case of rough seas, wet towels were used in the kitchen and dining room to keep the plates and cutlery from sliding around; an old but effective trick.

"Better keep the meals simple until this weather blows over," Kiya suggested. For safety reasons, cooking was suspended in rough seas, either by order of the captain or by the cook's prerogative. In that case, sandwiches were served until the storm was over.

"Gotcha," George said and went through a side door by the stove, which led to the pantry.

Kiya went across to the dining room and checked the level in the giant coffee urn bolted to the deck. Satisfied there was enough for a while, she went back across and realized that even though they should still be on the river, the wave action was already picking up.

Reaching up, she switched to WWJ Radio for the news. The transistor crackled with interference as she adjusted the dial: reports on the carnage in Vietnam, activities in Washington, and problems at the mayor's office. Then came the weather forecast, delivered by the baritone voice of the reader:

> *"The National Weather Service has posted a Gale Warning for the southern portion of Lake Superior, as well as all of Lakes Michigan and Huron through tonight. A High Wind Warning is in effect for Lakes Ontario and Erie, which could be changed to a Gale Warning, as the track of two storms in the Midwest becomes better understood. Small Craft Warnings are posted for all of the Great Lakes."*

The voice continued:

> *"Cloudy skies will dominate the Detroit Metropolitan area southward to Ohio and eastward toward Ontario. Snow will begin falling again this afternoon. Three to six inches are expected by midnight tonight, with additional amounts in upper elevations. The high today, thirty-eight; the low tonight, three. That's the forecast . . ."*

Kiya switched back to the FM dial. "I hope Ed knows about that," she said half-aloud. For some reason, she had a feeling of worry. Common sense reminded Kiya that Ed stayed on top of the forecast without any prodding from someone like the cook. As well, any changes would come over the ship's radio; several lake boats served as reporters for the weather service. All vessels shared this information between themselves on a regular basis, too, so it should get to Ed in good time.

"Down On Me" by Janis Joplin began to play as George emerged bearing several bagged loaves of bread. "Just like GM," he quipped, "assembly line time."

They laughed, and Kiya went to the refrigerator for sandwich fixings.

* * *

It felt like a homecoming for Aki as she and the gang sat at the back corner tables of Uma's. The coffee shop they'd spent so much of their time before, during, and after classes had evolved over the years, but the lavender front and black lettering of the shop remained the same.

Uma was a little older and grayer, and his paunch a bit larger, but he remained the same cheerful person Aki remembered. The shop gained fame and additional business when fans learned Aki and her bandmates were regulars here in their high school days. Uma was happy to see his old friends again, but he made no public reference to tonight's special guests.

Aki noted the crowd this evening was largely people around her age or younger. The unsuspecting audience knew not with whom they sat on this night as they downed their lattes and cappuccinos and watched the odd couple armed with an acoustic guitar and djembe on the small, raised stage.

Zendo never billed himself as being a member of the Blue Jean Buddhas, although he was certainly recognized as one of them. His and Eiki's set touched on the B-J-B's catalog, but mostly they played their own songs and others.

Aki and Ri sat at one of the tables with Hiro and Noriko, while Kenji, Megumi, and James shared another. *If only Kiya were here; I can't help but think that, even though I'm having fun. I know she would have wanted me to enjoy myself. Since my return from the Summerland, I feel as though I'm this close to finding Kiya . . . it's going to happen.*

Zendo and Eiki's years of singing at the monastery were retrieved like they'd never been apart. Onstage, the smiles the two had were more for the joy of their being together again, inasmuch as they enjoyed performing.

The audience sat in rapt attention as the two led the crowd through songs old and new. "Here's one I heard several years ago while I was in Canada," Zendo announced.

He began the intro to "Four Strong Winds," which Eiki followed with a quiet backbeat. Aki peered over her shades. Wrapped in her coat, she watched her cousin and his partner in this atmosphere, which really was the best place for Zendo's music. Completely professional, Zendo gauged the crowd's reaction and carried on despite noise or distractions that would have deterred others. He did not mention who was in the audience either, mindful of Aki's need for privacy, especially now.

Eiki's vocal step into the verses was seamless, and her harmony fit with Zendo. Aki knew when a singer meant the words they sang; no doubt, Zendo was of that ilk with Eiki again. Aki once more resolved that she and Kiya would be, too.

The one-hour set earned the duo a well-deserved round of applause. The small spots on the stage came back up; Zendo and Eiki accepted congratulations from the couple dozen patrons who stayed for the set.

They made their way to the back, where they received more kudos from family and friends. They sat with the others and had a brief discussion. Zendo and Eiki were invited to go to the Imperial as well but begged off. "Much to do tomorrow," Zendo replied, but he did not elaborate.

After goodbyes, everyone headed up the street for their cars. Ri had ridden with Aki. "Wind's picking up," Ri commented. "This will be a bad night."

"It seems that way." As they turned from Uma's parking lot into the street, Aki hit the preset on the radio for the news station. The main story was a storm that suddenly brewed in the Pacific and was now lashing Taiwan and the Chinese coast. The commentator reported, not without some gravity in her voice, that the storm was gaining strength and moving on Japan and had the potential to be upgraded to a typhoon. Tsunami warnings were also expected for low-lying areas.

"That storm's getting together fast," Aki remarked, and she turned on the windshield wipers. The leading edge was already on them; the rain suddenly fell hard, and they felt the winds strike the car.

"This is going to be serious."

Aki's eyes shifted as she drove. Ri stared forward, but her expression and the way she made that statement were not speculative. Aki noted how Ri's voice and her posture changed; the same way they had when she spoke of Kiya the other night . . .

As the cars made their way in the ever-gathering tempest, a man stood alone on a skyscraper in the city's center. No one who bothered to look up at the sky would have seen him, all in black and in shadow. Fingering the crucifix around his neck, he said quietly, "It is time. I am the Storm."

19

Dancing Barefoot

KIYA STEPPED ONTO the bridge, cups of coffee for Ed and the wheels-man in hand. The *Ecorse* was well out into Lake Erie and straddled the invisible line between Canada and the United States. She knew that in potential storm conditions, Ed would not leave the bridge, even when his turn on watch was over.

Ed stood at the windows to the right of the wheelsman, a new mem-ber of the crew Kiya knew only as Andreas. Ed had mentioned he was from Norway and served in that country's navy as well as on a number of merchant vessels.

Both men gratefully accepted the cups. "Thank you," Andreas, a tall, athletic-looking man with short blond hair replied in good but second-hand English.

"Yes, thanks, Kiya." Ed turned back to the windows and rolled out-ward, as the *Ecorse* had no windshield wipers. The result left the bridge colder than usual; the wind occasionally whipped spray inside, which covered the bridge telegraph, the rail, and the floor. Kiya noted how quickly the water glazed over upon landing.

She stood to Ed's right and gripped the rail to steady herself. "This'll be as good a test as any," Ed noted as he looked through his binoculars. "Things are going okay, but this storm's starting to pick up."

"We're ready down below," Kiya told him.

Ed nodded but said nothing. Kiya noticed his expression had changed. Setting his cup on the rail and leaning its top against the wall, he brought the glasses back up. "Port your helm," he ordered sharply, "ten degrees."

Andreas caught the urgency in the captain's voice before Kiya did. "Ten degrees, aye, sir," he replied immediately and spun the wheel. He looked down at the compass and reported, "Steering zero-seven-seven."

At a pause, Kiya looked up at Ed and asked, "What is it?"

"We're gonna get hit," Ed replied, pointing to the distant waves. "No Christmas trees! Close these windows," he ordered then moved around Andreas and began to crank the windows on the port side of the bridge inward. Kiya did the same on her side, but as she closed the last one, she caught a glimpse of the wall of water that had risen above the bow and blotted out the sky.

My God.

The wave that struck the *Ecorse* was many times higher than the boat itself. Ed's order to alter course had come not a moment too soon; he'd seen that the white "Christmas tree" tops of the waves were not there and turned the boat to face it, bows on.

Tons of water blasted across the deck and rushed up against the hatch coamings. Even with all lines, tools, and gear stored, the wave was still able to tear open lockers, wash away one of the lifeboats, and slam against the bridge windows.

The vessel lurched, and it was enough to knock Ed and Kiya to the deck. Andreas was able to keep his feet, but only by holding the wheel in a death grip.

Ed pulled himself up and brought Kiya with him by her arm. "Keep her on course!" he shouted as he crossed to the telegraph. He manipulated the handle to signal for half-speed, then reached for the rank of buttons near the radio and pressed the alarm. "Kiya, get below!" he ordered. Ed then grabbed the engine room phone. "Mike, what's going on down there?"

The emergency bell sounded throughout the *Ecorse* in the code well known to everyone aboard, save, perhaps, the inspectors busy taking readings and overseeing the boat's improved power plant.

Across the vessel, the sudden turn and strike by the wave threw men off their feet or out of their bunks. In the engine room, Mike was only able to stand by holding onto an overhanging rack. Seeing the telegraph change, he and one of the two assistants on duty moved quickly to reduce speed. "Tell those clipboard carriers to check for damage," he ordered one of the men. To the second, he shouted, "Make sure the rest of the crew is up and at 'em—we're gonna need help!"

Down in the galley, Kiya found the place in disarray. Dishes, plates, and cups had crashed to the floor, many of them broken. The radio was hanging by its power cord and dangling over the stove, and George was attempting to get to his feet.

Kiya went to his aid, her boots crunching on the wreckage. "You all right?"

"*Holy Christ,*" George replied in Italian, "*this isn't Superior! We shouldn't have these kinds of waves!*"

George reverted to Italian when he was under stress, and Kiya responded, "*Well, we do now. Let's get this cleared up.*"

"*Not yet, Kiya! That was a seiche wave! They always come in threes!*"

Kiya suddenly felt a terrible fear. *Three of those waves? There's no way we'll survive two more . . .*

Then, the second wave hit.

* * *

"Aki-chan, you made it!"

Mika gave a big hello to Aki as her companions entered the backstage area of the Imperial. The cramped quarters housed the headliners, a five-piece outfit, plus the five members of Mika's group. Mika picked her way through the crowd to give Aki a welcome hug. "I'd kiss you," she said, "but my makeup will get all over you."

"Don't worry," Aki replied, "we're all here, despite the weather." She told Mika that driving over was like riding through a car wash. "But we made it," she finished.

"That's so cool." Mika's face was pale white with a number of red, green, and black markings. Her stage outfit consisted of a black bra, long silk gloves, a tiny pleated black PVC miniskirt that only covered about half of her buttocks, fishnet stockings, and a pair of platform combat boots. Her hair was also tied out in two side ponytails with a third pointed toward the ceiling, frozen in place by spray.

Suya came over to say hello in his favored Goth makeup, as were the rest of the band. Pushing in behind Aki were Hiro, Noriko, and Ri. "It'll be a short set," Mika explained, "but about half is new material. And I'm pretty sure there won't be any riots, okay, Nori-chan?"

After a laugh, the guests headed for the wings from where they could see the small area that the Imperial called a stage. Somewhere out in the darkened club, not the mosh pit, were Kenji and Megumi. Aki recalled that the band had played this club in their earlier days, not long after that wrestling show at Korakuen. The club catered to a much younger, mostly underage crowd then.

Tonight, the subcultures had arrived in force: leather-wearing metalheads and punks; Goths all in black, their faces a deathly white; *Ganguro* girls in caked-on makeup, their hair dyed wild colors; drag queens and Club Kids whose hair, outfits, and makeup were statements in themselves.

The venue was at capacity when the lights went down. Mika stayed in the wings to let Suya and her mates go first, the latter of whom were met with an appreciative howl. The club manager took the mic at center stage and yelled some abuse at the crowd; this drew a torrent of boos and good-natured insults, but he seemed to like that. He then shouted Mika's name as an introduction and hurried off.

The second guitarist began to strum a guitar line, and the band kicked in behind. Mika made her way onto the stage to a huge cheer. These were her fans, and she enjoyed the adulation. She walked to the mic, pulled it to her while still in its stand, and began to sing in a low, sexually charged tone, of benediction, addiction, and connections . . .

Mika had the crowd before she had even sung. She slowly paced the front of the stage while she sang the lyrics to Patti Smith's "Dancing Barefoot." Smith was Mika's biggest inspiration, and her cover was pretty close to the original in Aki's opinion.

"She sounds a lot better," Hiro shouted due to the noise. Both Aki and Noriko nodded. Aki liked what she was hearing and seeing; at least Mika wasn't inciting the crowd this time around.

Mika ended the song by reciting a poem and leaning into the audience from a kneeling position while the female keyboardist sang the last lines. The first song went well, all agreed; then it took a turn.

As soon as the song ended to a huge cheer and round of applause, Mika rose, looked at the crowd, flashed an evil grin, and shouted, "To borrow a phrase: *I haven't fucked with the past, but I've fucked plenty with the future!*"

The crowd roared with delight, and Mika followed it with a poetic rant, complete with obscenities, political observations, and a few rather nasty gestures. She then did something else, which Aki didn't quite see, but everyone in the audience did. The wave of reaction got even louder.

Aki turned and saw the shocked, scandalized look on Noriko's face. "Did she—

"*—she did!*"

The band immediately tore into the next song, and the high-powered guitar attack on an original seemed to calm the crowd down. Mika and the band continued at an intense level for the next thirty minutes without a stop.

Hiro and Ri remained in the wings while Aki followed Noriko to the backstage area about halfway through the set. The headlining band was there with their manager; they looked nervous and upset. They obviously didn't know Noriko's connection to Mika and that the new arrivals spoke English.

Some of the members were concerned about getting arrested for whatever Mika had done out there, and at least two of them were furious about getting blown off the stage by what was supposed to be a mere support act.

Noriko found a seat and lit a cigarette. She was, in Aki's mind, a combination of shocked and pissed off. After a deep drag, Noriko said calmly, "I don't know whether to congratulate or kill the bitch."

Aki shook her head and sat beside Noriko. "I don't think it's that bad, Nori-chan," she said. "It doesn't sound to me like this crowd is easily offended."

"Let's hope not," was all Noriko would say as she continued to smoke.

"So, she flashed her breasts," Aki mused. "Worse has been done."

Noriko turned to Aki. "That's *not* what she flashed."

It took a moment for Aki to process that. "Oh."

The set ended with no police officers at the door. Mika led the band back; she, like the others, was sweaty but in a good mood. Ignoring the glacial stares of Noriko and Megumi, who'd come back with Kenji, she went straight to Aki and asked, "Well, how was it?"

"It had a lot of energy," Aki replied, telling as much of the truth as she dared. "And your voice is getting better."

One of the staff came back and shouted, "Encore, guys!"

Mika and Suya huddled briefly with their mates; then Mika came back to Aki. "Got an idea," she said. "Wanna come out and do it with us?"

Aki's eyes widened. "Do what? I don't know any of your songs."

"We know 'Love You Like Me,'" Mika replied. "I love the way you sing it. Look," she added quickly, "I know Kiya-chan isn't here, but I can do her part. Let's do it, for her and you."

Aki looked to Noriko, who had forgotten her initial anger with Mika, and said, "Yeah, do it! It'll be a big surprise for people."

"Do you want to, Aki-chan?" Megumi asked her.

Aki looked to her brothers; both nodded, as did Ri. "Do it," Hiro urged.

"Yeah," Kenji added, "we want to see it."

She turned to Mika. "Okay," she said and took off her jacket. "How do we want to work it?"

A quick discussion over the verses, and then the band filed back on to a good ovation. Two microphones were now set up at the front of the stage. Mika again went last, while Aki waited in the wings. She was shaking; nerves for sure, but also from a step she now had to take. *Wish me luck, Kiya . . . this one's for you.*

The keyboardist began the opening of "Love You Like Me." Mika stepped up to her mic. *"You traveled the world, lookin' for, lookin' for love, there ain't nothin' out there that you deserve . . ."*

A rumble from the crowd. Aki took a deep breath and walked on-stage to the second mic. *"Tell me I'm crazy, but I know what you're worth, and you'll keep coming back, 'cause baby I am your girl . . .*

"Can't nobody love you like me . . ." The stage shook as a result of the crowd's reaction, and Aki could feel it through her boots. The power

from the drums and guitars pushed her from behind; Mika took Kiya's high part and Aki tore into the second verse.

"I'll keep all your secrets, and I'll wipe your tears, I see all the scars on your broken heart, and if you let me in, I'll take you to the stars . . . can't nobody love you like me . . ."

Flashes were going off all through the club as fans used their smuggled cameras and cell phones to try and get a shot of Aki onstage for the first time in a year. Aki was only aware that she was back where she needed to be.

Mika looked her in the eye, and for a very brief moment, Aki thought Kiya had returned. *"Take my hand and surrender, I promise you don't get a fear, tonight you're gonna remember, there's nothing else better . . ."*

Aki's vision turned inside out: in that split second, she saw Kiya in some kind of trouble, a storm not unlike the one outside, reaching out for her. *"'Cause baby I'm in this forever . . ."*

Mika brought her back. *"I'll take your pain and wash it all away . . ."* The wail, the power chords, and Suya's double bass drums blasted Aki into the night.

"Can't nobody love you like me . . ." They belted out the final chorus; the keyboard outro came and went, and the club shook to the rafters with cheers and applause.

Mika took her mic and motioned to her guest. "Aki Sato!" she shouted.

"Mika!" Aki shouted into her mic and motioned to the band. A wave, a bow, and all were offstage.

Backstage, Mika hugged Aki and said, "Thank you, Aki-chan! But I think that was more for you than us," she added, "you needed that."

"I did," Aki replied, relieved in more ways than she could describe. "And thank you, Mika-chan. Thanks for giving me a chance. I owe you one."

As everyone involved with the band began to leave, the headliners' people were raising a new stink with the club manager. That representative, a well-dressed older man, was shouting at him in the narrow hallway about what had just transpired.

"What the fuck is going on!" he yelled in English as they passed. "You give us some kind of weird-ass performance band to support us! They do these things, and then they bring up some woman to pull out the show for them? And those freaks out in the audience! What kind of a club is this?"

"It's a *music* club, asshole," Hiro remarked in English and fixed the American with a dirty look. "Tell those *gaijin* poseurs if they don't like it, get out there and show what they got—or go home."

The man was speechless; Aki and the rest hid their grins as they walked out. Following an uncomfortable silence, the manager calmly replied, "I think that says it all. Get 'em out there."

20

Face to the Wind

THE SECOND OF the "three sisters" slammed into the *Ecorse*, and the boat again shuddered to its keel from the force of the water. From his position on the bridge, Ed McCarthy watched as the bow went under and then slowly pushed its way to the surface.

"Keep her headed into the waves!" Ed ordered Andreas. "What's the course?"

"We're on zero-six-six, sir," the wheelsman answered as Dave, the new first mate, clambered onto the bridge.

"Hold her on that." Ed ran into the chart room and motioned for Dave to follow him. The metal clips used to keep the charts in place on the table did their job. The mate began to pick up the dividers, pencils, and other materials from the floor.

As Ed pored over the document, he looked for landfall. Pelee Island was dead ahead. "Dave, what do you think? Should we try to get into Scudder on the north side," he suggested as he indicated its place on the chart, "or around the northern edge for some protection?"

"Scudder's no place to try for in a storm, Ed." Dave was a stocky bearded redhead of Irish descent; he was an old friend of Ed's, and a former master himself. He pointed to the chart and added, "We need to get to the other side; there's plenty of areas there if we have to beach."

"I agree." Returning to the bridge, Ed ordered, "Steer zero-four-seven degrees. We'll head 'round Pelee and find somewhere to anchor." He dismissed the thought of beaching the *Ecorse*, at least for the time being.

This was Ed's first command, and he was not going to lose it unless it came down to a choice of the boat or his crew.

Andreas held the wheel, and the *Ecorse* slowly moved onto the new course. The wind now blew from the southwest, behind them. Ed slid open the starboard door and leaned out as far as he dared. He ignored the cold spray that struck his face like needles. They appeared to be from that direction, but since the storm broke the winds were shifting, and they seemed to attack the boat from all sides. He'd heard the old tales about storms like these but never experienced such a phenomenon until now.

Ed went to the radar screen, but the backscatter made it impossible to read. He tried a different magnification and got the same result. He cursed under his breath knowing they'd lost radar. *One of those waves must have knocked it out.*

Back to the windows, Ed now scanned ahead with his binoculars. Visibility was down to less than a quarter-mile, but he didn't see any other vessels. That didn't mean they weren't out there.

Ed went to the telegraph and rang down for another reduction in speed. "We'll have the wind at our backs for a while, hopefully," he told Andreas. He peered again through the glasses and searched for the island; they'd have to run parallel to it for a time to avoid any shoals.

The engine room telephone buzzed. Ed grabbed it and heard Mike's voice on the other end. "We're taking on water," Mike shouted down the line. "Portside, amidships."

"Start the pumps if you haven't already," Ed ordered. "How bad is it?"

"Not a bad crack," Mike said. "It's right on one of the welds, and it's above the waterline. I've got the guys shoring it up now."

"Good, any other damage?"

"None that I can find, but we may be getting some water in through those old hatches. They haven't reported from the hold yet."

Ed turned to scan the deck. All seven of the wooden hatches were still in place and securely clamped down. As Mike alluded to, however, they came with the boat when the *Ecorse* first went down the ways. Replacing them would be a custom job, one the company did not want to pay for.

Maybe this storm will change their damned minds. "Anyone hurt?" he asked.

"Nope," Mike replied. "A lot of bumps and bruises, that's it."

"Okay." Ed hung up the phone and again took hold of the rail as he looked ahead. He could now see the dim outline of Pelee Island in the distance. They were near the northern point, and they'd have to turn farther in that direction to make it. So far, the old *Ecorse* was handling it, as were the crew. He allowed himself a moment as well to think about Kiya.

Down below, when it became obvious the third wave would not come, Kiya and George set about clearing away the mess. They quickly swept up the debris and spills, and Kiya prepared another urn of coffee.

They kept themselves braced as the boat rolled and pitched. She and George kept on with barely a word; they knew Ed and the rest counted on them as much as anyone else in the crew.

* * *

Aki drove home alone through the worsening storm. Her wipers were on full speed, but these did little to deal with the sheets of wind-lashed rain. She was traveling slowly, as were the other vehicles on the city's streets.

After leaving the club, Ri accepted a ride home from James. All seemed concerned about letting Aki travel alone, but she resisted entreaties to have someone go with her or for her to stay the night with them. Aki needed to go; as the night wore on, she knew something was about to occur. She would have to be alone when it did.

The radio news report confirmed it for her. The same news anchor reported that the storm hitting southern Japan was now officially upgraded to a typhoon. The nation's Self Defense Forces were being activated for evacuations.

"Authorities in Taiwan have reported numerous fishing vessels missing or lost in the heavy seas, and coastal areas report widespread damage and several deaths," the reporter continued. "The Chinese news agency Shin Hua is reporting damage of varying degrees along its coastline with a number of small vessels sunk or damaged.

"Government officials in Tokyo say damage is expected to be moderate to severe along the southern shores. Anyone living in coastal areas is urged to leave and to take steps to secure life and property.

"In another weather-related matter," the reporter continued, "the North American Great Lakes area is being hit by what forecasters there are referring to as a freak weather system. The merging of two storms over the Lakes region has produced hurricane-force winds, closing many of the major ports, the locks at Sault Ste. Marie, and the bridges between the United States and Canada . . ."

What?

"At least two major carrier vessels have run aground in Lakes Superior and Huron, and the US Coast Guard reports several small vessels in distress across the region. Forecasters say this storm is remarkably reminiscent of one that struck the Great Lakes in the spring of 1970 . . ."

This is it.

At a break in the weather, Aki put on speed and changed stations as she drove into her neighborhood. *I'm coming, Kiya* . . .

She dodged a downed tree limb as she drove down her street at full speed. Aki knew what she had to do; then, a crunching guitar and a voice she recognized came out of the radio, singing about the summer of love, a universe about to unwind . . .

Aki was no longer in her car; she didn't feel the wind and rain, yet it tore at her hair, her clothes, her being. All things vanished before her, but for the soundtrack; it called on Aki to reach out, touch the moon, the stars, face to the wind, and feel the freedom . . .

* * *

"I thought these things only happened in the North Atlantic." Andreas leaned over the wheel as he held out his coffee cup for a refill, which Kiya poured from a dented metal pot.

"Welcome to the Great Lakes, son," Mike replied as he queued next in line.

Ed laughed, an exhausted one, seated in his chair for the first time in hours. The *Ecorse* was anchored in a small cove on the eastern side of Pelee Island. The storm was finally blowing itself out; the crew had effected a temporary repair of that crack in the hull, but the boat would need to return to Detroit to finish the job.

Kiya came over to fill his cup for the third time as he looked out the open bridge window. Deckhands were re-clamping the cargo hatches and clearing away debris. Water had gotten in during the storm; there was more down there sloshing around than was comfortable, but the pumps were running and slowly getting rid of it. "What'd you think of that ride?" he asked.

"That reminded me of a typhoon," was all Kiya said; she looked beat but didn't complain as she and George kept the crew fed and fueled all through the storm.

"Weird one, too," Ed added.

Kiya looked to him. "How do you mean?"

"Well," Ed replied, "I've never seen a storm like that. Sudden ones on the Lakes happen, to be sure, but that came out of nowhere." He shook his head. "It was like someone conjured up the whole deal, the wind shifts, the wave action, all of that." He turned to face the windows. "I know that sounds superstitious," Ed admitted, "but I've never had an experience the like of that one."

Kiya nodded as she rested the coffee pot on the rail and re-gripped the potholder that protected her hand. "I do know," she replied. "When do we get underway?"

"Soon as the clipboard boys get done," Mike replied. "At least the engine did well. They seem happy about that."

"We'll need to get the radar fixed when we get in," Ed replied. "I've radioed ahead for a technician to meet us when we get home. Kiya, since things have calmed down, would you and George kindly get us up a solid meal? Think we could use it."

Kiya smiled. "Aye-aye, Captain," she said with a casual two-fingered salute. "Consider it done."

Ed laughed as he returned the salute. As she headed back down the stairs, Mike said, "Nice girl, Ed; great cook, too. How long before that boyfriend of hers shows up, you think?"

"Don't know." Ed leaned back in his chair. "She's waited a long time for the guy; she won't quit on him. Reminds me of what it takes when you love someone. I'd wait for Patti till the end if I had to. Kiya's shown me how to really do it, though."

"Can't say I know how that feels. Kind of different," Mike admitted, "seeing as how my missus is right at the door when I get in and all. It's a good feeling."

"You're one of the lucky ones, Mike," Ed said. "But then," he added after a pause, "times have changed."

The engine room telephone buzzed, and Mike picked up, as he was closest. "Bridge . . . all right, thanks." He hung up. "Looks like we're ready to go, Ed. We'll have to take it slow back to Detroit all the same to make sure the port side holds."

Ed grinned as he stood up. "Right, then," he replied. "Steam on the capstan, Mr. Lonegan. Let's take her home."

Aki opened her eyes. That song was still in her ears, a new world before her. Looking around, Aki found herself standing on a rock high above a huge lake, arms stretched skyward with the wind in her hair. The sun was shining, but a cold, brisk wind blew in off the water.

The rock she found herself on overlooked the lake. Aki thought of herself as a black sentinel as she stared out over this expanse of freshwater. She took in the scene over her shades: the lake was a deep blue and untouched by pollution. In the distance, she saw an ore carrier, one of the big ones, heading in for the bay.

Aki had never been here before but knew exactly where she was. Looking across Lake Superior, Aki had a commanding view of Whitefish Bay and could even see the Canadian side. A quiet, wild place this was, and she took it in.

Aki jumped from the rock, made her way down to level ground, and walked to the road. A late-model Dodge Charger, panel black in color, was parked there. She climbed in, fired the engine, and peeled out.

Heading south through a small town called Paradise, Aki turned onto Route 123 and put on speed. All she knew was she had to get to Detroit. Allowing her instinct and the car to guide her, Aki drove on, listening to the radio and someone singing about a journey to the center of the mind.

I told you I was coming, Kiya, Chiang or no Chiang. Hold on, my love . . . I'll be there soon.

21
Drifting

MEGUMI RESET THE overstuffed pillows against the headboard of the bed and lounged in her red velvet bathrobe. A good night all around from a management point of view, she thought. Zendo and Eiki's show had gone down well; Megumi was sure bookings would not be a problem. Whether their schedule would permit it, and if they even wanted to, was up to them.

As she made notes on her tablet, Megumi also thought about Mika's performance and how that ended. Mika had at least toned down the act; her singing had improved, and there'd been no repercussions from what she did onstage. Still, that girl was a handful; reading her the Riot Act was not going to do any good. If she'd learned anything, Megumi knew not to push certain people's buttons. Mika was one of those artists.

Aki's decision to join Mika onstage caused a gigantic ripple. Megumi's and Noriko's phones blew up with voice and text messages. The office voicemails were full, too. The press and social media were ecstatic that Aki finally resurfaced; video shot from phones and other devices at the Imperial garnered hits, comments, and especially likes. An online write-up of the show spent nearly half the article talking about Aki, and there was much analysis of her appearance and her voice. In addition, there was the lingering question of where Kiya was. Overall, however, the response was positive—Aki was back in the public eye—and had been missed.

Kenji walked in bearing two cups of coffee, the Sunday *Asahi Times* under his arm. "Here you are," he said as he passed her one of the cups.

"Thanks," she replied, and they kissed. After a sip, Kenji set about taking off his paint-smeared work clothes. "Sorry to tell you," he said, "but I may have to go in."

Megumi dug through the paper and took out the entertainment section. "Trouble at Mr. Ito's?" she asked.

"Not sure yet," Kenji replied. Down to his underwear (which drew a smile from Megumi), he pulled a pair of jeans out of a dresser drawer and sat on the bed. "That was a rough storm last night, and we may need to call some of the grounds crew out to clean up."

He picked up the TV remote and switched to the NHK network. Keeping the sound low, he continued, "Mr. Ito called a little while ago. Pretty wild in Singapore, he said, but the island didn't get hit too badly and everyone's okay. Looks like up this way wasn't so lucky."

He indicated the screen, which showed a harbor located in the southern part of the country. The footage panned along a dock area, showing fishing boats run aground or sunk at their moorings.

Megumi checked her cell again. "Aki-chan hasn't called back," she said. "The buzz is incredible from her cameo."

"Keeping the wolves from the door again, eh?" Kenji slid onto the bed and scanned the front page of the paper. There were more disaster photos, but at least the storm blew out quickly.

"I know she's just getting back into it," Megumi replied, "and that will take time."

"You know," Kenji said as he put the TV on mute, "Hiro-kun and I had a talk yesterday; I took the liberty of passing the gist of it on to Aki-chan."

Megumi turned and looked at her husband, her eyebrow cocked in imitation of a Sato family trait. "And?" she asked expectantly and with that cunning smile.

Kenji related the conversation. "They are both keen on the idea of putting the band back together. They want to do it," he added, "I think for different reasons, but they're both energized at the prospect."

The wheels in Megumi's head were already turning. "That'd be cool," she said guardedly. "I can see a lot of stuff from that." She sipped her drink, then slid herself closer to Kenji. "Still," she went on, "experience has taught me that the idea is one thing . . . whether or not they will all do it is another. I can't push that; it's up to them."

"It's therapeutic." Kenji put his free arm around Megumi and kissed her. "The one thing that helped us all was the music. Aki-chan needs it, and us, now more than ever. Going out there last night without Kiya-chan? Dad would say something like that requires courage but also growth."

Megumi thought for a long moment. "Do you think Kiya-chan is still out there in that alternative timeline or whatever it is?"

"I believe so," Kenji replied, "but Aki-chan knows that she has to move on with her life. Whether Kiya-chan comes back or not, she's doing what she must."

Megumi nodded; she leaned up, kissed her husband again, and said, "Those two embody love, the black and white, the yin and yang—that's what they are to each other. If one laughs, the other laughs; if one weeps, the other weeps. Aki-chan has lost the one person in her life; her reaction to whatever happened to Kiya-chan was normal. Aki-chan is still fighting, but I worry about the cost.

"I have felt so bad for them, and Kiya-chan's parents," Megumi went on, and her voice betrayed her shift in emotion. "For the latter, I feel like I've lied to them about the Amida, not being able to tell them what we know. I'm not sure they'd understand it. And I've felt the same, if not worse, for Aki-chan . . ."

Megumi put her cup aside. "I know how much you love her," she said quietly. "I do, too. Nori-chan was in tears when she called me after she'd caught up to Aki-chan. Then I saw her; she's been dying inside all this time, and we couldn't do a thing to help her."

She removed her glasses and covered her eyes with her hand. "I always try to remember as a manager that these are people, not products," she went on. "So many of our colleagues aren't like that, but I don't believe in making money that way. Nori-chan and I have a job to do; but at the same time, with or without the music I just want to see Aki-chan as herself again."

Kenji held his wife close. "You have always done what's proper, Megumi," he said. "I've never considered any of the decisions you've made on their behalf bad ones." He paused. "Well, there was that wrestling thing, but it did turn out okay."

Megumi tried not to laugh but couldn't help it. "I'm never going to live that one down, am I?" she asked as she looked up to her husband.

"No."

Both laughed. They kissed, and Megumi leaned against his chest. "I am so happy," she said. "I got the best man on Earth."

Kenji turned up the volume on the TV slightly as a commentator continued to discuss the damage from the fast-moving storm. "Nori-chan may beg to differ," he said, "but I'll happily accept that role." As he watched the screen, he asked, "You said Aki-chan hasn't called back?"

"No." Megumi sat up and leafed through the portion of the paper that interested her. "She'll call when she feels like it, of course."

"Look at that." Kenji indicated the screen, which showed what looked like a tanker run aground on a rocky shore. The big ship was getting a battering from the high winds and waves; a rescue helicopter was floating overhead, attempting to lift an injured person off in a stretcher.

"The American Great Lakes also experienced a similar storm last night," the newsreader said, "with numerous cargo vessels such as the *Bradley D. Warner,* shown here, grounding or otherwise suffering damage. Reports from Lake Huron were similar to much of what has been seen across the Pacific region.

"In addition," said the commentator, "discussion in American shipping circles as to the sudden formation of this storm, reminded all of one that struck the Lakes in 1970. That storm caused widespread but generally minor damage, yet the sheer ferocity of the storm and its formation led many veterans of the Lakes to consider the possibility of supernatural activity. However," the speaker went on, "these theories have never been given much weight . . ."

"Uh-oh," Kenji breathed.

"What?" Megumi asked.

"I know why Aki-chan hasn't called back," Kenji replied. "She's *there.*"

* * *

The Mariner's Church was quiet this morning. The main portion of the edifice was empty but for one person. Kneeling before the pulpit, he spoke quietly in Latin, crossed himself, and stood up. Chiang looked up at the brilliant colors of the stained glass and its beatific depiction. The church was Anglican in its tradition, but Chiang felt it made no difference. He carefully replaced the cross before his chest, slid his collar over the chain around his neck, took a deep breath, and exhaled.

"A most intriguing paradox."

Caught off-guard, Chiang spun around. Standing in the aisle, a few rows back, was a man, dressed the same as he. "A man who acts as he does yet has a connection to a holy man," Kazu observed as he stepped closer. "You still have something in you for this one."

Chiang nodded and slowly walked around to where Kazu stood. He kept his distance, however, at two meters. "My parents converted to Catholicism when I was an infant," he explained. "When the Chinese government cracked down on religion, we emigrated to Japan; but they remained faithful, as I have."

"I find that hard to understand." Kazu's expression was neutral; there was no anger or sarcasm in his voice. "Yet I have known men and women who have claimed such things but cannot bring themselves to, shall we say, 'walk the walk.'"

Chiang smiled that thin, emotionless smile. "You don't need to understand it, Kazu," he said. "I highly doubt you would, even if I had the time to explain it all."

He was about to pass when Kazu put his hand up. "Allow me to finish."

Chiang stopped. "Very well."

"This is a house of God," Kazu said, "and I have no intent on causing trouble of any kind here, or anyplace else, for that matter. But there is a connection between your faith and mine. I am here to give you a warning: stand aside from Aki and let her pass. If you do not, your worst fears will be realized."

Chiang's smile did not change. "Please explain."

"Think of it this way." Kazu put out his left hand and motioned to the side. "Here lie the gates of Hell." He then held out his right, making the same motion to that side of his body. "Here lie the gates of Heaven. It is a decision—one you must make."

Chiang considered for only a moment. "Thank you for your demonstration, Kazu," he said as he walked past. "Fear is something I have dealt with my whole life, and my afterlife. I am prepared."

Kazu watched Chiang walk out the main doors, which closed with a muted echo. He turned and gazed up at the figure of Christ, and those who surrounded him, for a long moment, then he headed for the door himself.

Pausing out front, Kazu looked in each direction. Chiang was already out of sight. Crossing the street, Kazu walked at a measured, mindful pace, hands in the pockets of his leather coat.

The sun shone, but the weather remained cold. The overnight storm was violent but quick; fallen limbs, leaves, and other scattered detritus covered the streets; some of the properties he passed suffered damage, broken windows, and some loose roof tiles, but otherwise, most were in decent shape. These things mattered little to those who had to pick it up, but for Kazu they were indicators.

His destination was a few blocks away, a small park. Kazu cut across the main path and moved into a more secluded portion. Seated alone on the end of a bench was a woman, also dressed in black, seemingly in meditation.

Kazu sat on the other end and looked forward. "I saw Chiang," he said quietly.

The woman did not move. "What did he have to say?"

"Very little. He remains resolute. My last warning has failed."

"You did not fail," the woman replied. "It is he who has. The time to act is now."

Kazu nodded. "The storm has sapped Chiang's strength," he said, "and his attempt to sink the *Ecorse* has come to nothing. It will take time for him to recover, which is why I believe he was at the church."

"So be it." Hiroko stood up. "Aki-chan is coming; the meeting must take place."

"You do realize," Kazu replied as he rose, "that the danger for all of us is loss. I have no fear of that, but I would like to know your thoughts on the subject."

"Loss is something we have all had to bear in our lives, and now," Hiroko replied, her face impassive. "I fear nothing. As we say, 'this we do.'"

She walked away in silence. Kazu watched until Hiroko was out of sight. He then turned and walked back the way he came.

* * *

The *Ecorse* plowed through the light chop at six knots. From the bridge chair, Ed felt the boat was holding up under the circumstances; its slightly lower ride in the water helped the vessel take the waves a little easier.

Despite a need for sleep, Ed determined to remain on the bridge until they reached port; Andreas was back on the wheel after a four-hour rest break. On deck, under Dave's direction, hands made further repairs from last night's storm and worked to re-clamp the all-important hatches.

The radiotelephone sounded, and he moved to answer. "*Ecorse*, Captain McCarthy speaking." After hearing the response, he said, "Affirmative; confirm request that a technician be on hand for radar repair, plus a full crew for docking. We have a couple of feet of water in the hold," he went on, "but the pumps are coping. The crack needs to be welded again, but dry dock should not be required. Engine overhaul is being termed a success."

Ed listened. At length, he replied, "Very good, thank you. *Ecorse* out." As he hung up, he mentioned to Andreas, "The port's been reopened. Lot of damage up and down the Lakes, and a couple of boats ran aground in Superior. Guess we got off light when you think about it."

Andreas nodded in the affirmative but said nothing. Ed returned to his chair. He could not get out of his mind the oddities of last night's storm. *The weather service rarely screws up like that. Had we any idea of what kind of storm it would be, I would've canceled the sailing. If we were loaded, we might have done better, ridden it out more easily.*

The Lakes are unforgiving, and that was the worst storm I've ever been in. I didn't say anything because the last thing you want to do is get the crew in a panic. Guys like Dave and Mike don't blink, but there are the younger fellows to think of.

Then there's Kiya. She's never been through things like that, but she's tough. I saw that in her from the start. Somehow, I can't stop thinking about her, in relation to all of this . . .

Aki tore down I-75 in the left lane. She'd driven nonstop, focused on the road and unconcerned about the scenery or other traffic.

She pulled out a photograph nestled against her wallet and gave a brief glance at it as she drove. The picture was of the two of them in evening wear, Aki in black, Kiya in white. They were holding one another, smiling more at one another than the camera.

Aki downshifted, put both hands on the wheel, and floored it. The Charger leaped forward with additional power. The closer Aki got to Detroit, the more certain she was Kiya would be there. Others, too; but at this point, Aki was determined that nothing, and more importantly, no one, would stop her.

22

Decision

DALE MCLEOD SAT before his desk at the Black Dragon. The boys were at work cleaning the store, stocking product, and seeing to customers while Dale busied himself with the paperwork of his varied enterprises.

The *Free Press* was on the desk; Max and one of the others had already pulled the comics and sports sections for themselves. The front page had a good shot of the wave action from along the shore last night. A strange blow, but those on the water seemed to have mostly made out all right.

He reached up and adjusted the volume of his marine radio. Despite being "on the beach," Dale still listened to the traffic and recognized voices of old mates from out of the ether.

"Hey, keep the music down a bit," Dale called toward the front. Behind the counter, Max lowered the sound of the Supremes so Dale could concentrate. He knew the *Ecorse* had its trials yesterday, and he'd worried about his friends on board, particularly Ed and Kiya.

Now it sounded like they were coming home. *Ed knows what he's doing,* Dale thought. *He got around on the backside of Pelee and rode it out 'til it was over. A real sailor, the genuine article, as my father would say.*

The damage reports that came through on the old boat were a cause for concern; some of those bloody hull plates had been patched, re-patched, and welded too many times for comfort. Then there were the ones still being held together by rivets. Ed indicated it recently, and Dale wondered if the company would finally break down and either refit the boat or perhaps put her up for good.

Dale hated to see any boat go to the breakers, but like the passing of a loved one, you had to accept it. The *Ecorse* was launched in 1917, during a boom of wartime shipbuilding. She'd served numerous companies and masters but always kept her name. Bad luck to change a boat's name was an old sailor's mantra and one Dale firmly believed. Fortunately, *Ecorse's* owners understood at least that much.

He stood up and took the local news section in hand. "Gotta take a leak," he announced to no one in particular. "Be right back."

Max stifled a laugh. For Dale, "right back" would be about a half-hour. Dale heard the radio being switched to the FM as he headed back. "Crosstown Traffic" emanated from the radio; he listened with amusement as Max sang the high backing vocals while Jimi Hendrix went on about so hard to get through.

The song blasted from the Charger's speakers as Aki turned down a side street near the waterfront. She was still being guided, but the tension inside her increased. Aki's eyes swept the street before her and searched among those who were on it. *Kiya's here, or she's been here. I haven't seen Chiang, but I feel his presence. Whatever the case, I'm close—very close.*

The car moved slowly along Atwater Street. Then the turn signal flipped on, and Aki moved the car into an open parking space. She killed the engine and removed the keys. Getting out, she found herself across the street from an old brick building with a black, gold-painted sign hanging above it. Two kids in wool coats were sitting on the front steps.

Here. Aki crossed the street. As she did, she noticed the two boys were staring right at her. They moved aside as Aki climbed the steps and entered.

Aki closed the door to the cold and looked over the wall of comics on the left side and the collection of other items as well. To her right, a blond-haired boy was on the cash register. He was looking at her, too; Aki sensed recognition.

On a practical level, Aki realized she must look very strange in this town: a Japanese woman, all in black, wearing leather, but Aki was used to people staring at her for one reason or another.

Max slid a stack of comics into a paper bag for the customer. "Thanks, see you again soon," he said as the customer passed Aki and left the store. The boy then came from around the counter. "May I help you?" he asked politely.

"Yes," she replied, "I'm trying to find an old friend, and I was told to look her up here. Perhaps you've seen her." She withdrew the picture from her coat pocket and handed it to Max.

The boy took one look at it and then at her. "You're looking for Kiya," he said.

Aki tried to hold in her excitement. "Is she here? Has she been here?"

"Just a minute," Max said and hurried to a doorway at the rear of the store. "Dale," he shouted, "get out here!"

"Taking the channel course, Captain," Andreas reported. "Speed at one-quarter."

"Good." Ed raised his binoculars. The waterway ahead was free and clear, the Ambassador Bridge in the distance. "Almost home," he said, "and about time."

Kiya stood alongside him. She was wearing her usual jeans and heavy flannel shirt; her scarf was loosely wrapped inside the collar. Her cap was pushed back on her head, her hair in a ponytail. "Nice to see that again," she commented.

Ed smiled. "I know," he replied, "I've been through some bad ones, but never have I been so happy to see the bridge like I am now."

She nodded as the radio crackled. "*Ecorse*, this is the *Washtenaw*, come in."

Ed reached up for the mic. "This is the *Ecorse*," he replied, "over." They could see the vessel in question on the other side of the bridge, downbound.

"This is Captain Wilkes. We got a problem up here," the reply came. "We've lost power, and we're anchored in the channel. You should pass us by okay; we're waiting for a tug."

"Any idea what happened, Ron? Over." Ed knew Wilkes, and the *Washtenaw* was one of the larger bulk carriers. Off mic, he commented,

"She's only about six years old; this is the first I've ever heard of 'em having this kind of trouble."

"Not a clue, Ed," Wilkes replied. "Everything just kicked out. At least it didn't happen right under the bridge or we'd really be in a fix."

"Well, glad you're anchored okay. Anything we can do?"

"No, but thanks. Hopefully we can sort it out before long."

"Okay," Ed said, "good luck. *Ecorse* out." As he replaced the mic, Ed motioned to the huge carrier on the opposite side of the channel. "Take a look at her, Kiya."

She followed Ed's direction. The *Washtenaw's* bow rose high above the *Ecorse*. The boat dwarfed theirs; it looked menacing, even from this distance.

"Lucky they dropped anchor where they did," Ed said. "It'll be tight for the bigger vessels trying to come out, or in. We'll stay in our lane; we should get by."

"I'll be right back," Kiya said suddenly.

As she left, Ed turned and watched her leave. Her tone of voice had changed. He turned back as Dave came in from the port bridge wing, and they discussed the approach as well as the *Washtenaw's* predicament.

Kiya passed through the kitchen and sidestepped George, who was preparing fixings for the coming meal. She knew George's gaze followed her as she passed through; he was wondering what was up.

She slid open the door to her quarters. Going to her bunk, Kiya slid her arm under the mattress and dug into a hole she'd found on the bottom side when she first came aboard. She pulled back her hand and withdrew a small roll of American currency. Since starting work on the *Ecorse*, Kiya kept her money either on her or in the hole. She chose not to open a bank account. Kiya either cashed her paychecks at the shipping company's bank or on occasion at the Dragon. Kiya stuffed the money into her jeans pocket, picked up a couple of personal items from the desk drawer, and made sure her notebook was secured inside her jacket. Putting that on, Kiya adjusted her scarf and left again.

* * *

Dale stepped out of the back room. Max's voice sounded more urgent than usual, and he passed a photograph to him. "This lady's looking for Kiya," he said and indicated the woman in black who followed him.

"I see," he replied, "thank you, Max; dismissed." Dale then turned his attention to the picture and one of those in it. "Let me guess," he said, "you're Akira."

Aki's eyebrow rose involuntarily, but she nodded. "I am."

"Dale McLeod," the man returned and extended his hand. "Good to meet you." The handshake was polite, but Dale could feel "Akira's" mood through this as well as see it in her face and posture. She was on edge.

"Tell me about Kiya, please," she said. "I've been looking for her for a long time."

"Indeed you have," Dale replied as he sat at his desk and offered a seat to Aki. "I was led to believe," he continued as Aki took the chair Kiya normally used, "that 'Akira' was a man. I think I understand why."

"It doesn't make much difference to us, Mr. McLeod," Aki replied.

"Please, call me Dale." He handed the photo back to her and said, "Since you've obviously come a long way, I'll tell you what I know. Kiya is serving on a boat called the *Ecorse*, and they should be on their way back to harbor as we speak. If you'll excuse me . . ."

He turned to the phone and dialed a number. Dale's name opened a door, and he was transferred to the dockmaster's office. After a quick hello and how-have-you-been to this person, Dale got the desired information. A brief thank-you later, and Dale hung up.

"Good news," he said as he turned back to Aki, "the *Ecorse* is coming up the Detroit River as we speak. They should be at the Ambassador Bridge in a matter of minutes."

Aki stood up quickly. "That's to the south, isn't it? I saw it on my way here."

"Yep. Take Jefferson south, and you'll see the turn for Canada."

"Thank you for your help," Aki said as she turned and rushed out of the store.

Dale walked to the door in Aki's wake. As he reached the front steps, he saw Aki jump into the Charger, fire the engine, and tear out into traffic.

The two boys on the steps looked to Dale, puzzled. Max also came out and stood with his boss. "Strange chick," he said.

"Yes, but being in love can make you act strange," Dale replied. He then went inside and returned to his desk. Turning up the radio, he sat and resumed his work on the papers before him.

Aki hoped she didn't run into any police as she blew through a stop sign and wheeled the Charger onto Jefferson. She floored the accelerator and raced past a series of slower cars and trucks. The radio station was playing Hendrix's version of "Wild Thing," which Aki was only vaguely aware of at this point.

Her heart pounding, Aki gripped the steering wheel tightly to keep her hands from shaking. From the moment Aki had arrived at the Dragon, she knew everything she hoped for in the past several months was coming to a head. Aki had to get to the bridge—and to the *Ecorse* before it docked. Aki wasn't sure why, but she knew she had to get there now.

The trip to the turnoff for the bridge only took a few minutes, but to Aki, it felt like a week. She cut right and downshifted as the Charger took the turn hard with a squeal of its tires.

Then, the bridge was before her; Aki stomped the accelerator and tore up the road. There wasn't much traffic, but either way, Aki was going to get there.

She slammed on the brakes at mid-span and jumped out. Aki ignored the honking of horns from the vehicles behind her as she leaped over the rail. She ran along the walkway until she was over the slow-moving boat that was sailing up the channel. There were no other boats in the water of any appreciable size coming from seaward; that one had to be the *Ecorse*.

"Reduce to slow ahead," Ed ordered.

Dave reached out and adjusted the telegraph handle. They watched as the Ambassador loomed over them, though Ed also kept one eye on the *Washtenaw*. Both her bow anchors were out, plus one at the stern. She looked secure enough, Ed thought, but he wanted to give her as wide a berth as he could without grounding on the Canadian side.

Kiya reappeared at this time. Ed knew the bridge was something she liked to see, whether sailing into or out of the harbor, but this time he saw something else.

Kiya stared up at the span, her expression blank. "You okay?" Ed asked.

"Yeah," Kiya replied. "It's just one of those days."

Ed scanned the horizon with his binoculars and then noticed that some of the deckhands were pointing up at the bridge. "Hey, look up there," Dave called.

Ed turned his glasses toward the bridge; then he saw it. "What the hell?"

Kiya turned. "What is it?" she asked.

"Take a look at that," he replied and handed her the glasses.

Kiya peered through them for only a moment, and Ed saw the horrified expression. "*Aki-chan*," she whispered, "*no!*" She thrust the glasses back into Ed's hands and ran out.

Ed looked again. Andreas was also looking up, shielding his eyes from the sun. "She's going to jump."

They weren't seeing things. A woman, dressed all in black, was standing on the bridge rail, gripping a metal stanchion for support.

"Reduce to dead slow." Ed's order was routine; caution going under any bridge was required. But before he could process what Kiya had said and what was going on before his eyes, he heard a sound come across the water, a sickening one.

A crack, like the report of a deck gun, then another. Ed looked straight ahead; he didn't need to see what was happening as the radio blurted out the warning.

"*Ecorse*, this is *Washtenaw*!" Wilkes's voice was urgent. "Our forward anchors have snapped! We're coming across your bow!"

All on the bridge watched as the bow of the fully-loaded *Washtenaw* began to swing to port into the channel. They could see the remains of the bow anchor chains, hanging useless from her sides. Without power, and her stern held by the remaining anchor, the *Washtenaw* turned across the river, right into their path.

"Helm amidships! Full reverse!" Ed's orders were automatic from years on the water, and he reached up to press the alarm button next to the radio. At the same time, Dave turned the telegraph handle to that position.

Those on deck stopped their work to look up at the bridge. They could see the outline of the woman in question, and someone wondered aloud if she was really going to jump. Then came the sounds of the *Washtenaw's* chains breaking, and most turned their heads in the direction of the sound.

The scene became even more bizarre as Kiya ran past them screaming, "Aki-chan! Don't do it!" She climbed onto the number one hatch and stretched her arms out as if to hold the mystery woman back. "Don't!"

The screw of the *Ecorse* stopped and then churned in the opposite direction as it tried to drag the boat back from a collision that would surely sink her. But even on a small vessel, inertia cannot be changed right away; the boat slowed yet continued forward as the bow of the *Washtenaw* loomed closer.

The order crackled over the boat's intercom: "Brace! Brace for impact!"

Above the river, Aki could hear the *Ecorse's* siren and see the men on deck, some running aft. She also knew something was wrong with the big boat on the other side of the bridge, though she could not see it. Aki focused on a small figure standing on one of the hatches, her arms seemingly reaching out to her . . . *Kiya*.

Aki could always pick her out, even from a distance. Gripping the stanchion, she took a deep breath and timed herself. *And I was always afraid of heights.*

"Are you sure you want to do that?"

Aki looked to her right. Chiang was standing on the walk a couple of meters away. "What you're doing is suicide," he said, an amused look on his face. "Are you sure?"

"Aki-chan! Do what you must!"

Turning to her left, Aki saw Hiroko standing an equal distance and angle away. "If your heart tells you to, Aki-chan, do it!"

Aki looked down. The vessel had stopped its forward progress and was now headed in the opposite direction.

She took a deep breath and shouted, "I'm coming, Kiya-chan!"

And she leaped out and into space.

23

The Last Battleground

THOSE ON THE deck of the *Ecorse* watched as the woman known only to one of their number shot down upon them. They stared in disbelief as she kicked her legs to remain upright, arms crossed, hands clenched to the shoulders of her jacket.

Kiya screamed as Aki's body flew down. She landed feet first on the number three hatch and smashed through it. The impact was deafening, and everyone hit the deck to avoid the flying shards of wood.

Racing onto the port bridge wing, Ed looked at the *Washtenaw*. She was still cutting across the *Ecorse's* bow, but his boat was now slowly backing away from the danger, as well as the bridge.

He had also seen Aki's leap. As Kiya and the men got to their feet, he ordered through the intercom, "Clear the hatch!" To the mate: "Full stop; drop all anchors! Call the Coast Guard and get someone below!" He then rushed down the ladder.

Dave moved to execute Ed's orders. He moved the telegraph handle to the "Engine Idle" position and ordered, "Keep your wheel amidships." He then pressed the buttons to drop the forward and stern anchors.

He grabbed the radio mic and switched to channel 16. "This is the *Ecorse*," he called. "We are inbound at the Ambassador Bridge. We have a vessel without power downbound in the channel, plus we have a jumper. Request Coast Guard and tug assistance immediately, I repeat, immediately."

Dave and Andreas watched the *Washtenaw*. The carrier now blocked both lanes, held from grounding by her stern tether. They looked on as crew members ran along the deck of the carrier to prepare lines and a storm anchor.

George now entered the bridge. "What's goin' on—" he began to ask then fell silent as he saw the big carrier across their bow and far too close for his liking.

"That's not the only problem. Somebody jumped off the bridge," Dave said without looking back. "She landed right on us. If you're not doing anything, get below. She'll be hurt if she isn't dead."

The deckhands dragged the remaining pieces of the shattered hatch from around the coaming, assisted by Kiya. As soon as there was enough space, Kiya pushed past them and threw herself over the side.

She ignored the shouts of her shipmates as she hung by her hands and looked down into the cavernous hold. She couldn't see, but it didn't matter. She let herself drop into the darkness.

A splash, and Kiya found herself lying in frigid water, of which there was still a fair amount in the hold, and she slowly pulled herself upright. The light from the open hatch shafted down, but Kiya couldn't see anything.

"Aki-chan!" Kiya shouted. No response. The lights in the hold were off, and Kiya knew she could not wait or go to turn them on herself.

In a panic, Kiya dropped to her hands and knees in the water; Aki might be unconscious. Splashing in a circle, she slowly worked her way through the dirty water despite its iciness. Her heavy clothing quickly became a sodden, leaden weight on her body. She shouted Aki's name again above the idling engines and the sounds of the anchors dropping out of their housings. There was no reply.

Freezing and now frantic, Kiya swept her arms and moved in a wider circle, repeatedly screaming Aki's name. *She couldn't have drifted away that far. She's got to be here!*

Then her hand brushed against something. Grabbing hold, Kiya pulled it to her. It was a leg! As Kiya dragged herself up Aki's body, she found her facedown in the water.

With all her strength, Kiya turned Aki's body over in her arms and pulled her head to her chest. At that moment, the lights came on.

* * *

Ed began to climb down the ladder to the hold. He saw Kiya on her knees in the water, holding the strange woman and screaming, "Aki-chan? Baby, I'm here! I want to go home! What do I do? Tell me what to do!"

He splashed into the water, wading forward as best he could to get to Kiya and the woman who lay lifeless in Kiya's arms. As he approached, Kiya turned to him. Her hair was wet and across her face, and he saw the wild look in her eyes.

"Ed, forgive me!" she cried. "Thank you for everything! Give Dale and George my best!" She again turned to Aki, brushing her wet hair out of her face. "Aki-chan," she shouted, "I want to go! Now!"

Ed watched in the dim light as Aki's left hand slowly came out of the water and touched Kiya's arm. Before him, the two women vanished.

The anchors bit into the bottom of the river at that very moment, and the *Ecorse* shuddered; the backward motion slowed. The sudden shift of the vessel that followed threw Ed off his feet and into the water.

"Let's go!" George led the way down the ladder; he jumped into the water and made his way toward Ed. Behind George were three crewmen, one bearing a portable stretcher, another a first aid kit.

George helped Ed to his feet, and the captain leaned against the hull. He grabbed one of the ribs of her keel for balance as he tried to clear his eyes. George and the other men were looking around; two of them shone their flashlights off the water, then around the hold. "They're not here," one of them said.

Ed clung to the metal and looked down at his other hand. He was holding Kiya's cap; somehow, he had ended up with it in his grip.

He stared at the soaked item, uncomprehending.

* * *

It's not over.

Kiya was shaking from the cold and her wet clothes. She was still on her knees, holding Aki to herself. Aki did not move, but Kiya held a hand to her chest and found her heartbeat.

Looking around, Kiya had no idea where she was. They were inside something, but the room had no walls, and she could not see a ceiling, either. It felt like being inside a huge planetarium; there was that odd feeling of being in space. There was a pale light coming from above, a spotlight upon them.

Kiya then noticed the markings on the floor. For a radius of about five meters around them there glowed a green circle, drawn by what she didn't know. They were in its center.

She turned her attention to Aki, who was beginning to stir. Kiya gently stroked her forehead and face. "Aki-chan," she whispered, "it's me. I've got you."

Aki looked so thin and tired, Kiya thought. There was a slight cut above her left eye, and blood was trailing in a line from it. Then her eyes opened.

Aki stared up into Kiya's face; she was trying to process seeing her lover in this condition, and in clothes meant for a man. Aki tried to speak but could only cough as water from the boat came out of her lungs. She turned her head to the side and spat out the horrible-tasting fluid that was in her.

Kiya held Aki's head up to help her breathe; Aki felt the hands, and those arms holding her again, but she didn't have time to enjoy them. "I don't know where we are, Aki-chan," Kiya said.

Regaining her breath, Aki tried to sit up but cried out and sank back; her voice echoed through the strange room.

Kiya held her securely. "Where does it hurt?"

"All over." Aki raised her head. "Kiya," she whispered, "help me up."

Kiya slowly brought Aki to her feet but had to support her. Aki had trouble standing; her left leg was unsteady and couldn't bear weight. Shivering, she held to Kiya and said, "I know where we are. This is the Last Battleground."

"The what?"

Aki tested her leg, and she cried out again. Favoring her right, she placed her hands on Kiya's shoulders. "I'm sorry, Kiya," she said, "but you can't help me with this. Whatever happens, don't get involved. If we're going to be together, I have to do this. Trust me; get outside the circle."

Kiya didn't want to let Aki go but did as she was told. "Aki, what is going on?" she asked as she backed away. "What are you talking about?"

"He's here," Aki replied as she stood one good leg in the center. "The man who tore us apart, and has torn others apart, is here. It's me he wants; or part of me. And I'm going to give him all he can handle."

She swept back her damp hair, which dripped freezing water along with her soaked clothing as she turned around the circle. "Chiang! I know you're here!" she shouted. "You want it so bad, come here and get it!"

Aki seethed. She knew her expression, coupled with her physical condition and that of her clothes, must have made her look fearsome. Kiya looked stunned by the transformation.

"This is what you wanted, huh?" Aki yelled into the space. "Well, you've got it! Come get what you want! Bring it on!"

"A fighter to the last." Chiang stepped to the edge of the light, on the opposite side of Kiya. "I must congratulate you, Aki. You have accomplished your goal of being together with your, ah, lover. I hope you take pride in what you went through to get her back."

"It's not pride," Aki replied, facing him. "It's love. Something you know nothing about."

"Oh, I do," Chiang said. "And I must disagree. The love I have and know is perhaps different than your own, but they contain common threads. But let us not talk semantics; we are here for one reason: the Amida. You know why I desire it."

"But how much is enough for you?" Aki demanded. "You just want more and more of it. How much more do you need, how much more pain do you have to cause before there is enough to do what you want?"

Chiang took a step forward into the circle. Aki took one backward but kept herself between Kiya and Chiang. "Kiya was a tool that I had to use in this case," he said. "To get to you and your pure power. You have judiciously used the Amida over the years of your life. It is in this wiseness and discretion that your power remains so strong. That is why I seek it, in order to return to Earth as a man and carry out what a man must do."

"That's not how this works," Aki replied. "The Amida is for us to learn, to discover what we can about ourselves, to make us and the world around us better. It is to learn from history, not repeat it."

"Do not preach at me." Chiang's expression changed to a darker one. "It is unfortunate in this matter you remained obstinate," he said. "For that, I had no choice but to bring you here. I'm afraid your friend is going to have to witness *this*."

Chiang made a quick step forward. At the same moment, Aki pushed off on her right leg, and the two clashed in the center of the circle. Chiang's hands went from Aki's shoulders to her face, and he gripped her head in his hands.

Aki tried to move her arms under Chiang's to break the hold. Chiang was stronger than he looked; his hands felt afire, as the energy that ran through them began to drain what strength Aki had left in her.

Kiya ran to them and grabbed Chiang's arm. "Stop it!"

Chiang pulled his arm away and struck Kiya in the face with a knife-edge blow. The force of it sent Kiya off her feet and threw her near the edge of the circle.

Their bodies shifted, and Aki was forced to her knees. Chiang bent over her; his hands felt as though they would crush Aki's face in them; the maniacal expression on his face grew into a grin, and his eyes started to glow.

Pain tore through Aki's body; she could not break Chiang's hold. To her right, she saw Kiya; she lay on the floor, and blood dripped from her mouth as she stared in horror.

"Don't interfere, Kiya!" she shouted. "I know what I'm doing!"

Chiang seemed to turn into a demon, his eyes changed their glow from white to red. Spit dripped from his teeth and lips; he made a sound, like that of an animal. His face was exultant; he had what he had sought for so long.

Then Aki got to one knee. She seized Chiang's wrists and began to stand; Aki no longer felt pain.

She looked up to the light and shouted in a thousand voices: *"Now!"*

24

"This We Do..."

AKI'S CRY BROUGHT an immediate reaction. Kiya watched as four black forms dropped from the darkness above and seized Chiang. The look on Chiang's face went from ecstasy to shock.

Aki fell back; Kiya raised herself on one elbow and stared, amazed at the people in black who came to Aki's aid.

Zendo was holding Chiang by one arm; a stocky, longhaired woman Kiya recognized held the other. Another, who looked just like Aki, had Chiang by the hair, and a small man with a long mane gripped Chiang's neck in some sort of nerve hold. Chiang was now unable to move, fixed by the hold the four had on him, as well as whatever energy was coming out of them.

Then a flash; all fell to the floor, save Chiang, who remained on his knees. From her prone position, the lookalike called, "Aki-chan, the time is now!"

The room fell silent. Kiya sat up; she watched as Aki slowly rose, a wet, disheveled crone. To Kiya, her face was as before, but there was a frightening look to it now. Slowly and with great effort Aki brushed her wet hair from her face, then examined the blood from the gash on her forehead.

Barely able to walk, Aki now limped forward to Chiang, her breaths heavy and guttural. She grabbed Chiang's dangling cross in her blood-covered hand. She did not rip it from Chiang's neck but held him on it like a leash.

"Do you believe in God?" Aki's voice was quiet and even but belied a rage Kiya had never heard from it before.

Chiang's voice trembled in response. "Yes," he whispered, his bravado gone.

"Then let's see what else you believe in," Aki said as she closed her hand around the cross and the glowing inner irises of her eyes opened. "Let's go to Hell."

There was no light, no sound, no evidence of life could Aki detect. Before her, Chiang remained on his knees. She could not see Chiang; but as Aki still held him by his cross, she knew he was there and that he could no longer harm her, Kiya, or anyone else.

"So, this is Hell," Aki said quietly, "your personal hell. Darkness; nothingness. How interesting; your worst fear realized is nothing. It is a pity, the choices you have made. But now, the combined forces of the Black Watch and myself have made things right. You did not account for others sacrificing themselves for me, did you?"

She let the cross fall from her hand, and Aki heard it strike his chest with a thump. Chiang's head lowered to the floor, and she heard the metal clatter in contact with it.

Aki backed away three steps. "I, however, can feel no sorrow for you," she said. "You have damaged me; you stole from me the one person I love more than anything else, more than even myself. You have caused untold suffering in how many others, I do not know, nor wish to know. I can do only one thing: forget you."

In the shadow, Chiang raised his head slightly. He was holding the cross in both hands to his chest, praying in what sounded like Latin.

Aki turned and walked away. *"Here,"* she whispered, *"lie the gates of Hell!"* She did not look back.

A moment later, she found herself standing back in the circle. Kiya was sitting on the floor, being attended to by Hiroko and Ri. Kazu and Zendo stood on either side.

Before Aki could speak, her stomach muscles wrenched, and she fell to her knees. A hot liquid forced itself up from within, and her insides gushed out of her.

She felt Kiya and Hiroko come to her side. Her hands on the floor, Aki continued to vomit. Blood, bile, and what little food she'd had of late forced themselves out of her. Aki could feel the sickness around her hands, and her hair lay in it; she retched, and still more came from her.

"What's going on?" Kiya asked Hiroko, frightened. "She's dying, isn't she?"

"No," Hiroko replied. "She is losing the Amida, for herself and for all of us. It will be over soon."

The pool of blood and offal from Aki's insides spread to cover the whole of the circle as she gasped for breath. Aki could not control it; she felt like she had been beaten over her entire body. Then she coughed one last time, and the remainder finally dropped from her lips. Before she could fall into it, Kiya took Aki in her arms and rested her lover's head and upper body against her thighs.

Aki coughed and gasped for air. Her head spun as tried to breathe. Then she felt Hiroko take her hand. Through her blurred vision, her mother leaned in.

"It is all right, my child," she said quietly. "The Amida has been lost, but you have yourself, the one you love at your side, and you will go home. You and I shall not see each other again until you reach the Summerland."

She leaned over and kissed Aki's forehead. "I love you, Aki-chan, as does your father. Please give our love to your brothers. We are forever proud of all of you, and we will watch over you."

Kazu now stood at their side. "Please give my best to them as well," he said. "I await the day we can all play together again," he added and smiled.

Aki managed to wipe her eyes; she looked past her mother and Kazu to Zendo and Ri. "Why," she asked, "why didn't you tell me?"

"That was not our place or time," Ri replied. "There was, and is, no need to mention it, here or elsewhere."

Zendo nodded. "We must return to the mundane world," he said. "We'll see you when you get back." The two turned and walked off into the gloom.

"It is time for us to go as well," Hiroko said as she stood up. "We have completed our mission; we, too, can go home."

As Hiroko and Kazu turned to walk away, Aki called weakly, "Mom . . . thank you. You and Dad did so much for us . . . why this, too?"

Hiroko turned and smiled. "This we do," she said, "but we also do for the ones we love. Farewell, Aki-chan and Kiya-chan, but not goodbye."

They, too, walked out of the circle; the blood and remnants from Aki and the others had drained away; the circle was now gray and only its outline remained. The stars once again shone here, and Aki envisioned the way into the tesseract.

Aki felt Kiya's arms tighten about her. She looked up into those brown eyes, flooded with tears that plowed wet furrows along that face.

"It's over, Kiya," she whispered, "but not for us."

Kiya lowered her head to Aki's. She held Aki to herself and sobbed aloud. Aki took Kiya's arm with her remaining strength, and she felt Kiya's body rock with the emotions both felt.

After what seemed like several minutes, Kiya said in a shaky voice, "I knew you'd come, Aki-chan. No matter what, I knew. I just had to wait and hold on."

She lifted Aki's face to hers. "I love you," she whispered. Wiping the blood away from Aki's mouth, Kiya kissed her, long and hard.

Aki closed her eyes, feeling the kiss that she'd longed for, Kiya's tears falling onto her face. The strength of lips and mouths fed off one another; for Aki, the feeling of this moment was the same as they'd always known, even now.

As it ended, Aki whispered, "I've waited so long for that."

Kiya nodded. "Me, too."

"But my breath must really stink right now."

With all that had gone on before, both laughed a little. "It matters not," Kiya told her.

"Let's go home," Aki said.

Kiya smiled. "Yes, please, Aki-chan; take me home."

Aki pulled Kiya to herself, and for one final time, the room slipped away.

* * *

Words and lyrics passed through Aki's subconscious mind, ones about a lovestruck Romeo and his Juliet. She remembered Hiro liked the guitarist; Kiya came up with a piano version, and they did the song during the *Lotus Flower* tour. Time as well, that, too, came up, perhaps that was why . . .

Aki slowly became aware she was naked. She lay in a certain bed with a familiar set of sheets and comforter over her skin, awakening from a long sleep.

Then came the feeling of someone brushing out her hair, gently working through the tangles. Opening her eyes, the pale blue ceiling of the room came into focus, then the walls.

Looking to her right, she saw Kiya in her blue silk chemise, legs drawn up beside her. "Hey, you," she whispered quietly.

"Hey." Aki smiled back, unable to move. "Are we home?" she asked.

"Yes, we are." Kiya laid the brush aside and pulled down the hem of the short dress. She lay down over the covers beside Aki; she stroked Aki's face and kissed her cheek. "How do you feel?"

"I'd like to get up," Aki replied, "but that feels so nice right now."

Kiya smiled and kissed Aki's lips and lay with her. Aki closed her eyes again; she allowed herself to enjoy the feeling of Kiya's fingers touching her, her face against her own, her body alongside.

After some time, Kiya said, "Let me help you." She carefully rearranged the pillows, then lifted Aki's upper body into a reclining position without any assistance.

"Your arms," Aki remarked. She placed a hand on Kiya's shoulder and felt the muscle there. "What were you doing on that boat, shifting cargo?"

Kiya chuckled. "Cooking, believe it or not," she said, "but I had a lot else to do."

Aki looked over to the floor where their clothes were piled in a sodden, discarded heap. "How did you end up there?" she asked. "I've got so much to ask you."

"I have as many questions for you," Kiya replied, "but I need a bath, and I think you do as well. Let's take one together, and we can talk, okay?"

Aki smiled. "Okay."

As she shuffled down the hall assisted by Kiya, Aki decided she hadn't broken any bones, but every limb and joint ached. "I can't believe you jumped," Kiya remarked, "but that shows how much you love me, I think. Doing all you could to get to me."

"If you didn't know I loved you before then, Kiya," Aki said with all sincerity, "you do now," and both laughed.

In the large, gleaming bathroom, Aki leaned her nude body against the dual sink while Kiya heated the tub to the right temperature. She watched Kiya get things ready for the shower and could not but enjoy being in her presence again. "You had quite a life there for a while, didn't you?" Aki asked.

"Yeah," Kiya replied. "I lived in another world, but I had help. By the same token, I hope you don't mind I made some calls in this one."

"To whom?"

"Mom and Dad first." Kiya walked toward Aki as she pulled off her nightdress. "I so needed to hear their voices again. Claudio broke down and cried over the phone. I've never heard that before."

Aki smiled as she admired Kiya's body, toned from her work on the *Ecorse*. Then there was her brown hair, even longer now, but especially the face, the smile, and the brightness of Kiya's eyes.

"It's love and emotion all wrapped up," Aki said. "We've missed you so much."

"I am anxious to get caught up," Kiya replied, "but first I want to get caught up with you." Her arms around Aki, Kiya held her close and said, "When you feel strong enough, I want to love you, Aki, the way you deserve to be loved. I owe you my life, my real life. You gave it back to me."

Aki rested her head on Kiya's shoulder. Her fingers moved along Kiya's back, and her hands traveled up the smooth curved torso and down past her hip, over her buttocks and thighs. Kiya remained thin, but now there was a layer of muscle all along her woman's frame . . .

Her arms suddenly wrapped around Kiya. "Gomen," Aki whispered.

"Why are you sorry?"

Aki raised her head and looked into Kiya's eyes. "I didn't tell anyone," she said as her voice began to break, "but I confess, there was a period where I lost faith. I feared I'd lost you, Kiya, lost you forever and couldn't get you back. I feared that I'd killed you, and I didn't know what to do."

"No apology is necessary." Kiya held her more tightly and replied, "You never lost faith, Aki. You didn't give up; you came for me. I will be forever thankful that you brought me home."

"That was my responsibility," Aki replied. "I could not leave you in the Amida; I didn't know about Chiang and what he wanted. He used you to get to me; I've gone nearly mad trying to find you, but I don't care. It's done, and I brought you home."

The hands, rough from work, slid along Aki's face and lifted it again. The eyes looked into Aki's; the nose rubbed against hers. In spite of herself, Aki giggled as Kiya joined her in that emotion and kissed her. "You did," she whispered, "and I'm grateful, even for what I went through."

"How?" Aki asked.

"Aki," Kiya began, "for the first time in my life, I was totally on my own. I've always had someone at my side, or behind me. I had Mom, then Claudio, you, everyone around us. Out there, I had to make all my own decisions. I was helped, but I had to start with nothing and work and make my way in a place and time I knew nothing about. I grew up there, Aki. I learned to live without my parents and without you—I proved to myself I could do it. I'm a stronger person now."

"You always were strong," Aki replied, "but I understand you. I had to learn to live without you. I didn't do very well at that, I'm sorry to say. But I had to find you—I had to do what was right."

"And so you did." Kiya looked behind herself. "The water awaits," she said.

The two kissed, embraced, and felt their skin against one another. *"This now is the love . . ."* Aki sang quietly.

"Where have you been all this time?" Kiya sang back.

"Find us, here and now . . ." Kiya reached over to the wall and flipped a switch. Only the mini lights around the tub remained.

In the semidarkness, the two washed one another beneath the shower; then Kiya helped Aki into the bath. They took their places beside each other, kissed, and melted with the heat into the other's arms.

Aki closed her eyes and let Kiya hold her. They were home.

25

Reunions and Remembrances

AKI LAY AGAINST the back of the bed, propped up by the pillows. Lying in her arms, in a way welcome after so long, was Kiya. Aki did not wish to move again, at least not for a long while.

The love Kiya promised came right after the bath, and despite her ordeal, Aki forgot her pain when the two slid beneath the covers. All they'd saved for one another over the course of nearly a year came out through the next several hours.

Time meant nothing, and neither cared that the sun came and left. At times aggressive, at times gentle, Kiya made good on her promise. Aki did as well, and satisfaction came the way they both craved it.

At its end, both were exhausted but knew this emotion from any time the two became one. Aki brushed aside Kiya's hair and felt the warmth of her lover's being merge with her own.

Talk came in the afterglow as the two brought each other up to date. Aki was fascinated by Kiya's experience, intrigued by Dale and his "gang," as well as Ed, George, the *Ecorse*, and all the friends Kiya made in that other world. The stories of her time on the water, the storms, and the things she saw in this period gone by were like one great tale, but not a tall one by any means.

Kiya was interested in knowing how her family held up but also how everyone else was. She was especially pleased about Akito and Kala and moved to know both thought of her. Hiro's blues recording and Mika's show were also of interest, but the sharing of each other's own writing was a priority.

Both sat up in bed, reading; Kiya's notes had survived the water. They listened to one another's ideas, sang some of the lines, and made further notes. "These lyrics," Kiya said, "about seeing? We need to get them into a song; they're beautiful. It would be a great new one to put out there."

Aki agreed. "I think it good to have at least one or two new songs," she replied, "when we get the band back together. I think everyone wants to, and I have some thoughts on how the show ought to at least start. I've been thinking about this, and it must be done in some form."

"I want to hear," Kiya said and leaned toward her in anticipation. She was again so close, and Aki joyfully took in her aura. "Tell me," she went on. "I don't care how long it takes; we've all our lives now."

Kiya slid atop her and pressed Aki down into the bed. The strong, lithe body covered Aki, who drew Kiya down into a long, loving kiss.

"We do, indeed."

* * *

"Is everybody in?" In his spare uniform, Ed stood at the head of the dining table aboard the *Ecorse*, the full crew mustered before him. The boat remained at anchor in the river, at the head of a line of vessels that waited to get inbound. On the other side of the bridge, tugs were still shifting the *Washtenaw* back into the channel.

Her power had returned nearly as quickly as lost, according to a befuddled Captain Wilkes. Another few hours would be required before she could move out into the lake, turn, and head back to port for the replacement of her anchors. Behind the boat was an equally long line of river traffic.

As for the *Ecorse*, the last of the water was finally pumped out. Once back at her slip, repairs could begin to return the boat to service. At this moment, however, Ed had something more important to contend with.

The men, mostly young, sat or stood around the room, waiting. He began, "For those of you that are new to this crew, this is going to seem very strange, what I am about to ask of you. If you have any questions or concerns about this, feel free to air them here. There'll be no judgment of you, either by me or anyone else."

He paused and saw that the men were attentive. "The incident that took place today," he continued, "is something I don't think any of us have fully been able to comprehend. I know what I believe I witnessed, but I'm still not sure how to describe it. The Coast Guard will investigate what occurred on the *Washtenaw*. That appears to be a separate incident from the one I'm going to speak to you about. I am talking about the woman that jumped from the bridge.

"I know she went through the hatch and into our hold," Ed continued. "Most of us also witnessed our cook, Kiya, go in after her. We need to get our stories straight; no one is going to believe that two women went down into the hold of this boat and disappeared. I, most assuredly, would not. That being said, I would like to bring to the new crew's attention the situation surrounding Kiya."

Ed paused. "In the short time she was on board this vessel," he explained, "Kiya was not only an exceptional cook and a hard worker; she became a good friend of ours. She waited a long time for someone named Akira to come for her. I believe that the woman who jumped from the bridge was that person."

He sipped from his coffee, then leaned his hands on the table. "I can't explain how this happened," he continued. "The company wants answers, as do the authorities. I feel for the sake of this boat, this crew, and for Kiya especially, we need a plausible story. I propose this: the woman who jumped from the bridge landed on the hatch, then went overboard. That makes it a Coast Guard job in terms of finding her. If they don't, then they don't. As for Kiya, since we were so close to our berth, I will say she left the boat on her own accord with no forwarding address. Men and women alike have passed through numerous boats on the Lakes, sometimes for only one passage. Let us say that is the case here."

Ed looked around the room and Andreas raised his hand. "Yes?"

The wheelsman stood up. "As the eldest of the non-officers of this crew," he said, "I have been asked to speak on behalf of them in this matter, Captain. While some of us did not know Kiya as well as you, we understand the high regard you and the others had for her. With that in mind, and considering the unusual nature of the situation, I believe we would be prepared to put that story forward. If I may say," he added, "our feelings could be summed up as such: who would believe us if we told the truth?"

There were some chuckles, but the sounds among the crew were those of agreement. Ed nodded gratefully. "Thank you, Mr. Nilsson," he replied, and Andreas sat back down. "As I say," he went on, "investigators are likely going to visit the boat and will have questions. If you weren't on deck and didn't see it, you didn't see it. For the rest of you, make sure you stick as close as you can to the story; I trust you all are aware of what we have here."

The men nodded or verbalized in the affirmative. "I thank you for your commitment," Ed said as he summed up. "In time, this will pass; at the very least," he added, "we'll have a hell of a story to tell our grandkids about."

Everyone laughed at this. "All right," he said, "return to your stations." Ed remained standing as the crew filed out; Mike, Dave, and George remained behind in their seats. As he refilled his coffee cup, Ed asked, "You think that'll fly?"

Mike shrugged. He removed his Tigers cap and ran his hand through what was left of his hair. "I dunno, Ed," he replied. "Crazy things have happened on the boats over the years. People still see the *Bannockburn* on the Lakes, same way they see the *Flying Dutchman* around the Cape."

"No evidence," Dave added. "I mean, no evidence that the woman was still on board, and Kiya's leaving, it should go okay."

"We'll have to make it," Ed said, "as there's no other way to deal with it. George, make sure Kiya's stuff is out of her cabin. I feel that she knew something was coming, whether consciously or otherwise I can't say. But she was ready to leave."

George nodded. "I gotta ask, boss—what'd you see down there? When I got to you, you looked like you really had seen a ghost, and I ain't joking."

"I may have," Ed replied. "I know what I saw, but it's something I can't even put into words."

Ed left the room and climbed to the bridge. He greeted the mate and wheelsman on watch; the former reported all hands were in place. Ed acknowledged and stepped out to the port bridge wing, where he looked aft at the line of nearly three dozen boats, large and small, anchored behind the *Ecorse*.

Looking forward, Ed watched as the tugs continued to move around both sides of the *Washtenaw*, the carrier nearly back on station. He stood alone as he sipped his coffee and thought of events that had occurred within split seconds of one other. *I guess all mariners are superstitious in one way or another. How all that happened just as it did: the woman on the bridge,* Washtenaw *losing both her anchors, Kiya behaving like that, there had to be a reason.*

Then what happened down in the hold; I'll never be able to explain that to anyone. But I do know for sure of one thing I saw down there: the way Kiya held that woman, everything about it told me that was unconditional love.

Ed reached inside his coat with his free hand. He withdrew a photograph, which he had carefully dried out; he had found it floating in the water in the hold. He looked at the picture and noted how Kiya and the other woman stood beside one another, how close they were, and how good they both looked. Kiya's cap was still drying down in his cabin; he at least had these two things by which to remember a special and enigmatic friend.

Looking over to make sure the mate and wheelsman were occupied, Ed raised his cup skyward. *Goodbye, Kiya. I'll miss you; I hope you and Aki found your way home.*

* * *

The piano downstairs was being played by a well-remembered set of hands as guests mingled in a house that had been silent for too long. Reuniting and music were the orders of the day, with the former taking precedence.

Motoko and Claudio were first to arrive, and the reunion with their daughter was as joyous as expected. Watching Kiya run out to the carport to embrace her parents was as moving for Aki as it was for them.

Inside, as there was still time before others arrived, Aki and Kiya resolved to tell them the truth about the Amida. Much to their relief, the story did not upset Kiya's parents, nor did it fall upon deaf ears. Both Motoko and Claudio were understanding and fascinated by Kiya's adventure.

"We knew," Motoko said, "something unusual happened to you, Kiya-chan. We were sure you would never have left us without some kind of message."

She then looked to Aki with that same motherly expression. "I must tell you," she went on, "that I knew there was something different about you, Aki-chan. I felt that energy in you from the first time we met. You reminded me so much of your mother, and in that way as well. I do understand."

"I do as well," Claudio added. "It all sounds so strange, but we've learned that such things occur. All that matters is that you are home, Kiya-chan."

"I admit," Aki replied, "I was terribly selfish when it came to Kiya-chan, but I also had that obligation. I hope others will be as forgiving."

"There is nothing to forgive, Aki-chan," Kiya replied. Her hand held Aki's through the entire conversation, and the other went over theirs. "We don't have to tell the public a thing—if they don't accept our absence, too bad. It's our lives.

"This was an experience like none I've ever had," Kiya went on. "I have learned so much about myself but also about Aki-chan." Her arms went about Aki, and she kissed her. "I am truly fortunate to have someone who will do anything for me."

Aki blushed and leaned her head on Kiya's shoulder. "As you would for me."

Kiya's parents both smiled. "A match made in Heaven, no?" Claudio asked his wife, who only nodded.

The later meetings included big hellos from all, and an emotional one from Akito and Kala. Both were happy to see their aunt again; they were surprised when Kiya scooped both of them up and onto her shoulders with no effort.

"Oba-Kiya, you got strong!" Kala observed as she looked at how high up she'd been raised.

"I am stronger," Kiya told her, "in many ways."

The reunions with friends and bandmates were equally happy. Ri turned up as well; when Aki and Kiya made to quietly thank her, the woman just smiled. "Thanks are not necessary," she said. "I acted when called upon—this we do."

Food always played a big role in the band's rehearsals, and Kiya insisted on working some of the kitchen magic she'd learned on the *Ecorse*. It was mostly American-style fare, but all ended up well fed.

Downstairs, before the music began, the band held a meeting. Aki decided to tell the whole story: she explained the Amida. As bizarre as it may have seemed to some, those who had not known accepted the story.

"I always thought you were a little out of the ordinary, Aki-chan," James said with a grin. "That just lent to who you were—and are."

"It explains a lot," Suya admitted. "As nice a person as you are, Aki-chan, you struck me as closed off, but not in a bad way. This explains all of it."

"Yeah," Mika added, "we knew you had a secret, or a thing that had to be protected. But you did that to protect all of us; we did our best to do the same."

"You did," Aki replied, "and I thank all of you for that. The hardest part," she went on, "was never the music or anything that came with that. For myself, I had to protect this part of me; the more people knew of it, the more vulnerable I would become, but especially those around me."

She looked to Kiya. "Kiya-chan needed to know the truth," Aki continued, "for we should have no secrets. I try not to blame myself for what occurred in the tesseract, but I've learned a hard lesson—never take for granted what you have, in this world or any other."

With that dealt with, Aki and Kiya then moved on to the band. "It's been discussed by some," Aki said, "but we feel the full band needs to return. We all seem to miss the days when we gathered, had fun, and played the music that meant the most to us."

"Nori-chan and I have gotten nothing but questions about it all," Megumi said. "We know what to say about Kiya-chan's return but not what was said here. We're with you on getting it back together—but in your own way."

Kiya added, "For the current band, we have the question of new members. Aki-chan and I discussed it, and at least for the return show, we would have you involved."

She had indicated Mika, Eiki, and Ri. "You are all here," Aki said, "and you belong with us. This is about fun but also about our friends."

As they each considered it, Aki added, "And Kenji-kun—we would love to have you back as well. The door is open and always has been."

Kenji smiled as he held Akito on his lap. "I'd like that," he said, "but do you need a harmonica or a flute on every song?"

Through the laughter, Mika said, "You can sing backup, too, Kenji-kun, I've heard you. Speaking for myself, I'm honored, and yes, I'm in. I'll gladly do whatever you would like me to."

"I shall as well," Eiki replied and bowed. "It would be an honor."

All eyes turned to Ri. "The piano bench belongs to this person," she said as she nodded to Kiya. "But I can dust off my old synth," she added with a knowing grin. "I'd love to do it, and I thank you for the opportunity."

"One more," Aki said. "Hiro-kun, I love what you have done with those new recordings. If you three wish to go solo, tour on your own, no one will stop you."

Hiro shrugged. "Well," he replied, "it'll be a while before those songs are completely ready. James-san has a lot of mixing to do, and there's all the other stuff that goes with that."

He looked around at the faces before him. "I am ashamed to admit it," Hiro said, "but I had to look beyond the band and consider a future, one I wasn't sure of. The layoff let me take some time to do some thinking."

"Go on," Aki encouraged; she saw the doubtful look on his face.

"I must tell you," Hiro said to Aki and Kiya, "I missed you both, not just as bandmates, but family, too. We got on a treadmill these past few years; as proud as I am of all we've done, I started to feel like I was going to work."

The group considered Hiro's words, and most seemed to agree, if not at least understand. "I never was jealous of how you did with *Lotus Flower*," Hiro continued, "you did your own thing, and you made it happen. You became better artists. While you were doing that, I had to get back to my roots."

There were chuckles, but Aki got what Hiro was saying. "You went back to the blues," she replied, "and there's nothing wrong with that. I think we all will go our separate ways one day—but right now, I just want to play again with the people who mean so much to me. That's all of you."

With unanimous agreement, work began on the music, the lineup, and ideas that Aki and Kiya had. While they had the framework in mind and led the discussion, they actively sought ideas from the others and collaborated as one.

Megumi and Noriko began putting out feelers and making arrangements. Rehearsal space could again be found at Kitaro; the rest of the logistics and planning began to be laid down in Aki and Kiya's living room. The kids played upstairs, the grown-ups downstairs.

With Kiya on the piano and Ri on the former's synthesizer, the first "rehearsal" took off. While most were a bit ragged on certain songs, it soon came back. Tunes from the three B-J-B albums, covers, and new songs all made their way into the mix.

Following the meeting, Kiya brought Claudio out to the patio. She looked up at the man whose hair had grayed slightly but remained the sharp-dressed, dignified yet self-deprecating man she called her father. *"Dad,"* she said in Italian, *"may I speak with you?"*

"Of course," Claudio responded and smiled.

"This whole story," Kiya asked, *"it's not all crazy to you, is it?"*

Claudio shook his head as they sat at one of the tables. *"Not at all. Your mother, as she said earlier, knew from the beginning that Aki-chan had some special qualities to her. These I mistakenly thought were of this world only."*

The two chuckled and Claudio went on, *"Motoko-san understood, as only a mother could. She knew that there was trouble in this 'Amida,' by the fact you vanished and by Aki-chan's departure from here."*

Kiya reached out and took her father's hands. *"I am so sorry,"* she said. *"I felt terrible I could not get in touch with you. I was afraid for you both; I was so worried about how you'd take this."*

"There is nothing to apologize for," Claudio replied with a fatherly smile. *"What occurred was not your doing; once we were certain, Motoko-san*

and I did what everyone else did—we kept our faith. In Aki-chan, as well as in you, and in ourselves. We knew that things would come about as they were meant to."

Kiya nodded. *"There is another matter,"* she went on. *"I'm worried for Aki-chan. You see how she looks; she is so tired, but Aki-chan is too good to say anything about it. This ordeal I fear has cost Aki-chan her strength. I don't know what to do about it. I don't want her wearing herself out if she can't sing or perform anymore."*

She felt her father's hand as he caressed her cheek. *"Aki-chan does look fatigued,"* he admitted, *"but over all the years I've known you, and Aki-chan, I have seen incredible strength. It is in both of you; you have helped each other through the hardest of times. It's your love that is each other's strengths, Kiya-chan. The way you have healed one another in the past, God willing, you will do it again."*

Kiya smiled and leaned over to kiss Claudio's cheek. *"I love you, Dad,"* she whispered. *"I think you're right, but then, you always are."*

"Not about everything," Claudio replied as he kissed Kiya back. *"I am reminded of this by Motoko-san, when need be."*

Father and daughter shared the laugh and held onto one another.

The parents left not long after, but the session went on well past midnight. The rest filtered out until Aki and Kiya were alone. Down in the basement, Kiya went over a piece that had come up briefly in the session. "Before we go to bed," she asked, "can we try this out?"

"Sure." Aki sat beside Kiya at the piano; she began to play it slowly, and Aki sang: *"If I ask myself, my answers are not words, I merely turned to you, and I know . . ."*

"Draw it out," Kiya encouraged, "the last line." Aki nodded and continued: *"First time I saw your face, the smile you gave me, the look in your eye, and that was all . . ."*

Kiya played through the chords; everyone had liked the new song and dove into it with their ideas. She nodded to Aki as she sang it again, with prods to "keep it lower; then, up here . . ." Aki didn't mind the direction, and with each improvement, her excitement rose. That meant they were on the right track.

"The magic is still there," Kiya said quietly after the song ended.

"And the music is as well," Aki told her. "You especially have picked it all back up. Are you sure you didn't play while you were out there?"

Kiya shook her head. "No. It came back, just like being brought home."

"Either way," Aki said as she put her arms around Kiya, "I remain amazed by you, Kiya-chan, and everything you do."

She took a breath, and Kiya slid her arms about Aki. "You wish to say more."

"Yes." Aki smiled and looked into Kiya's eyes. "This song," she said, "is my new love letter to you, Kiya-chan. I never was able to put into words how *much* I love you; I want to think I did it this time."

"You did." Kiya's arms pulled Aki to herself, and she kissed her lips. "You wrote at a time when you must have felt desperate," she said, "and you remembered what not only brought us together but held us together, even when apart. I'm so thankful."

Aki's eyes misted. "I see everything I need to see," she replied, "and we do belong as one. I don't care if that sounds silly or sugar-coated, it's the truth."

"That's okay," Kiya told her. "Like you said a long time ago: it doesn't matter how it looks. It matters how it *feels*."

She kissed Aki once more and said, "Our love feels right. It always has."

Aki nodded, and the two kissed, holding to it as they held to each other.

26

What Did You See?

THE ACTIVITY AROUND the Nippon Budokan was intense as the hour approached for the Blue Jean Buddhas' return to the stage. For the principals, the eight previous weeks were a whirlwind of rehearsals, plus a concerted effort to keep a lid on what was going on.

The band rehearsed at Kitaro, but even with tight security on campus, fans and the media soon learned about it. Megumi and Noriko kept the press thinking, the little information they released ambiguous. No press conferences or talk show appearances were held; Aki did not want them, nor did anyone else.

In a meeting at the rehearsal space, most agreed a theater-style show would meet the demand yet still be intimate enough. "I don't want to play in a dome," Hiro declared in reference to the replacement for the old Korakuen Stadium. "The sound just isn't right in that place," he went on, "and I think everyone wants to see the band, not some bugs in the distance."

The choice of venue came down to the Budokan. Built for the '64 Olympics, the venerable hall hosted numerous sporting events but was famous for its concerts. The B-J-Bs had played there; the Beatles, Bob Dylan, Cheap Trick, and so many others had performed and recorded live albums there. The arena could be set up as if it were a large theater, and the sound system was more than passable.

While all ignored the press reports and social media chatter, they could not but be impressed by the determination of some of their fans. Demand for tickets was staggering; online agencies reported sellout of their allotment in a matter of minutes. Those willing to try their luck the old-fashioned way camped out at physical ticket offices a week in advance. All the nearly fifteen thousand seats available would be filled on the night, plus the standing-room-only sections.

As per usual, the band arrived at the arena hours in advance. There was no support act, and a soundcheck was conducted while the crews that would document and record the performance got their pre-production work in. Everyone then repaired to the backstage area for dinner and to rest and relax.

For Aki, she could not do the latter. She spent time playing with Akito and Kala, as did Kiya, and she went over in her mind all the things she'd need to do and think of that night. As she did so, Aki drifted between the dressing rooms to see how the others were doing.

Nerves were in abundance, and everyone dealt with them in their own way: Zendo and Eiki led a meditation session for band members, crew, and staff; Suya went through a series of stretches and calisthenics before a preshow shower; James took a nap stretched out on a couch; Kenji sat in a corner and worked on a pencil sketch; Mika was in an armchair, her boots up on the coffee table while she read a manga, and Ri took a walk around the building to get the feel of the place.

Hiro was in the tuning room, a small, quiet space for the guitarists to tune their instruments. Aki found him sitting there; his Telecaster was in a stand, along with the white Fender Strat that served as his backup electric. The ancient slide guitar was also there, plus the Martin acoustic. His tuning complete, Hiro was seated in a sort of silent communion with the axes.

"You okay?" Aki asked.

Hiro smiled as Aki sat beside him. "Yeah, I'm good; just thinking."

Aki smiled back. "Might I ask what of?"

"A lot of things." Hiro laced his fingers before himself as he leaned forward. "I am glad we've a moment alone, Aki-chan; I wanted to tell you that I'm totally behind you and Kiya-chan. I meant it," he went on, "when I said that the fun needed to come back. I've found it again with the guys, but this is where it all began."

Aki nodded. "I've wondered," she replied, "about how it all went the past several years. When the focus of the band became myself and

Kiya-chan, I worried about how you would handle it. I never heard you complain," she went on, "but in the back of my mind, I had to wonder."

"Afraid of hijacking my band?" Hiro grinned as he asked the question.

"To some extent," Aki admitted.

"How could I be upset about that? You and Kiya-chan took the pressure off me."

"In what way?" Aki asked, surprised.

"I wasn't ready for all this." Hiro motioned around the room. "I don't think any of us were, but when the band took off, Aki-chan, I was scared to death. I was afraid my deficiencies would show. Having the cameras on you and Kiya-chan most of the time let me do the work I needed to do. That's what I meant about how you two became so much more—you grew. I did as well; I'd like to think I became a better musician because of it. And I hope," he added, "a better person—not that jerk I was as a kid."

Aki laughed and threw her arms around Hiro. "We're not that old!" she exclaimed. "Hiro-kun, you are a better person," she said. "You are the spine, no, the soul of this band. You wanted to do this more than any of us; your love of music pushed all of us but in the right direction. We'd never have done any of it without you; Kiya-chan and I would never have had the experience to become Lotus Flower. I love you for it, and I'm as proud of you as everyone in this family is." Aki then added, "Mom and Dad are proud of you, and Kenji-kun, too."

"That's good to know." He'd heard the whole story of Aki's experience in the Summerland and her reunion with Hiroko; Hiro had seen and done enough to know it was true.

Finally, curtain time arrived. The band lined up in the wings of the hall, and they could hear the buzz of the audience. They'd played to bigger crowds in the past, but this was the comeback. "Just remember," Zendo said quietly to all as they joined hands in the dressing room, "this is for fun, for the fans, and for us. Send them your love, and they will send it back."

In the semi-darkness, the band filed to their positions. The crowd began to applaud and cheer as they saw movement in the shadows onstage. Suya climbed to his drum kit at the center; to his left and slightly below, Ri settled in before her keyboard and organ setup. Kiya's grand piano and keyboard were to Suya's right on the stage floor. To Ri's left, Kenji, Mika, and Eiki took their places at the backup microphones on a riser.

James set up on the floor in his usual spot to the right of Suya and strapped on his signature bass. Hiro was to his left and in front, Tele over his shoulder, and Zendo stood between them, his Taylor acoustic on and at the ready.

The spotlight slowly came up on an old-fashioned microphone at center stage; the fans knew this one, and they cheered. Footlights slowly faded up, and the shadows of the band could be seen on the stage.

Their cheers grew louder as Zendo played a slow progression. The strings sounded magnified by a chorusing effect. Then, from behind either side of the drum kit, two women made their way onto the stage, one in a short black dress, the other in white.

As they joined hands in front of Suya, the crowd came to their feet and the cheers turned to a roar. As if in a trance, Aki and Kiya stepped to the mic.

Looking at each other, the two smiled. *"Where did the time go?"* Aki sang, *"How could it be that long ago?"*

"We remember it so well," Kiya returned, *"the stories we could tell . . ."*

"Where did the time go?" Aki asked again.

"Where did the time go?" both sang.

A pause, and Zendo began to play another piece. James added an understated bass line, and Ri did the same on her synth. Without thinking about it, Aki and Kiya slid their arms around each other's waists and began to sing an old song about how love was strange.

The audience applauded at the opening lines, but this version was different without the hokey call-and-response of the original. Some knew the arrangement was reminiscent of the version recorded by Everything But the Girl. Aki and Kiya were fans of the duo and loved this one. It fit the message they wished to send out.

The Budokan fell silent. Over their harmonies, Aki and Kiya could hear the quiet percussion and lead guitar coming from Suya and Hiro respectively; the band was one in the performance.

At its end, Kiya walked to her piano over the applause. She immediately played that intro, and the stunned crowd awoke. The spotlight shone on Aki, and her hand went around the mic. *"You traveled the world, lookin' for, lookin' for love . . . there ain't nothing out there, that you deserve . . ."*

The crowd roared; once more, Aki was on the big stage, with the world watching. She felt the power of the music behind her, the fans in front of her, and that which came from above and below. *"Can't nobody love you like me . . ."*

The explosion of the band, the lights and effects, and the roar of the crowd electrified Aki. On her heels, she held the mic and tore into the song. Behind her, the band and its sound were seamless. Kiya took the high range; Aki picked up the chorus again, and they wound that song down as before . . .

Aki stood alone as the crowd response struck in a wave. The concert had started well; now Aki hoped she could get through this next part.

"Arigato gozaimasu," she said as the crowd noise died down. "First," Aki went on, "we would like to thank all of you for coming out tonight and for supporting us over these years. Many things have occurred in the past several months, and without getting too much into detail, allow me to say I have changed a great deal, as we all have."

There was more applause. "Tonight," Aki said, "we will present to you the music that has defined the Blue Jean Buddhas, plus some new songs. The message we wish to convey to you tonight is this: we have decided to play the songs that mean the most to us, the ones that inspired us to play and sing in the first place."

There was stronger applause, and Aki smiled as she looked around to see all were ready. "I feel like singing the blues," she said with a grin.

A roar from the crowd, the click of Suya's sticks, and they were off.

There were strange bedfellows in the select upper box of the Budokan. This one provided a front-and-center view of the stage, reserved on this night for dignitaries and guests of honor. Motoko and Claudio sat together holding hands. Beside them, a former sumo wrestler, his wife, and four of their children watched in admiration. The eldest was working tonight, head of the road crew.

Megumi and Noriko's parents were there, as were Mika's and Suya's families. In the next row back, amongst the record company executives, fellow musicians, press, radio, and TV personalities, sat a man in formal evening wear.

Mr. Ito smiled as he watched the performance. During an instrumental portion of this song, he leaned over to his wife and said, "I have always enjoyed hearing our friends as they stretch themselves. They are doing it again, Sumi-chan; it is needed after so long."

His wife nodded in agreement as their teenage children looked on and listened, thrilled as anyone else this night.

The evening saw the Blue Jean Buddhas take the fans on a tour of their history: those first songs of the old days came out once more: Zendo led on "Four Strong Winds," Kiya sang "If I Could," with Aki joining her at the piano, and they dipped into the blues catalog for "Walking Out of San Francisco" and a rousing cover of "Green Onions" in which Hiro and Kiya "dueled" on their instruments.

The night included an unplugged set, as Aki, Suya, and Eiki brought out their tribal drums. Everyone came down and sat around center stage, except for Ri, who took Kiya's spot at the piano for a number of tunes. Aki's vocals on "Nighthawk" got a huge response, while Hiro sang "He Left Me His Guitar" and "Got the Blues." Kenji added harmonica to these, and each earned a big hand.

Then came "Aki's Song," and the crowd response was louder on this than on any other selection so far. Kenji played flute while Aki and Kiya sang as they had so many times before; the rest of the band added sparse accompaniment.

The last song of this portion was the new one that Aki and Ri had arranged. Everyone returned to their places but for Aki, Hiro, and Kiya. *"When we were stars . . ."*

Aki felt her way with the song over the past few weeks. Hiro mirrored Ri's chord choices, while Zendo took an understated lead. *"The world was open to all of us, all things at our command . . ."*

At unusual times, especially when performing, Aki would have flashbacks, and tonight was no exception. *"When we were stars, we flew beyond the heavens, it was ours for the taking . . ."*

Aki remembered the early years of the B-J-B's career; from first on the bill to signing, to those initial hits and the stardom that followed. The song recalled for Aki the times they'd become important, when people opened doors for them, carried their bags, and accorded them VIP treatment.

"Stars are born, stars fade, stars fly high, come crashing down, stars live and stars die . . ." All that had passed over the months was going through her mind at this point, but it hurt her no more.

"In the end I still wonder . . . were we ever stars at all?" Aki could not but steal a glance at Kiya, who caught it and smiled back. *Yes, we still are in our fans' minds . . . I'm all right with it now.*

The set continued with more songs by the full band, until near the end, when the band came out of a mournful "Silent Tears" to a fervent response. Immediately, they tore into "Time Won't Let Me," which brought the crowd back to full energy. Aki waited until the applause died down again. One of the road crew moved Aki's microphone and stand to the side and handed her a wireless mic.

"Thank you once more," she told the crowd. "It's a little late in the game, but we will now offer you one more new song."

More applause. Aki paused, a little longer than she should, but she needed to gather herself again. "This was written a few weeks ago," she explained. "I have struggled for many years to put into words how much I love one person in my life."

The *oooh* of the crowd swelled as Aki turned to Kiya. She sat behind her piano, eyes wide in anticipation. "This is my new love ode to Kiya-chan," Aki announced. "It is called, 'What Did You See?'"

The lights went down. Mika ran a wooden dowel around the edge of the metal singing bowl into its microphone. The tone it gave off sounded through the arena.

"I am searching, deep with-inside myself, to understand these things I feel . . ." Aki sang to a silenced arena, and the universe, *"they are not fantasy, what then, are they?"*

The band kicked in: Suya's backbeat, a minimal baseline from James, and dual rhythm guitar from Hiro and Zendo slid under Aki's voice. Ri again replaced Kiya at the piano; she had left the stage.

"If I ask myself, my answers are not words, I merely turn to you, and I know . . ." Aki sang to the audience. *"First time I saw your face, the smile you gave to me, the look in your eyes, and that was all . . ."*

Wireless in hand, a spotlight lit Kiya's way as she crossed the stage to join Aki. *"I didn't plan this out, still broken from before, never would have tried, where would I start?"*

Aki switched her mic to her left hand and reached out with her right. She caught Kiya's free hand in hers, turned, and faced her; these lyrics were for her. *"What did you see in me, what made you strip away, all your insecurities and the fears that kept you down? Why was I the one, what made you reach for me, and tell me you loved me . . ."*

The music faded at the last line; Aki looked into Kiya. *"Whatever did you see?"*

The second verse was more of Aki's recollections of that first day; the moment Kiya took her hand, how good it felt, and how much both wanted one another when apart. The music rose in urgency once more in the second bridge as Kiya again took over. *"You did not pursue me, the mirror from behind, when you opened up yourself, and I turned to find . . ."*

At full sound, the band took Aki and Kiya back into the chorus. Holding each other's hands, Aki poured her lower, more insistent voice into the chorus. *"What did you see in me, did you see yourself, recognize the pain, that I could no longer hide?"*

Kiya took the second half this time: *"Is it what you wanted most, someone to say they knew, who loved you anyway, whatever did you see?"*

Aki's heart raced. She clung to Kiya's hand and sang the final bridge, which Kiya returned like a chorus: *"Now the years have gone by, there's more left to live, I won't lose you this time, I promise, just tell me . . ."*

Aki could hear the band, the backing voices, and even those in the front row being overcome. She didn't care; tears blurred her vision. Kiya, no less emotional, wailed in her upper range as Aki repeated the second chorus, then the first.

Then it stopped. All that remained was the singing bowl. Aki pulled Kiya to her. Face to face, before all, covered in sweat, tears running down her face, Aki quietly sang the first three lines of the intro again, then added, *"What did you see?"*

"What did you see?" Kiya responded.

The world went silent but for Aki's final whispered question to Kiya: *"What did you see?"*

They kissed and fell into one other. Aki broke down, as did Kiya, their cries drowned out by the cheers of a grateful and loving audience.

27

When It's All You've Got...

ED MCCARTHY STOOD on the bridge of the *Ecorse*. The boat was back at the dock; she would sail again in the morning for her regular run into Lake St. Clair. There was no watch, and Ed took the time alone up here, though he wouldn't be for long. Heavy tread on the steps caused him to turn as a familiar stocky figure walked through the chart room onto the bridge. "Permission to come aboard, sir?"

The captain grinned. "Permission granted, Dale," he replied. The two shook hands. "It's been too long." He added, "What brings you out here?"

Dale looked ready to put to sea again in his customary mariner's rig. "Oh, I don't know," he said as he looked around the bridge. "Something told me I should drop in tonight; not quite sure what."

"Well, I'm glad you did."

"So how is the old *Ecorse* these days?" Dale asked. "See you got some new plates on the starboard side."

"Yeah, finally," Ed replied. "After that storm at the beginning of the season, the company finally decided to fix things. Did a good job, too; we also got the once-over, after that near-miss. Want to check it out?"

"Love to," Dale said with a grin.

"Before we do," Ed suggested, "let's get some coffee."

As they headed down the stairs, Dale said, "I heard that whole thing with the *Washtenaw* on the radio as it happened. Sounded like a hair-raiser."

"Indeed," Ed admitted, "then that strange woman, and all that other stuff."

Dale asked with a chuckle, "I guess you've heard the talk about the 'Phantom Lady of the Ambassador Bridge'?"

"I have," Ed replied as they laughed, "and the guardian angel image of her lends well to the charmed life the *Ecorse* has lived."

In the galley, Dale was introduced to George, now promoted to cook. A steward was located through the union hall; he would join the boat in the morning. As George poured coffee for himself and the others, the three sat down for some discussion as the radio played the Temptations at a low level.

During the talk, strange feedback blocked out the signal. George got up to adjust the dial, and the sound diminished.

What replaced it made them all stare. There was a back echo and an almost shortwave quality to the sound—and then they heard the voices.

"Where did the time go . . . how could it be that long ago?"

At the next stanza, all three men slowly turned to look at the radio, then each other, then back to the box. "It's Kiya," George said.

"And the one we know as Akira," Dale added.

As the brief song ended, Ed smiled. "An answered prayer," he said as the three raised their cups. "They made it home."

The three sat and drank, listening to a radio concert they knew was for them and them alone.

* * *

The end of the set had the crowd on its feet. The roar was deafening, but Aki didn't hear it.

She didn't care how long this took; tears still pouring from her eyes, Aki held Kiya with what strength she had left. "I love you," she shouted in Kiya's ear.

"I love you, too." Kiya was as uncomposed as Aki.

They kissed again and held on. The cheering did not stop as the rest of the Blue Jean Buddhas came down to surround them at center stage. Aki looked around and saw what she needed: the smiles on all their faces, especially those of her brothers and the knowing ones from Zendo and Ri. Aki was home again, for real.

They formed a long line, and all took their bows as the crowd chanted the band's initials. Some fans came down as close to the stage as security allowed and tossed bouquets of flowers onto it.

All congratulated one another as they went offstage and into the dressing room. Backstage, the press was waiting along with a few others who'd sneaked in. Representatives from the record label were there and already discussing with Megumi the possibility of releasing the concert both on CD and DVD. At least one said the last song had to be a single.

Aki didn't hear any of it; she and Kiya both needed the few minutes before the encore to dry their eyes, get their makeup fixed, and compose themselves. Quickly, they confirmed the plan and returned to the stage, save for Aki, who remained in the wings.

The spotlight focused on Hiro, and he hit the first few notes of a song on his Tele. The band kicked in behind Hiro as they played a haunting version of "Sweet Dreams."

The instrumental was one that Roy Buchanan, Hiro's initial inspiration for guitar, often played. Hiro followed Buchanan's arrangement of the piece but added his own soulful twists, plus a light step on his wah pedal. As the B-J-Bs did with others' songs, they made them their own but with respect to those that came before.

At the edge of the stage, Aki looked out into the crowd, from the floor seats to the upper levels of the arena. She saw a cross-section of Japan: there were adolescents, teenagers, college students, and young adults. Some had probably been fans of the band and now had kids; they were here, too. There were older folks as well; Aki was sure they weren't all from the music business, either. Megumi and Noriko ensured the front rows of seats went to fans.

The song ended with an extended solo from Hiro, and the crowd was again brought to its feet. Hiro grinned at Aki as she passed him on her return to the stage.

"Thank you so much," Aki said as she stepped to her repositioned mic, and the crowd hushed. "Once again, it has been a wonderful night, and I hope you have enjoyed it as much as we did."

The crowd cheered, then quieted down again as quickly. "I don't know," she went on, "what the future will be for the Blue Jean Buddhas. All I know is, we will continue to make the music we love; music that stirs emotions, inspires and, I hope, heals in its own way. We will continue to do it in the way that is best for us, and that is from the heart.

"That last piece, 'Sweet Dreams,'" Aki continued as the applause died down again," has significance for my brothers and me. Our late mother was a fan of Patsy Cline, the woman who sang it so many years ago. I have often said or hoped that everyone has at least one of those—one sweet dream—in their lifetime."

Aki fought off another break in her voice and continued, "I have been fortunate, for I have had more than I deserve." She looked over at Kiya, who was trying to hide her smile and blushing face. *That is so cute, especially right now . . .*

Covered in sweat, Aki kicked off her heels. "I want to feel you," she challenged, breathlessly, "when we do this one."

She looked around the black starry space of the Budokan; musicians, family, friends, and an audience that remained on its feet and wanted more. "Oh, yeah . . ." Aki teased.

Hiro responded with that guitar line, and the crowd roared. "Everything's gonna be all right!" Aki shouted.

"I'm a Woman" thundered out into the night as Aki removed the top part of her mic stand. Through her bare feet, she felt the stage vibrate as she sang the line, growled, and shouted the lyrics.

The walk took her the width of the stage. Aki no longer felt the floor; sweat glistened in her hair, on her dress, and across her skin. As she neared Hiro, her brother stepped out, and he did another solo.

As he did, Aki pointed to Kenji, who was near Zendo and playing harp. Kenji walked over; Aki placed herself between her brothers and belted out the title. Grooving in time to the slow, powerful rhythm, Hiro and Kenji played and soloed back and forth. All lights on them, the band churned the underlying musical path as Aki felt the closeness of her true family, and those close beside, once more.

The last lines, a powerful howl from the harp, the guitar, and a wash of cymbals, and the song ended in another cacophony of cheers. Aki could only smile as her brothers retook their places. "Thank you one more time," she called. "This has been amazing, but we must leave you now."

A drum kick, and Zendo began the familiar opening rhythm. Hiro added the power chords, and they were off again on the Poco song. It hadn't grown old; the crowd remained standing and sang along, much as they had done throughout the night. Zendo took the first verse as before, while Aki handled the second, and the backing vocals again swelled by several thousand.

Hiro's fiery guitar solo, the repeat of half of the first verse by Zendo, and an organ solo from Ri stretched the tune out until the final guitar line broke it down to just the rhythm. Then Hiro changed a setting on his pedalboard and picked out the beginning for "Sweet Home Chicago." Fifteen thousand pairs of hands clapped, feet stamped, and all provided extra percussion for one final song.

Then it was all over. Aki stepped to the edge of the stage with the rest of the band for a final bow. She waved to the crowd, took Kiya's hand, and the two walked offstage. *We rushed to try and get out of there, but it wasn't easy; after another round of congratulations, we showered, changed, and slipped out a side entrance. The limo just for us we thought was a bit much, but Megumi and Noriko really did think of everything. They knew the two of us would want to go home.*

We were dropped off at the house; we went inside and made tea. We sat together on the deck and watched the moon and stars for a while before going inside to make love. I know, not quite the rock 'n' roll lifestyle, but that never mattered much to me or to Kiya. The show was wonderful, and there will be more to come.

There will always be obstacles in our lives, but none shall be as daunting as the ones we've faced, separately and together, this past year. Having done this, we proved something to each other but also to ourselves.

As I lie here tonight in Kiya's arms, I think of my mother; I thank her, my family, and my friends. They represent strength, but I know now how much I have.

I love you, Kiya-chan; Sweet Dreams.

About the Author

TORY GATES has produced books for the Young Adult and Contemporary Fiction world since 2013. He takes readers to exotic locales, everyday places, and brings to life characters that are relatable and real, while addressing real-life issues.

Tory is the author of the Sweet Dreams Series, a trilogy of works that combine time travel, Japanese culture, and the power of music. *Searching for Roy Buchanan*, *Call It Love*, and *Shake Hands With the Devil* are all available on Brown Posey Press, the fiction imprint of Sunbury Press Books. He is also the author of two other Brown Posey releases, the award-winning *A Moment in the Sun* and *Live from the Café*. Tory's first book, *Parasite Girls*, was released on Amazon and Smashwords.

A broadcaster with more than thirty-five years of experience, Tory is a journalist, presenter, and producer. He can be heard on the Radio Pennsylvania Network and the Brown Posey Press Show, an interview program for independent and self-published authors. Tory is also known as "DJ`Riff," host of "The Music Club," a blues program for the London-based Radio-Airwaves Station.

A native of Vermont, Tory lives in Harrisburg, Pennsylvania, with a cat named Kao, and can be found anyplace that serves good coffee!

www.ingramcontent.com/pod-product-compliance
Lightning Source LLC
Chambersburg PA
CBHW030516020726
47494CB00004B/1113